34134 00045077 2

Leabharlann

D1587852

FS LIBRARIES

*Reflections*

MONTREAL
TRUST

*Reflections*

# JO BANNISTER

WESTERN ISLES
LIBRARIES

F30325187

WITHDRAWN

First published in Great Britain in 2003 by
Allison & Busby Limited
Bon Marche Centre
241-251 Ferndale Road
Brixton, London SW9 8BJ
*http://www.allisonandbusby.com*

Copyright © 2003 by Jo BANNISTER

The right of Jo Bannister to be identified as
author of this work has been asserted by her in
accordance with the Copyright, Designs and
Patents Act, 1988

This is a work of fiction and all characters, firms, organisations and instants portrayed are
imaginary. They are not meant to resemble any counterparts in the real world; in the unlikely
event that any similarity does exist it is an unintended coincidence.

This book is sold subject to the condition that it shall not,
by way of trade or otherwise, be lent, resold, hired out or
otherwise circulated without the publisher's prior
written consent in any form of binding or cover other than
that in which it is published and without a similar condition
including this condition being imposed upon the subsequent
purchaser.

A catalogue record for this book is available from the British Library

ISBN 0 7490 0695 1

Printed and bound in Ebbw Vale,
by Creative Print & Design

The author of over twenty acclaimed novels, JO BANNISTER started her career as a journalist after leaving school at sixteen to work on a local weekly newspaper. Shortlisted for several prestigious awards, she was Editor of the *County Down Spectator* for some years before leaving to pursue her writing full-time. She lives in Northern Ireland and is currently working on her next novel. *Reflections* is the third in a series featuring Brodie Farrell, Daniel Hood and Jack Deacon.

# Chapter One

After the man stormed out, trailing clouds of fury and despair, the woman took a moment to compose herself. A moment was all she needed. She had dreaded losing her youth, her looks, her waistline and her ability to turn heads merely by entering a room, but there was this compensation: she no longer cared what other people thought of her. She had never been a slave to public opinion; now she acknowledged it only for the pleasure of outraging it. If she went too long without giving offence she tried harder. As long as she could still turn heads, by one means or another, she knew she was alive.

Except that, in the diamond core of her being where she was as ruthless with herself as with everyone else, she cared what Robert thought. She knew she owed him better than this. Those who presumed to judge her were one thing, she had no reservations about frightening their horses. But her husband was a good man, a kind man, and he'd tried to make her happy. His failure was less a reflection on him than on her.

The faint flush that their argument had brought to her cheek had subsided before the door, slammed in his departure with all the force of Robert Daws' substantial frame, had done trembling. Serena gave a faintly wistful sigh. Anyone witnessing the scene would have thought she enjoyed humiliating him – that she'd taken pleasure and satisfaction from throwing her infidelity in his face. And it was true that things had been quiet lately, and a good knock-down, drag-out fight got the blood flowing in a way that few other things did. But pleasure? – no. Beneath the brilliant, brittle, reckless facade there was still a significant portion of Serena Daws who was her husband's wife before she was anything else. Because, despite her monstrous behaviour towards him, she did actually care for Robert.

He didn't know that. How could he? – she did everything in her power to hide the fact. She treated him with a scorn of which pretty young men were only a symptom. How could he know that none of them meant more to her than sweat-stains on a crumpled sheet? That she courted them not for their own attributes – their pretty faces, their strong young bodies, their arrogant adolescent lust – but precisely because of the effect they had on her marriage. Robert was a success-ful man, a wealthy man, widely respected for his business acumen – a leading light of a world to which she had no access. And Serena wasn't prepared to be merely a decora-tion on his arm. Serena never played second fiddle to any-one.

In company she referred to him as The Grocer. It need not have been offensive. Grocery was his trade as it was his father's, and he had no reservations about admitting it. He *liked* groceries, wished he got the chance to wear his white coat more often. It was the price of success: you turn a hand-ful of south coast shops into a national chain with a London head office and you hang up the white coat and immerse yourself in balance sheets. But a grocer was what he was, what he was proud to be. It was Serena's particular genius that she could turn the word into an insult.

Like the insults, the flirting began as a game. When on social occasions she caught him cloistered with other cap-tains of the packet goods industry, discussing transport costs and import regulations and the latest moves in the Banana Wars, she retaliated by homing in on the most attractive man present. Then people would chuckle, and someone would nudge Robert, and he'd bow out ruefully from the debate on raisin futures and pay her some attention. At that time they both went home satisfied: she content in the admiration she attracted, he in the envy he did.

Somewhere along the line the game developed a mom-entum of its own. When Robert became inured to her flirting it became necessary to do more than flirt; when secret lovers lost their power to hurt him she began to flaunt them. They became locked in a cycle of pain and punishment that neither seemed able to break. That neither could see for what it was: two people who actually still loved each other increasingly unable to demonstrate the fact.

Now they were reduced to this: playing parts in a pantomime. Serena wasted her time bedding boys she didn't want in order to hurt the man she did, and Robert pretended to be indifferent right up to the point where he lost all control.

Oddly enough, that was the moment at which they might have stepped back from the brink: when Robert came out of the kitchen with tears streaming down his broad face and a carving-knife snatched from the cutlery drawer in his hand. Perhaps if he'd tried to stab her; if she'd screamed; if they'd suddenly seen what they were doing to one another. But even at that point he sublimated his rage to a harmless gesture. His clenched fist rose and fell, rose and fell, sweat pouring down his cheeks along with the tears as he reduced her paintings to gaudy ribbons.

And Serena laughed. In the heat of the moment she was proud of that heartless laugh. "What's that meant to achieve?" she demanded. "Stab *me* – kill me. Go after Nicky if you think he'll stand still long enough. But a picture? Dear God, Robert, it's only a bit of paint and canvas. There are a dozen others in the cupboard; and if there weren't I could run up another tomorrow. They're not great art, they don't take months of painstaking work. They just take a few brushes, a bit of paint, and someone with a body worth looking at."

Her head lifted arrogantly. "Or is that why you find them so offensive? Am I only supposed to look at you like that? I have news for you, my dear. I *never* looked at you like that."

Which was when he choked on a sob, and threw the knife at her – not like a weapon but as he might have thrown a cup; it clattered harmlessly on the floor at her feet – and turned and hurried away, his cumbrous body denying him even the consolation of a dignified departure.

11

The voice of Serena's heart cried to her to go after him; warned her she'd gone too far this time, urged her to make amends while there was still a chance – if there was still a chance. But it was a small and muffled voice and she ignored it. Her blood was up, and she was still surfing the adrenalin-wave of the passion she'd provoked.

She looked at the ruined canvas and chuckled bleakly. At least by savaging her latest venture into life-painting he'd saved her the embarrassment of hanging it. Serena had no illusions about her skill as an artist. Her technique was good but she didn't inject enough soul into her work ever to graduate from the ranks of the merely competent. Perhaps she didn't have a soul. She painted not because she admired the results but because she enjoyed the process.

She wandered through the studio, picking up brushes and tubes of paint thrown or spilled in the excitement, and regarded the damaged canvases thoughtfully, wondering if any of them was worth the trouble of repairing. Objectively, she thought not. But then, Robert would come back; and he'd come into this studio in the little cottage behind their house; and Serena could wring a last drop of satisfaction from the episode by watching his face when he saw the boy who cuckolded him back on the easel in all his youthful glory.

She plucked idly at the coloured streamers, remembering the animation – the fury, hatred and despair – in her husband's ruddy face as he slashed. It was the most energy she'd seen him expend in years. Though the painting wasn't worth the trouble of repairing she would do it. The silver wouldn't be hard to replicate, and flesh-tones she always had available. And that was about all the thing was: a young man's body sprawled on a silver sheet, reflections chasing one another through the folds of fabric and flesh. Technically it was accomplished. But even painting her lover she couldn't seem to instil much passion into it.

Thinking of the boy – his wariness, confusion, infatuation,

compliance – brought a tired smile to her perfectly defined lips. She knew herself too well to pretend she loved him. She basked in his inexpert attention, relished the bunch and slide of hard muscles under his perfect skin, enjoyed the urgent thrust of his body into hers. But none of those was the reason for what she'd done. Her only purpose in seducing a pretty, sweaty teenage labourer had been for its effect on Robert. Her husband was genuinely the only man who mattered to her.

The cottage door creaked. She wouldn't yield him the satisfaction of turning to face him, went on tidying up in a languid, desultory way. "Something you forgot to say?" There was no reply. Her shoulders lifted in a cynic chuckle. "I hope you're not waiting for *me* to apologise."

Then she turned, expecting Robert's tears. Instead she saw the glint of steel: the knife she'd left lying on the floor. Perhaps she should have put it away when she had the chance.

But she didn't feel threatened. She laughed aloud, dismissively. "Don't be absurd! Put it back in the kitchen drawer before someone gets hurt. This isn't a tragedy, it's a farce."

It wasn't the first time she'd misread a situation, underestimated the pain she'd inflicted or the helpless power of the despair she'd invoked. But it was the last.

# Chapter Two

Hugo Daws had exhausted every other avenue when he turned into Shack Lane, a stone's throw from Dimmock's shingle beach, and stopped in front of a curtained window displaying a few discreet testimonials and a slate inscribed *Looking For Something?* The policeman in charge of the case had sent him here. Daws no longer lived locally, had never heard of Brodie Farrell, wasn't persuaded that the answer to his dilemma lay behind a burgundy velvet curtain in an unregarded sidestreet of an unfashionable seaside resort. But he was desperate and would try anything before he admitted defeat.

He had nothing to lose. A little time, a little money perhaps. He was not concerned about making a fool of himself. No one, looking back on these events, would pause to chuckle because Hugo Daws had been reduced to consulting a private detective before abandoning his nieces to council care.

Athough on a Wednesday morning in September there were more seagulls about than tourists, he was unable to park in Shack Lane. He left the hired car on waste-ground round the corner and walked back. As he walked he told himself it wasn't seedy so much as authentic. Original. Some of these buildings were three hundred years old. So, he suspected, was some of the paintwork.

At least Brodie Farrell knew how to use both paint and polish. Daws wielded the bright brass knocker on the burgundy front door and waited.

A woman opened the door: a tall woman in her early thirties with a cloud of dark hair pulled back from her brow and brown eyes that scanned his face for a second longer than he considered polite. "Can I help you?"

"I'm Hugo Daws," he said, "here to see Mr Farrell."

The woman regarded him a little longer, the ghost of a smile on her lips. "I'm Brodie Farrell."

Daws blinked. He'd lived in South Africa for twenty years – the feminist revolution had passed him by. The doubts he'd had about coming here returned with a vengeance at the idea of a female private detective.

He cleared his throat to cover his confusion. "Superintendent Deacon suggested I see you. He didn't warn me – "

"Warn you?" The voice was educated and ambivalent. He wasn't sure if she was laughing at him or about to throw him out.

"I mean ... I was expecting Humphrey Bogart."

Brodie Farrell chuckled softly and held the door wide. "Sorry to disappoint you. Jack Deacon said you might call round. Come in and tell me how I can help."

He followed her through a tiny ante-room into an office that was hardly any bigger. It held a desk, a chair, a small sofa and a filing cabinet.

Brodie saw him weighing up her premises. She said candidly, "It was all I could afford when I started up last year. But the business is doing well and now it's not big enough. I'm trying to acquire the building next door so I can knock through. In the meantime, all I really need is room for a computer and a telephone. A lot of my work I don't do in the office."

"What kind of work do you do, Mrs Farrell?" He'd spotted the wedding-ring.

"What did Jack Deacon tell you?"

"He said you find things. Does that make you a private detective?"

She shook her head, the dark hair tossing. "No. I don't lurk in alleys, I don't bug telephones, I don't follow people to see if their evening class is actually an assignation with a person of the opposite sex. It's like Jack said: I find things. Things that people have set their hearts on and haven't been able to track down. A painting by a particular artist, a piece of

15

furniture from a particular period, a silver inkwell to match a set. Going from one dealer to another until you found it would take months and cost you a fortune. I deal with the dealers all the time, I leave them a list of what I'm looking for and they call me. Sometimes it's bigger things. You want a house that meets particular criteria and the estate agents can't show you anything? I'll find you one that wasn't even for sale until I talked to the owners."

She saw his expression and laughed, a clear laugh like a wind-chime. "No, of course I don't threaten them! There are other kinds of offers you can't refuse. I closed one deal by moving the vendors into something smaller now they were getting older, making all the arrangements including finding a new home for two Bearnese Mountain Dogs. You try getting that sort of service from an estate agent!"

Hugo Daws was still frowning uncertainly. He was a man in his mid-forties, tall and rangy, and Brodie saw from his tan and his warm coat that he was used to a milder climate. "It isn't a thing I need finding," he said. "It's a person."

A shiver ran down Brodie Farrell's spine: not so much fear as the memory of fear. Her lips pinched to a thin line. "Inspector Deacon" – she hadn't got used to his promotion yet – "didn't tell me that."

Daws looked puzzled. "Am I missing something?"

Brodie rubbed an eyebrow with the side of her hand in a wry gesture. "Nothing you should have known. But Jack Deacon knows I don't look for people, and why. The last time I did it someone got hurt. Maybe it wasn't my fault, but it wouldn't have happened without my help – my skill, if you like. I swore I'd never risk it happening again."

"I see." Daws blew out his cheeks, defeated. "Well, I understand your position. If Mr Deacon had told me I wouldn't have troubled you. Only, I really don't know where else to go, and I'm running out of time."

Brodie regarded him levelly. Behind the stillness of her expression her brain was running calculations. It wasn't much like last time. Deacon had sent him because he thought she should make an exception for Hugo Daws. He knew and respected her views on the subject. His involvement was as close to a guaranteee as she could hope for that Daws was on the level.

Anyway, no harm would be done by listening to him. She gave a conciliatory smile. "Maybe I'm jumping the gun. Tell me what you need, Mr Daws, and I'll see what I can do."

The man paused for a moment, wondering how to say the unthinkable, the unbearable. He decided that quick was better than slow. "My brother murdered his wife. He stabbed her thirteen times with a kitchen knife, then he disappeared. I have no idea where he is or when he'll be found, but I do know he's in no position to look after his two daughters."

A little tic twitched on his cheekbone. It was the only indication that he was talking about his own family. "My wife and I flew up from Johannesburg as soon as the police contacted me. But I have a business and people depending on me, I can't stay much longer, and the girls can't leave the country until matters are settled here. I don't want them going into care, but the only family they have apart from me and Peris is their mother's sister, and she and Serena seem to have lost contact years ago. That's who I want you to find. If she could look after them for a few weeks, then they could come to South Africa with us. We'll give them a permanent home. It's what happens to them in the short term that concerns me."

Brodie had heard about the case, of course – the public details that were carried in *The Dimmock Sentinel* and the bits that Jack Deacon had dropped over late-night coffee in her flat when he was too tired to be discreet. She didn't mind him unburdening himself when the alternative was going home with his mind too full to sleep. Heading a murder inquiry only sounds glamorous: in practice it's long hours full of hard work, dead ends, frustration, anxiety and pressure.

Jack Deacon was luckier than some in both his superior

and his sergeant, but neither would share in the criticism if an investigation went pear-shaped. The buck stopped with Deacon, and there was no one he could confess his worries to if he didn't bring them to her. When Brodie was married to a solicitor he did the same thing; but there was this difference. Nobody blames the solicitor if a killer remains free long enough to kill again.

So much of what Hugo Daws had steeled himself to say she already knew; including the answer to her next question. She asked it because it would help her to understand where he stood in all this. "Is there any question about your brother's guilt?"

Hugo shook his head grimly. "Not much. No one saw him do it, but that's about all. The girls heard their parents arguing and saw Robert slash Serena's painting with a knife. The fight was about a young man – unfortunately she didn't settle for just painting him. The children were scared and ran off. When they came back half an hour later Serena was dead and Robert had gone. They called a neighbour and he called the police."

So the family weren't trying to believe in a passing maniac who stabbed Mrs Daws and kidnapped her husband. If they could be realistic about the situation it should be possible to help them without getting drawn into their tragedy. Either she would locate the wife's sister or she wouldn't, but no one would expect her to make everything all right again. No one could do that for the Daws family. The best they could hope for was finding a way to live with what had happened.

A good start would be finding Serena's sister. Without knowing anything about her, Brodie was confident she could track her down. People were generally much easier than things. They left a paper-trail wherever they went.

"Mr Daws," she said, "because this relates to a serious crime I'll need to check with the police that I won't be getting in their way. If Inspec ... Superintendent Deacon's OK with it I'll take it on. So what can you tell me about Serena's sister?"

18

Relief wiped some of the creases off Hugo Daws' brow, but not all of them. "Not much, I'm afraid. I've never met her. Her name is Constance, but whether she's still Constance Ward or if she's married I don't know. She's a couple of years older than Serena – thirty-nine, maybe forty. The family were local, they had a house at Peyton Parvo, but it was sold years ago and all the older generation are gone." He gave a rueful smile. "It's not much to go on, is it?"

Brodie didn't like making what she did sound too easy, but the man was desperate for reassurance. "It's surprising what you can find when you look in the right places, Mr Daws. I can't give you a guarantee, of course, but if you're a betting man you might risk a little flutter. Leave it with me for a couple of days. When I speak to you again I'll have a better idea how feasible it is and how long it's likely to take. How long can you stay in England?"

Hugo shrugged under the coat that would have seen him through a Dimmock winter and looked rather absurd in mid September. "Not much longer. I'm an architect, I have clients and colleagues waiting for me. But my wife's willing to stay for a couple more weeks in the hope that something can be sorted out."

Brodie nodded. It was one thing to say you should drop everything in an emergency, another actually to do it. Hugo had come six thousand miles at a few hours' notice to try to help his nieces. Perhaps he thought he could have done more but Brodie didn't. She thought he'd done all that could reasonably be expected of him. "Where are you staying?"

"Sparrow Hill. My brother's house." He jotted down the address and phone-number: as he passed her the note he saw surprise in her face. "The girls wanted to stay," he said defensively. "They've lost so much already, they didn't want to be homeless as well. And the – murder – didn't happen in the house. It seemed less disruptive to stay than to move them elsewhere."

Brodie nodded her understanding. "There aren't any

absolutes in a situation like this, are there? You just have to go with what feels right; and failing that, what's possible."

The man stood up, extended his hand in a way that wasn't fashionable when he last lived in England. "Thank you for your time. I'm feeling a bit more positive already." He started to turn, then stopped. "Something occurs to me. It's a long shot but you might be able to help. I need a tutor for the girls. Serena was teaching them – putting them into school now would be a major trauma, but they can't just do nothing."

Brodie smiled brightly. "I bet Jack Deacon didn't tell you to ask me that."

Fresh misgivings etched themselves on Hugo's brow. "No, he didn't. Why?"

"Because I have a friend who does that sort of work, but he's not Superintendent Deacon's favourite person. Not for any reason you need worry about – it's purely personal. They're two quite different types of men and they've never been able to see eye to eye. But I could tell Daniel about your situation, see if he can help, if you like."

Hugo pursed his lips, momentarily embarrassed. "I'm sorry, you've rather taken me by surprise. I was looking for a woman – perhaps a retired schoolmistress?"

Brodie nodded again. "If you'd prefer. I don't know anyone off-hand but I can make enquiries. Though I have to say, man or woman, you'll be doing well to find someone as well qualified as my friend Daniel."

"Why do you say that?"

She hesitated a moment. It was no one else's business; except that maybe, just a little, it was Hugo's. And it wasn't as though it was a secret. "Because Daniel knows about pain. It makes him the ideal person to help your nieces deal with theirs. Listen, why don't you meet him? If you'd still rather hire a woman he'll understand. But when you talk to him you might agree with me that you've been lucky to find him."

"Daniel?" said Hugo doubtfully.

"Daniel Hood."

# Chapter Three

Brodie rang the number of Marta's flat, above her own. Daniel was lodging with Brodie's Polish neighbour while his house was rebuilt. Since Marta was a music teacher working from home it wasn't an ideal arrangement, but it was the best they could think of at short notice. They'd imagined he'd be under his own roof again by the end of the summer. But four months after the fire Daniel was still waiting for his roof to go on.

No one answered the phone, so Marta was shopping and Daniel was down at the shore. Brodie reached for her jacket. "This way, Mr Daws. He's probably arguing with his builders – let's go and cheer him up."

A short walk took them down Fisher Hill to the Promenade where they turned right towards the pier, a finger of black timber pointing sullenly out to sea. Brodie indicated the tar-boarded netting sheds. There used to be three of them: now there were two and a building site.

"What happened?" asked Hugo.

Brodie considered. "Some people blamed him for something that wasn't his fault. They burned him out."

The tall man broke his stride and stared at her, appalled. "This is the man you're recommending as a tutor for my nieces?"

She bristled slightly. "Daniel did nothing wrong – ask Jack Deacon. Or if it makes you nervous, forget it. It's nothing to me, I'm not his agent. He's a friend, that's all. And a good teacher, and a good man."

Hugo thought for a moment. Then he shrugged awkwardly. "I suppose, while we're here, we could say hello."

Dimmock was not one of the south coast's leading resorts. It couldn't boast miles of sandy beach, smart hotels or a marina full of gin-palace cruisers. It had a stony shore, a derelict pier and a crazy golf course, and the general feeling was that anyone who wanted more excitement than that should be in Acapulco.

It also had, until comparatively recently, a small fishing fleet. The boats were launched by tractor straight from the beach. EEC grants and factory fishing put an end to that, so now all that remained were a rotting hulk by the pier and the netting sheds, two-storey structures built on the shingle just out of reach of the fifty-year wave. Four months ago the one nearest the pier had provided a pleasant flat with unrivalled sea views for a single man unburdened by too many possessions.

Now it provided him with not so much a hobby as a magnum opus – the restoration of a traditional building using materials that satisfied both the eye and the Building Control Officer, in the hands of builders whose answer to every problem was, "Whack a bit off that breeze-block."

There were half a dozen men on the site this morning but Brodie had no difficulty locating Daniel. Partly because in any group of men he was likely to be the shortest; partly because of his yellow hair, bright as sunshine; but mainly because of something it was hard to put into words. He was a twenty-seven-year-old maths teacher with the gentle manner of a curate and the stature of a fifteen-year-old boy, yet somehow he had a presence. He stood there on the stony shore, spare frame wrapped in an old guernsey, yellow hair batting in the breeze against the thick round lenses shielding his pale grey eyes, and Brodie felt she should be worried about the tough, bluff, street-wise builders walking all over him.

But she wasn't, and the reason was that Daniel Hood could hold his own against anyone not actually armed with a shot-gun. He was intelligent, articulate, and as quietly determined as a raindrop is to reach the sea. If he said he wanted Scandinavian pine for the weatherboarding, Mr Wilmslow of Wilmslow Construction might as well stop arguing that a lick of black paint on larch-lap would look the same and start telephoning Norwegian timber-merchants.

"Daniel."

He heard her above the hiss and chink of the shingle and turned, his plain round face already framing a smile. Brodie beckoned. "Mr Daws and I are going for a coffee. Join us – he may have a job for you."

He looked interested. Then he looked at his work-grimed sweater. "I'm not dressed for eating out."

Brodie sniffed. "Actually, I heard Claridges had dropped their plan to take over *The Singing Kettle*."

Daniel grinned and they trooped across the promenade together.

Daniel read *The Sentinel* too. He knew who Hugo Daws was as soon as he began his account. "How can I help?"

"Mr Daws needs a tutor for his nieces," said Brodie. "Their mother was teaching them at home."

"How old are they?"

"Juanita's fourteen," said Daws. "Emerald's eleven."

Brodie bit down on a laugh. But Daniel had taught a Marilyn Monroe – children's names had long lost their capacity to surprise him. "Are you thinking of this as a permanent arrangement?"

Hugo shook his head. "I want to take them back to Johannesburg when I can. It shouldn't take more than three months, it might be less. But it's too long to leave them to their own devices. It's not even the education they're missing, it's the lack of structure to their day. I think it would help to restore some semblance of normality."

Daniel thought so too. "I've no one coming for tutoring at the moment. It's too early in the school year: parents don't start panicking till after Christmas usually. The only thing I have to do is keep an eye on progress across the road. Otherwise I can fit in with whatever hours you have in mind."

"According to the girls, they work for four hours in the

morning and finish at lunchtime," said Hugo. "Your afternoons would be your own."

Daniel nodded amiably. "Then I'm at your disposal. I'm a maths teacher really, but I can cover the physical sciences up to GCSE, and given a few hours with the textbooks I could keep them ticking over in the rest of the curriculum. Except sport: I know nothing about sport. And cooking. And languages too, actually, but I'll have a go. If their French is better than mine they can teach me. If you want to give it a try."

From the pause that followed it was clear that Hugo still had reservations. He was honest enough to say what they were. "I was really looking for a woman. You know, with them being girls ... "

Daniel nodded again. "That's reasonable. I taught mixed classes, I still take pupils of both sexes, but if you'd be happier with a woman I'll ask around, see who's available."

It was almost impossible to talk to Daniel Hood for any length of time and not like him. Hugo was already wondering if his reservations were anything more than bigotry. "Can I ask where it was you taught? And why you left?"

Brodie looked away. But it was an entirely appropriate question that Daniel was willing to answer. "Dimmock High School. I was there for almost a year – talk to the principal before you make a decision. I quit because of an accident that left me with a stress problem. I hope to go back sometime."

"An accident?" Hugo suspected he was being rude, but he was responsible for the well-being of two young girls and before he left them with anyone he wanted to know they'd be safe.

Daniel smiled gently. "I bumped into a sadist." He explained what had happened; at least, as much as had been in the papers.

They continued talking over the coffee and scones, and it struck Brodie that although the job had not formally been offered, in fact the deal had been done. She was glad. She thought it would be good for Daniel – not only financially, though she knew the rebuild was proving an economic strain, but in terms of easing him back into full-time employment. She believed it would be good for the girls too. They were inside a nightmare: who better to guide them through it than a man who had rebuilt his own life, brick by brick, recently enough to remember how?

Daniel said, "We'll need to clear it with the girls. Are you going back there now?"

Daws nodded. "Do you want to follow me up?"

"I don't have a car."

The tall man blinked. Of course, he came from a land where distance was measured not in miles but in hours or days. "All right, I'll bring you back when we're finished."

"And I'll come over tomorrow morning," said Brodie. "I need to look at Serena's belongings for any clues to Constance's whereabouts." She checked her notes. "Poole Lane. That's off the Guildford Road, yes? – a couple of miles out of town."

Hugo nodded. "There's a farmyard opposite the drive. Once you turn in you'll see the house."

"A big house, is it?" asked Daniel. His experience of big houses hadn't always been happy.

Hugo shrugged. "Fairly big. It was a good house in its day, but the land was sold off generations ago and it went quietly downhill for a hundred years.

"When Robert – " He stopped, as if just speaking his brother's name had been a breach of taste. Then without prompting he set his jaw and continued with what he had been about to say. Brodie respected that. She knew it took more guts than simply changing the subject. "When Robert turned a modest family business into a retail empire he did the place up. But I don't think he's done much with it recently. The paint's beginning to flake again."

"Was it your family home?" asked Brodie.

The tall man nodded again. "I grew up there. When our mother died twelve years ago Robert decided to keep the

25

place and moved his family in. That was the last time I was home until ... this ... happened."

"It must have come as a terrible shock," said Brodie quietly.

"It did," Hugo said simply. "But I've wondered since if it should have done. I knew they weren't happy. I knew Robert was driven to despair sometimes. He's a quiet man, a gentle man, but even gentle people can be pushed over the edge if someone's determined to do it.

"At first I didn't believe it. I couldn't imagine the circumstances that would make a murderer of my kind, considerate brother. Now I've come to terms with the reality that Robert stabbed his wife, but I still can't get my head around the fact that by doing so he abandoned his children. Whether he skipped the country or stayed and went to prison, that was the inevitable result of what he did. He thought the world of those girls, and they of him."

"Perhaps he was just too distraught to think through the consequences," murmured Brodie. "He felt betrayed and struck out in blind anger. If there hadn't been a knife handy he'd probably have slapped her face. Of course he's responsible for what he did, but not for the situation he found himself in."

"He killed her!"

"I know. But he's not the first decent man to do something terrible. We think murder is the ultimate crime, and in a way it is. But it doesn't need a criminal to commit it. A momentary loss of control and a handy implement – a kitchen knife, a golf club, a flight of stairs – and someone's dead who ought to be getting a severe talking-to, and someone who ought to be getting tea and sympathy is a killer. I can't imagine resorting to blackmail, extortion or robbery. I *can* imagine striking out in pain and fury and finding myself on a murder charge."

Hugo Daws met her gaze. He wasn't sure if it was the truth, but if it was a lie he appreciated it. "I was fond of

Robert. I still am. I know what he's done can't be mended or forgiven, but I can't bring myself to blame him. I blame her."

"That's what families are for," agreed Brodie. "Loving unconditionally. Believing in us when we're least worthy of it."

Until quite recently Jack Deacon's idea of a social life had been a pint after work with Charlie Voss. Mostly they did this when he needed someone to bounce ideas off and the overtime allocation didn't stretch to doing it in the office. He thought Detective Sergeant Voss was unaware of this. In fact, Voss not only knew what was going on but actively encouraged it. In order to hear Superintendent Deacon think aloud about an investigation he'd not only have stayed late without being paid, he'd have brought the beer.

Getting to know Brodie Farrell had expanded Deacon's horizons immeasurably. They went out for meals, went home for coffee; occasionally she dragged him round an art gallery or to the theatre; occasionally he dragged her on a three mile walk across the downs, at the end of which he was just getting into his stride and she was exhausted. She hadn't seen him as an outdoors man. He was a Londoner, as she was, despatched to Dimmock by superiors who, since they couldn't stop him being offensive, had thought to put him where there was no one important to offend. He'd caused considerable irritation at Divisional Headquarters by solving some high-profile crimes and winning promotion.

Not that Brodie was the first woman he'd known. He'd had girlfriends before; he'd even married one of them. That was a long time ago and he wasn't keen to repeat the experience. For living with he was pretty well satisfied with his cat, a vast malevolent tom called Dempsey.

But it was a nice change that sometimes when his phone rang it wasn't someone's brief uttering veiled threats, or his own superiors uttering overt ones, but an attractive intelligent woman seeking his company for lunch.

27

Even in the middle of a murder inquiry a man has to take nourishment. He opened Voss's door and said, "I'm going for something to eat. I'll be back in an hour. If you need me before that – "

"I know," said Voss, nodding his ginger head. "The little French place in Bank Lane."

Deacon smiled complacently. "I was going to say, tough."

He had a fair idea why Brodie wanted to see him and she quickly confirmed it. "Hugo Daws called with me this morning. He wants me to look for Serena's sister. I said I'd have to check with you first."

"By all means," said Deacon, buttering his roll. "If I had the time I'd look for her myself. I don't want him to take the girls out of the country – they're my witnesses, I need to be able to talk to them; when I find Robert the court will want to hear from them. But I don't want to see them in care either. No, you find their aunt if you can. If I can help I will."

"I thought I'd go up to Sparrow Hill tomorrow and take a look at Serena's things. She may have some old letters, photographs, something like that."

"We didn't find anything helpful. But then, that wasn't our priority. Go ahead, we're finished at the house."

"No mysteries left, then?"

"Only where Daws is holed up. But he's a businessman, he has a lot of contacts both in England and abroad. I don't doubt he could get himself smuggled out of the country if he wanted."

"Shades of Lord Lucan."

Deacon's upper lip curled. He'd been a policeman for more than twenty years but he'd never learned to be philosophical about the ones that got away. "He wasn't my case."

Brodie tried not to smile. He had no sense of humour where his job was concerned. She said, "You didn't tell me he wanted a tutor for the girls."

He shrugged. "I thought he'd tell you."

"You could have mentioned Daniel. You know he needs the work."

Deacon pushed his big body back in the chair and eyed her speculatively. "Brodie, do you want to have this argument again right now? Or shall we put it off till we've more time and less of an audience?"

"You're not fair to him," she said evenly.

"So you keep telling me. Look, I know he's a friend of yours. Damn it, I like the man myself. But he's not – reliable. I'd be uneasy leaving children of mine in his care, and I wouldn't advise anyone else to."

Despite her best intentions Brodie felt her hackles rise. "You have no reason to feel that way. Daniel Hood has never hurt a soul in his life. He's taken punishment himself rather than see other people hurt. I would trust him with my life, and my daughter's life."

"I know he's a good man, Brodie. But he makes bad decisions, and whether or not he means to he puts other people at risk. He's put you at risk, and Paddy. And if Robert Daws comes back for his daughters I don't want Daniel to be all that's in his way. I don't want to lose my witnesses because a man with more ethics than common sense stayed to talk when he should have grabbed them and run."

# Chapter Four

"I don't know what you'll make of them," confessed Hugo as he drove out of Dimmock towards the green hem of the downs. "God knows I'm no expert – Peris and I have none of our own – but they don't strike me as entirely normal." He cast a troubled glance at the man beside him. "I shouldn't be saying this, should I? Not if I want you to take the job."

"If you want me to take the job," said Daniel patiently, "I'll take it, unless the girls want you to keep looking. As for how they seem, it's a miracle they're still functioning at all. Their father murdered their mother almost in front of them. They were the last to see Serena alive, the first to see her dead. Their world was destroyed in the space of a few minutes."

"I hadn't forgotten," said Hugo, quietly reproachful. "And if that's all it is, then fine. Of course it's been traumatic; of course they need time to get over it. It's just, they don't seem traumatised so much as – detached. I find it quite intimidating. They look at you as if you're trying their patience just by being there. As if you've turned up at an important meeting with the wrong papers."

Daniel chuckled. He'd been a teacher all his working life, knew that children had many different ways of disturbing adults. Those that weren't punishable were the hardest to deal with. Sometimes even experienced teachers became paranoid, no longer saw children but little blazered aliens plotting world domination. "Did you know them before this happened?"

Hugo shook his head. "We came over for my mother's funeral, but Juanita was only a toddler and Emerald wasn't even born then."

"Their mother's decision to teach them at home was perfectly valid – the law requires them to receive a suitable education 'in school or otherwise' – but there are drawbacks.

Funnily enough the standard of teaching isn't usually one. Anyone willing to put in time and effort can do a perfectly adequate job. What's harder is to duplicate the gradual accumulation of experience. Kids learn most of their social skills at school, through the constant interactions with other people – children, adults, friends, strangers, people they like, people they don't.

"They get an understanding of how the world works which home-educated children don't always have. They tend to be hot-house flowers: flourishing in their own environment, prone to wilt out in the cold hard world. Many of them have problems with self-confidence. Maybe that's what you're seeing in your nieces. They know things are never going to be the same again, and they don't know how they'll manage. Keeping their distance, staying aloof, makes them feel safer."

Hugo glanced at him again, this time with respect. "You're good at this, aren't you?"

"I never wanted to be anything but a teacher," said Daniel simply. "No, that's not true, I wanted to be an astronaut but I'm too short-sighted. Teaching isn't about knowing the subject: it's about knowing children. What motivates them. What worries them. How to guide them from where they are to where they need to be."

"If you find out what motivates these two," said Hugo glumly, "you might let me know."

Serena Daws hadn't seen educating her own children as the easy option. She'd done it properly. She'd furnished a room on the second floor of her house with a big deal table, a computer and shelves groaning with books. There was a blackboard, a projector, and a map of the world covering most of the end wall that had been renewed as recently as the previous year. Mrs Daws had taken her obligations seriously, at least where her daughters were concerned.

The younger girl was sitting at the table drawing when

the two men came in. The older one was perched on the window-seat, looking out over the garden with studied nonchalance.

Hugo performed stilted introductions. At fourteen Juanita was a tall strongly-built girl with long chestnut hair that fell in waves down her back. Emerald, at eleven, was not just younger but also smaller and fairer, a mousy little creature with a sharply pointed face and bright blue eyes.

Daniel knew better than to be chummy with them. More than most, these children would be acutely sensitive to insincerity. He didn't try to shake their hands but left his own in his pockets and nodded gravely. "I'm pleased to meet you."

Both girls nodded back, Juanita staring off over his left shoulder, Emerald peering up at his face with disconcerting directness. Neither offered a word of reply.

He could deal with dumb insolence, but actually he didn't think it was that. He suspected they were feeling desperately insecure and trying not to show it. They weren't just meeting a new teacher. They were meeting their first new teacher ever. They had no idea what was expected of them.

They might have been relieved to know that Daniel had very few expectations, was here not to judge but be judged. If he could help them he would; if he couldn't he'd let someone else try. He agreed with Hugo, that re-establishing a routine would be a positive move and that lessons could provide a framework around which normality would grow. But right now it wasn't fractions and French verbs they needed help with so much as getting through one day, and then getting through the next.

If they had reacted to their tragedy with screams, bed-wetting and smashing the furniture they'd be seeing a child psychiatrist now. Because they had internalised the horror, relying on one another for support instead of turning to those around them, there was the danger that they would appear to be coping better than they were. Daniel was full of admiration for them. In the circumstances, anything short of babbling insanity was a major achievement. But he also knew that you can't lock up that much rage and grief forever. At some point they would need to release it, and facilitating that was a job for which he was neither trained nor qualified. But he did have personal experience to rely on.

Still defensive about his wards, Hugo felt obliged to break the silence. "Mr Hood could come and tutor you if you'd like that."

Juanita said distantly, "Fine." Emerald said, "OK." By a narrow margin they were too polite to say that they couldn't care less, but the message got through just the same.

Their uncle looked worried, but Daniel chuckled. "Wrong question. If you ask, 'Do you want to work or not?' the answer's obvious. You should have said, 'Do you want to work with this guy, who seems like a push-over, or will you risk me hiring an ex-military policewoman who'll have you standing to attention and singing the National Anthem every morning?'"

Hugo grinned. Daniel caught a quick, curious glance from the older girl. He looked round the school-room and then out of the window. "It's a nice room. But until we decide to do this, maybe we'd be better on neutral ground. Why don't we go for a walk? You can show me the garden."

Outside everyone relaxed. Hugo fell back a step, pretending to inspect the hydrangeas. Emerald appointed herself to the rôle of guide. "Sparrow Hill is a Georgian house, built in 1805 for Edward Foster who was a merchant. What's a merchant?"

"Someone who buys things cheaply that other people are prepared to buy dear," said Daniel.

Satisfied, she carried on. "There are five bedrooms and four reception rooms but only one bathroom, so the early bird catches the hot water. Originally the house was surrounded by a thousand acres of land, but most of it was sold after the First World War. When the three sons of the Foster family died in the Second World War the house passed to a nephew. That was Grandpa Daws, and he left it to Daddy." Her little face clouded. "I don't know what'll happen to it now."

Daniel said quietly, "I'm sorry about what happened. I know I can't replace your mother, even in the schoolroom. I don't intend to try. But I would like us to be friends. And if it's what you want too, I'd like to be your teacher."

Juanita was drifting along beside them, at a carefully judged distance so that she could ignore any conversation that didn't interest her and join in any that did. She shrugged. "Whatever."

Daniel's pale eyes creased behind his glasses. "A little enthusiasm would be nice, but I guess 'whatever' is better than 'no'. Juanita's an interesting name. Is it Spanish?"

"No," she said shortly.

Even in normal circumstances a fourteen-year-old girl carries a rag doll on one arm and a baby on the other. Her hormones are telling her she's a woman, her parents are telling her she's a child. Her physical structure is changing daily: if mood-swings are all those around her have to deal with she's handling puberty pretty well.

He tried his luck with the other one. "And Emerald's a gem."

The younger girl rewarded him with a toothy smile, and got an elbow in the ribs for her pains. "Actually," she confided, sparing her sister a hurt look, "we don't much like our names."

"They're pretty," said Daniel, "but perhaps a shade decorative for everyday use. What would you rather be called?"

"Johnny calls me Em," volunteered the eleven-year-old. And then, somewhat superfluously, "I call her Johnny."

"Is that what you want me to call you?"

They traded a glance. "You can do," said Johnny indifferently.

"What do we call you?" asked Em, peering intently into his face again.

34

He almost asked, "What did you call your last teacher?" But the answer was too painfully obvious, and they sure as hell wouldn't be calling him Mummy. "When I taught in school they called me Mr Hood, but with just three of us it might sound a bit silly. I'm happy with Daniel if you are."

"Daniel in the lion's den," said Em with a grin.

"Not an original observation," murmured Daniel, "but sometimes that's how it feels."

Johnny eyed him mockingly. "Don't you like teaching?"

"Of course I like teaching. It's why I'm here. But it's not easy. Even with just three of us I'm outnumbered. I can't make you learn anything, but if you don't it's my job on the line. I need your help, your goodwill, much more than you need mine. If this doesn't work out it's my failure, not yours."

Johnny gave that some thought. "You mean, we could sack you?"

Daniel laughed. "Not unless you're planning on paying my wages. But you could make it impossible for me to stay."

Again the swift exchange of glances, the trade in messages no one else was meant to read. Em said diffidently, "I don't think we'd do that. Would we, Johnny?"

Johnny gave a negligent shrug. "I'm not making any promises. But we can give it a try."

"All right," said Daniel. "Good."

He and Hugo sorted out the details. "I'll check the times of the buses," said Daniel. "Is it OK if we fit school hours around them?"

"Of course," nodded Hugo. "But it's a hell of a walk from the bus-stop."

Daniel grinned. "People with cars think it's a hell of a walk to the bottom of their drive. It won't take me ten minutes from the Guildford Road."

"And from where you're living to the bus-station?"

"About the same."

Hugo shook his head in disbelief. "You'd walk forty minutes a day rather than learn how to drive?"

35

"I can drive," protested Daniel. "I just don't have a car. I've never felt the need."

"Suppose I hire a car for you?"

"Suppose you let me worry about getting here?"

Hugo laughed. He'd been worried about his nieces before he got here, and increasingly in the time he'd spent with them. A lot of that worry had now lifted off his shoulders. He suspected they'd met their match in Daniel Hood. He only looked like a push-over. Behind that round, amiable face and the thick glasses was a surprisingly resilient young man.

Another thought occurred to him. He turned it over a couple of times but couldn't see any drawbacks. Or only one, and maybe he was being over-sensitive. "You're living with a friend, yes? While they repair your house?"

The word "repair" hardly covered it but Daniel nodded.

"There's a cottage at the back here. Why don't you move in? It'd save you time and shoe-leather, and by the time things are sorted out here maybe your house will be finished."

A few weeks, he'd said. Daniel couldn't see Mr Wilmslow being finished in a few weeks – sometimes he didn't think he'd ever finish, that he'd haunt the place in perpetuity – but if nothing else it would give Marta a few weeks' respite. She had taken him in without question, but none of them had expected the work to take so long. Now he was trapped between imposing on her further or causing offence by looking for a cheap hotel. But if his work required it she could enjoy his absence with a clear conscience.

"Fine," he said. "Knock the rent off my wages."

"Have a look round the place," suggested Hugo, "tell my wife if there's anything you need – towels, blankets, whatever. I'll get her to stock the fridge for you."

Daniel hoped the girls would show him the cottage. But they claimed business elsewhere and vanished round the side of the stone house.

It must have been a beautiful house when Edward Foster built it; Hugo said it was again after his brother renovated it; but it wasn't now. It was starting to look neglected. Too many winters had got under the paint on the window-frames, and there was a scum of green algae like a tide-mark on the walls. Perhaps if there had been more love in the house it would have rubbed off. Now it was too late for Serena and too late for Robert; but the house could recover, given a little care and attention, and so could the children.

He found the cottage by himself. The plank door was unlocked: inside it was clean and bright, well-furnished and recently decorated. There was a living-room and a compact kitchen on the ground floor, two bedrooms and a tiny bath-room above.

The front of the living-room was just that, chairs and a sofa, a gate-legged table and a television. But the back wall had been replaced by french windows, letting the light flood in. It was Serena's studio: here were her paints, her easels and her canvases.

For a moment Daniel regarded them from across the room, reluctant to intrude. But he couldn't live here without doing just that, and perhaps this was what the family needed: someone with no baggage moving in and simply living there, diluting the tragedy in the minutiae of daily existence.

Because this was where Serena died. Daniel hadn't realised before, and if Hugo Daws hadn't exactly lied he also hadn't been entirely frank. Now Daniel was here the newspaper reports made sense. This was where Robert Daws stabbed his wife thirteen times and let her bleed to death. Someone had cleaned up but eight days ago the floor was still wet with it, the air sweet with the stench, and the ribbons of slashed can-vas lay thick about her.

Daniel wondered how he felt about that. He didn't believe in ghosts. He didn't think that bricks and mortar could see and hear and remember. He didn't think that what happened here a week ago was reason to avoid the place forever more.

But if Hugo had warned him at least Daniel wouldn't have asked the girls to show him round.

He went looking for the tall man to tell him so.

# Chapter Five

Following the sound of a radio Daniel entered Sparrow Hill through a back door and found himself in the kitchen. A woman was bent over the worktop, sleeves rolled up over muscular forearms the colour of mahogany, applying herself with gusto to the contents of a mixing bowl.

Daniel cleared his throat. "I was looking for Hugo."

The woman turned to him with a smile. The face matched the arms: strong, broad, dark and capable. She was taller than him and twice as far round, with her hair piled high and tied with a coloured cloth. "You must be Daniel," she said. "I'm Peris – Hugo's wife."

"Hello." He offered his hand, saw the flour on hers and hesitated. They both laughed.

"Taken as read," she suggested. "You do much baking, Daniel?"

He shook his head. "I'm a great heater-up of packaged food. My friend Brodie bakes occasionally, mostly when she's angry. She says it gives her something to thump that won't thump back."

Peris chuckled. "That's English women for you. In Africa, if you can't cook you not only go hungry, you go lonely." She looked around. "Hugo. He came through a minute ago – I'm not sure where he was going. You could try the attic."

"The attic?" Daniel's brow was puzzled.

"He and Robert grew up here, all their old toys are still there. The second night we were here I lost him for an hour, and that's where he was – up in the attic, brushing the cobwebs off the rocking-horse, patching up the puppet theatre."

Daniel perched on a handy stool. "It must have been strange for him, coming back in these circumstances."

Peris Daws regarded him evenly. "It was. Strange and difficult. This was his home, then it was his brother's home,

39

now he's back and Robert's on the run. I think he's afraid Robert will resent him for that."

"I'm sure Robert's grateful someone's looking after his daughters. He must have been worried sick after he came to his senses." Daniel hesitated. There were things he wanted to know – needed to know if he wasn't to risk hurting his pupils again – and it occurred to him that Peris might find it easier to talk than her husband would.

She saw him deliberating with himself and prompted him. "Daniel?"

"Can you tell me what happened? I know what was in the papers, but they can't always give much detail. It would be useful to know what you know, what the girls know. I won't be giving evidence in court, it doesn't matter if some of it's only supposition. But I'm going to be working with two traumatised children and I don't want to say the wrong things. For instance, if Hugo had told me it was Serena's studio, and therefore where she died, I wouldn't have asked them to show me the cottage."

Peris's eyes narrowed for an instant, then she nodded. "That makes sense. You might as well know, as much as we can tell you. What do you know already?"

"That Robert stabbed his wife. That she was seeing another man. That the girls found the body. And now, that it happened in the cottage."

Peris sighed. She left her baking, towelled off her arms and came to sit beside him. "Everyone knew about Robert and Serena. I understand they were happy once, but they hardly went anywhere in recent years that they didn't leave either separately or in a temper. Most people blamed Serena, but then she was easy to blame. Flamboyant, you know? If she wasn't the centre of attention she'd do something to make sure she was.

"There was a string of young men. I don't how much they meant to her, but if they meant much you'd have thought there'd be fewer. She didn't stay long with any of them: she *did* stay with Robert. I suspect they were Serena's way of saying he wasn't paying her enough attention."

She rocked on the stool like a hen settling on eggs. "Robert's a nice man. I'd have said he was a good man. He worked hard, and he gave Serena everything you can go into a shop and buy. In spite of that, they weren't a good match. Serena craved glamour, and Robert was never glamorous. He's ten years older – she was thirty-six – and he seems older than that. He's quiet, sober and industrious, and he spent the day making expensive decisions and all he wanted was a nice family to come home to at night. What he had was Serena: perfectly groomed, beautifully dressed, capable of turning every head in a big room, still wanting him to dance attendance on her the way he did when they were courting. Punishing him when he was too tired to."

She used her affairs as a goad, Peris said. There was no shortage of men who would spend time with her, and she used them, discarding them when her point was made. "That was almost the saddest thing. The man this was really all about was Robert."

And the second saddest thing was that as Serena got older the men got younger. "The latest was nineteen, for heaven's sake! Young enough to be her son. Robert annoyed her, and she went down to the bottom of the drive and seduced the first thing to walk past in jeans. Nicky Speers – he works at the farm across the road. I don't blame him for any of this. How many nineteen-year-olds *could* resist a beautiful, sophisticated, wealthy woman waving her knickers at them? She said she wanted to paint him." Her opinion of that hung unspoken in the air.

"But she was an artist," ventured Daniel.

Peris looked at him speculatively. "Did you see her paintings?" Daniel shook his head. "No," said Peris, "I don't think they're in the cottage now. Hugo took them up to the attic. Come and look."

Daniel met her gaze fearlessly. "Mrs Daws – are you inviting me upstairs to see your etchings?"

Some cliches don't travel. It took her a moment to understand. When she did she laughed out loud and slapped his shoulder hard enough to rock him. "You should be so lucky!"

Hugo heard footsteps on the wooden stair and met them at the top. "Is everything all right?"

"I want Daniel to see the paintings."

He looked as if he might object. Then he shrugged and stood back, and Peris led the way to the last of three attic store-rooms where a rack of canvases leaned against the wall, hiding their faces. She waved an arm in invitation. "You tell me if she was an artist."

Daniel turned the top four canvases to the room. Then he stood back, quietly observing. He didn't claim to be an expert but he reckoned to know the difference between a good painting and a bad one. And now he understood Peris's difficulty. Serena Daws had been a good painter. She had not been a good artist.

"Technically," he said at length, "they're superb. She's deliberately set herself challenges – capturing different textures, and the play of light on this silvery fabric – and met them all. And the flesh-tones: there must be twenty shades blending in that boy's skin. But ... "

"Yes?" said Peris softly.

"There's no soul in it, is there? No attempt to capture his personality. She doesn't care about his personality. She's meticulous about recreating the physical image – they're almost photographic – but you end up knowing nothing about either the sitter or the artist. Which is bizarre, because – " He looked up, carefully. "Well, this is him, isn't it? Her lover."

Hugo's voice was low. "Yes, that's him. That's the boy who wrecked my brother's life and made virtual orphans of my nieces."

Daniel wasn't sure it was fair comment, but perhaps fairness was too much to ask just yet. "I thought Robert slashed the paintings."

"Just the one that she was working on. She had a lot of paintings of Nicky Speers, all of them like this. After I found them in the cupboard in the studio, finally I understood. Until then I hadn't really believed Robert had done what he was supposed to have done. He isn't a violent person – in any conflict he was always more likely to be the victim than the aggressor. But when I found these I could see how even a gentle man could be pushed too far. I think, for the few minutes it took, he was literally insane. I think she drove him mad."

Daniel looked at the painting again, trying to see something human in the flawless specimen on the canvas. After a moment he started to. Not in the swelling muscles, honed by physical labour and recorded in a detail that was more scientific than loving; not in the perfect nineteen-year-old body rendered decent by an errant fold of the silvery fabric positioned so calculatingly that he managed to look more naked than he would have stepping out of his shower; but in the eyes. They were brown, deeply set, sensitive, and afraid.

Daniel touched the paint and found it hard, weeks old. When Nicky Speers posed for this painting the affair was new, the excitement high, the coming tragedy yet to cast its shadow over them. But even then, at a time when he was sufficiently captivated by Serena Daws that he was not only bedding a woman seventeen years his senior but also sitting for her – or sprawling, like the centrefold from a top-shelf women's magazine, pushed and prodded into an essay in soft pornography that stripped him of his dignity even more comprehensively than of his clothes – even then he was afraid of her. He knew what she was capable of. He was riding the tiger partly for the thrill but mainly because he was already too scared to get off.

Daniel straightened and turned the paintings to the wall again. "We'd better put them back in the cottage. The girls probably play up here too."

43

Hugo had the grace to look embarrassed. "I didn't want you stumbling on them."

Daniel shrugged. "Rather me than the girls."

They bundled them up in an old curtain and took them back to the studio. If the girls saw, they stayed out of the way. Once the canvases were back in the cupboard where Hugo had found them Daniel gave his employer a reproachful look. "You might have told me this was where Serena died."

"I should have. I – " Hugo shrugged awkwardly – "still don't find it easy to talk about."

"Peris was telling me what happened. I need to know the facts if I'm to help the girls deal with them. Can you finish the story?"

"How far did you get?"

"She told me a lot about your brother and his wife, not about how Serena ended up dead."

"Robert stabbed her," said Hugo briefly. "Thirteen times. And smashed the phone so she couldn't call for help."

Daniel winced. "How much did the girls see?"

"They heard shouting and peeped over the windowsill. Robert and Serena were fighting over" – he nodded at the cupboard door. "The girls knew what it was about. Serena hadn't tried to be discreet – they'd met here in the studio while the girls were in the house. They knew exactly what had been going on."

Hugo swallowed. "They say Robert was crying. That he disappeared into the kitchen and came back with a knife. When he began slashing the painting Serena flew at him, beating him with her fists. At that point the girls got scared and ran away.

"When they thought the drama would be over they came back. They found Serena dead in a pool of blood with the smashed phone beside her. They ran over the road in hysterics. Philip Poole couldn't get any sense out of them so he came to see what had happened. Then, of course, he called the police.

"That's about it. I'm sorry I wasn't straight with you. Would you rather not stay here now?"

"It's not that," said Daniel. "I just needed to know the truth. I know talking about it's painful."

Hugo nodded tersely. "It's awful. I love my brother – I still love my brother – but I really keep hoping the police will call and say they've got him. Not because I want to see him punished, but while he's missing everything's in limbo. We can't begin to sort out what happens to the girls or the house or anything. He's an innocent man until proved otherwise, and that can't even begin until he's found. Or gives himself up. That's what I'm praying for. But it's been eight days. If he was going to, surely he'd have done it by now?"

Daniel thought so too. His silence was answer enough.

"Grocery is an international business: Robert has contacts all over the world," said Hugo. It wasn't a boast. "They're bound to include people who, if he said he needed to flee the country, could whistle up an executive jet and have him safe abroad within hours. Maybe that's what happened. Maybe he's sitting by a kidney-shaped swimming pool right now, sipping a daiquiri and chuckling over the mess he's left behind."

"Is that what you think?"

Hugo flicked him a haunted look. "No. If he turned to someone in desperation and that was what they suggested, he may have gone along with it. But wherever he is, however safe he feels, what he's done will be tearing him apart.

"You never met my brother so this will sound pretty stupid, but Robert's a good man. A man you couldn't help but admire. Not because he was successful in business and made a lot of money, but because he was the soul of decency. He always was, even when we were boys. He was three years older than me so maybe it's partly hero-worship, but up to last week I thought he was the most honourable man I ever knew. I was proud of him. He was sure as hell too good for Serena. The only thing she wanted from him was his credit card. It broke my heart to see him wasted on flashy trash like her."

Hearing himself he stopped abruptly, flushing like a schoolboy. "I'm sorry. Whatever she did she's paid for, I shouldn't abuse her now she can't fight back. But I can't help the way I feel. She did this. He wielded the knife but she put it in his hand. She made a killer out of a man I thought the world of, and I'm afraid I'm never going to see him again."

"He may come home," said Daniel softly. "Once the dust settles and he realises there's no future worth having until this is dealt with. It may take weeks or even months. Whoever helped him will try to talk him out of it, it'll take time for him to know his own mind. But perhaps an honourable man would rather pay the bill than slip away down a back alley."

Hugo nodded. Contrary to his expectations, talking had actually eased the burden. "Unfortunately I can't wait weeks. I'm getting panicky e-mails from my partners: I'm on a plane tomorrow. Peris will stay till the end of October in the hope that Mrs Farrell will find Constance."

"She's very good at what she does," said Daniel. "If anybody can find her, Brodie will."

"She speaks highly of you, too." Hugo ventured a slow grin. "Are you two some kind of a number?"

Daniel considered. "No. We really are just friends. We haven't even known one another that long. It's just, you know how you click with some people? You spend an hour together and it's like you've known them half your life? We clicked."

Hugo still didn't understand. "Then *why* aren't you a number? She's free, and you are. Unless – "

He didn't finish the sentence, but the thought went all the way. Daniel laughed aloud. "No, I'm not gay. There isn't a reason, only that's not the deal. She's my best friend; I may be hers. I think maybe a real friendship is too precious to risk by trying to turn it into something different."

"All right." But it was plain that Hugo was still perplexed and probably always would be. "How did you meet?"

For a moment he thought Daniel was changing the subject. "When you asked her to search for Constance, did she tell you that she didn't look for people?"

"Yes. She wanted Superintendent Deacon to confirm my bona fides before she went ahead."

"Did she tell you why?"

"She said she did it once and someone got hurt." Then his eyes, normally snug in their sun-trained wrinkles, widened.

Daniel smiled. "Yes. That was me."

Hugo wasn't sure he'd got this right. "She found you for people who wanted to hurt you. They hurt you so much that you had to give up your job. And this is the woman you call your best friend?"

"None of it was Brodie's fault," Danel said quietly. "They lied to her. She was their victim too."

"But – "

"I nearly died," said Daniel forcibly. "When I woke up, she was the one sitting with me. She told me what happened. Her part in it. Can you imagine the courage that took? I've never stopped admiring her for it."

Hugo shook his head in wonder. "I can't imagine being able to find that kind of forgiveness. I can't even find it for my brother. I wish I could."

"You will," said Daniel. "It takes time. You're still in shock. When it stops being news and starts being history, you'll get a sense of perspective. You'll be able to place responsibility without allocating blame."

"I doubt it."

"You have to. If you're going to look after your nieces you can't afford to stay angry with either of their parents. They'll never see their mother again, but they may eventually get their father back. If they've spent a decade hating him it'll be a lost opportunity. If there's any way to preserve communications between them you have to do it. And if you let the girls know how you feel, that Serena got her just deserts, they'll feel guilty about still loving and missing her. They need you to take a step back. To refrain from judgement.

"I'm not saying it'll be easy. But it could be the difference between those girls growing up with a bearable sorrow, and never getting past the rage and bitterness and confusion. They're too young to see it for themselves, but in order to reconcile those feelings they'll need to be able to accept both parents and the mistakes they made, and love them anyway if they still can."

He found Hugo staring at him as if he'd sprouted an extra head. "What?"

Hugo coughed to cover his confusion. "Nothing. I'm sorry. I expect you're right. Er – when we first met, and I wasn't convinced you were the right person for this job? I was wrong."

# Chapter Six

In the morning, after Brodie had taken Paddy to school and checked the office for messages, they piled Daniel's belongings into the back of her car and she drove him to Sparrow Hill. Peris had offered to collect him, but Brodie had work there too.

"I'm pretty sure they'll have thought to check her address book," said Daniel mildly. "If Serena had Constance's number they wouldn't have needed your services."

Brodie nodded. "I know. But there'll be a lot of old friends and acquaintances in that book, and some of them may have kept in touch with both sisters. But most people haven't the nerve to phone fifty strangers asking who they do and don't know, and asking again until they get an answer they believe. That's why I'm worth my fee. I don't care who I offend."

It was true: most people are too polite to be good at research. When she first moved into this field, which was when she was still working as a solicitor's clerk, Brodie had been embarrassed too. She was a well-brought-up young woman who found it hard to quiz total strangers. But she discovered that most of them were polite too, and if they could help they would. The only time they got aggressive was when they had something to hide, and that brought out the hunter in Brodie. Embarrassment gave way to cunning.

She dropped the back seat of the car and lifted the tail-gate. "How much are you taking with you?"

"Everything," said Daniel. When she saw his belongings lined up at the front door she realised it was a stupid question. Apart from the telescope, everything he owned was in one suitcase, and the suitcase was hers. He'd bought some clothes since the fire, and replaced the telescope and some of the books. He had no furniture, no equipment, no personal treasures of any kind. Nothing of his previous life had survived.

Losing his telescope caused him the most grief. It would also be hardest to replace. He'd made it himself, and it had taken time and facilities he couldn't duplicate in Marta's spare room. Eventually he would build another, bigger and better; until then he'd acquired a second-hand reflector whose mirrors were in good order even if the frame had seen better days. It was an alt-azimuth and he really wanted a motorised equatorial mounting; as against that, he could afford it. In astronomy the bells and whistles come pricy. Brodie suggested waiting until he could get what he wanted, but he seemed to think the universe would forget how it worked if he left it to its own devices for too long. Start contracting; develop a blue shift; go off in a huff and collapse in a Big Splat.

For the same reason he couldn't imagine spending even a few days at Sparrow Hill without his window on the stars. He unscrewed wing-nuts and disconnected struts until the telescope folded its scuffed legs like a tired flamingo and tucked itself meekly into the car. Daniel had already worked out that the terrace outside Serena's french windows would give him a firm footing and a commanding view.

Driving up Guildford Road Brodie asked what he'd made of the girls.

Daniel thought for a moment. "They're holding together by sheer willpower. The older girl's withdrawn, the younger one's too bright. They were right there when this thing blew up, they took the full impact; but when the dust cleared they sat up without a mark on them. They don't know how they're supposed to feel. I don't know if they've even begun grieving yet. I think they're still in denial."

Brodie frowned. "They must know what happened?"

"Of course they do. But they daren't admit how devastating it was. It changed their lives forever, practically and emotionally, but they're trying to ignore that. Compartmentalising:

putting it in a box and leaving it shut. Pretending it was no big deal so it can't go on hurting for too long.

"But it was a huge deal, and the repercussions will run for the rest of their lives, and when they start to confront it the grief and the fear will be overwhelming. At that point they'll need professional help, and I don't mean with calculus. I hope that by then we'll know each other well enough, they'll trust me enough, to tell me what they need."

Brodie glanced at him, affection laced with concern. "The things we get involved in! Daniel, don't – " She stopped.

He looked at her. "What?"

She drew a deep breath. "There's a lot of pain in that house. Don't get so close to the children that they end up dumping it on you. You were hired as their teacher: not their guardian, their shrink or their priest. You can't make everything all right for them. If you try they'll let you shoulder as much of the burden as you can carry – and when you fold under it they'll despise you. Keep a professional distance. It's in their interests as well as yours. I don't want to see you damaged by this."

His eyes were disappointed. She knew better than to meet them, to expose herself to their gentle, heart-stopping reproof until she heard herself apologising when she knew she was right. She knew Daniel. She knew his weaknesses, one of which was giving himself too generously to answer other people's needs. Time and again he failed to hold enough in reserve to protect himself. The danger of him doing it now, of trying so hard to protect these traumatised children that he'd be torn apart by the shrapnel, was both real and imminent.

"Don't do that," Brodie hissed in her teeth.

"Do what?"

"Look at me like that! Like I'm Snow White's wicked stepmother. Of course I want what's best for the girls. But I want them to get it from people who can help them without getting drawn into the tragedy. Your heart's in the right place, Daniel, but you never know where to stop. It's like being a blood-donor. It's a great, generous, humanitarian thing – unless you give more than you can spare and end up in a body-bag, which is plain stupid. Help them by all means. But don't let them feed off you."

Now he was annoyed. The fair brows gathered behind the bridge of his glasses, and if they'd been on foot he'd have drawn himself up to his full five-foot-seven. "I've never heard such nonsense! They're not vampires: they're two frightened little girls, and I'll help them any way I can. Just as – heaven forbid she should find herself in a similar situation – I'd try to help Paddy. Don't tell me to keep my distance: it's contact those girls need. If I was afraid to make contact I wouldn't be going there now."

They drove the rest of the way in silence.

Peris met them in the courtyard. "I thought you might need a hand." She looked in the back of the car. "I see I was wrong."

"I haven't a lot of worldly goods just now," explained Daniel.

Peris watched in puzzlement as he extricated the folded telescope. "What *is* that?"

"Daniel's teddy bear," said Brodie nastily, "he never goes anywhere without it. Mrs Daws, could you show me Serena's room? And anywhere else that she kept personal papers?"

They left Daniel to move in and set off for a tour of Sparrow Hill.

Serena's bedroom was on the first floor. It was clearly her bedroom, not hers and Robert's: the paper was a pretty floral, the curtains and bedspread bought to match. There was a double bed but one dressing-table, one chair, one wardrobe. There was no evidence of a man's presence anywhere in the room.

The dressing-table drawer was full of cosmetics. "Is there a study or a library somewhere?" asked Brodie. "With a desk she may have used?"

"This way." Peris took her downstairs to a small room at the side of the house overlooking the garden. It was another intensely feminine room: a small chintz sofa, a velvet slipper-chair and a delicate bonheur-de-jour for writing at. A silver frame on top held a picture of the girls on ponies.

Brodie opened the desk and began leafing through the pigeon-holes. She was searching for a diary, an address-book and any letters Serena had kept. When she had built a tidy pile on the writing surface she said, "Can I take these with me?"

Peris gave a slightly bemused shrug. "Sure. The police have finished here. But there's nothing about Constance. We checked."

"I know. But if I contact all these people, one of them may know where Constance is. Or know someone else who may know."

"How long's that going to take?"

Brodie wasn't going to tell her the truth, which was a few hours – she didn't pretend that what she did was difficult but there was no need to rub clients' faces in just how easy much of it was. She said, "I know time's an issue. Hopefully I'll have spoken to most of these people within a few days. I may have found Constance by then, or at least have got a line on her whereabouts. But don't be discouraged if it takes a little longer. It's surprisingly hard to disappear in this country. I'll find her before you need to go home.

"Of course, there's no guarantee she'll do as you ask. She might not want or be able to take on Serena's girls, even temporarily. Have you thought what you'll do if she says no?"

Peris sighed. "It won't be our decision. There are proce-dures to go through, paperwork to do, legal requirements to meet – we can't just buy a couple of extra plane seats and take them back with us. If Constance can't take them before I have to go home, the girls will go into care. We're hoping it won't be for too long and they'll come and join us when they're able to. But it's not something any of us is comfortable with."

She found a shopping-bag and Brodie shovelled the papers into it. Then she checked the room to make sure she'd missed nothing.

She found herself looking at the photograph on top of the desk again. She frowned. "When was this taken?"

Peris leaned over her shoulder. "Can't have been long ago or the girls would look younger."

"Then why are they wearing bowler hats? Adults can please themselves, but children have to wear proper riding-hats that meet modern safety standards." She knew this because Paddy wanted to start riding.

They studied the picture together: two girls in tweed jackets and baggy jodhpurs mounted on a couple of sharp-looking ponies. The truth dawned on both women at about the same time.

"Those aren't our girls," said Peris. "That's Serena, aged about twelve. It's twenty-five years since that picture was taken."

Brodie nodded. "And if that's Serena, the other girl is probably Constance. I'll take this too – it might help."

"Do you want to see the studio?"

"I'll stick my head in, see if Daniel's finished playing with his telescope."

Peris chuckled. "That's a nice young man you've got."

Brodie laughed too. "Yes, he is a nice young man; but he's not mine. We're just friends. I don't know why people find it so hard to believe."

"Me neither," said Peris, and though Brodie looked at her hard she managed to keep a straight face until the younger woman turned away.

Brodie dropped the bag in the car on her way across the courtyard. She let herself into the cottage. "Making yourself at home?"

Daniel wasn't alone. The french windows were open and

he was out on the little terrace making fine adjustments to the telescope. He hadn't so much as unpacked his toothbrush but he was coaxing the finderscope on the side of the reflector into alignment with the main mirror. She'd seen him do this often enough that she didn't need to ask. The two girls, on the other hand, were fascinated, perched on the drystone wall and craning their heads to follow every delicate movement of his fingers.

When Brodie said drily, "Every peeping Tom should have one," all three of them started. The girls looked at her warily. Daniel sighed and started making his minute adjustments again.

Now Brodie understood why Peris had seen the photograph in the study without realising the girls were not her nieces. They were amazingly alike. The younger girl was the spitting image of her mother at the same age – the sharp little face, the bright eyes, the unruly shag of floss-fair hair – while the elder had the same strong, determined face and long dark curls as her aunt. Slap bowler hats on their heads and no one would know the difference.

They were looking at her as if she were intruding.

Daniel introduced them. "Brodie, I'd like you to meet Juanita and Emerald Daws. Girls, this is my friend Mrs Farrell. She's looking for your aunt Constance."

They didn't even try to be polite. Em turned her back and Johnny said coldly, "Well, she isn't here."

Brodie's eyes narrowed. Because she was often the tallest person in any company, men included, she didn't usually wear heels; but she could walk as if on the highest, sharpest stilettos ever forged. She crossed the studio and framed herself in the french window, taking possession of everything inside and out with one deliberate glance. Then she slid her gaze unhurriedly sideways till it pinned Johnny to the wall. "Go and put the kettle on, there's a dear, while the grown-ups talk."

Colour raced up Johnny's cheeks. She lurched to her feet

and struggled to get the words out. "I'm not the servant! Peris does that." She flounced out, Em riding her wake like a pram-dinghy behind a schooner.

Brodie sat down demurely on the freshly vacated wall. "That's better."

Daniel clung onto his patience. "You're not making things easier."

"It's no part of my job to make things easier for a pair of little madams who, however unfortunate their predicament, desperately need to learn some manners."

"No," said Daniel quietly. "But it is part of mine. If not to help me, why are you here?"

"I'm looking for anything of Serena's that might be useful. I wondered what there was in here."

They went back inside. Daniel stood in the middle of the living room, looking round hopefully as if asking for volunteers. Brodie began a systematic search that involved opening every drawer and every cupboard.

She found papers in a wooden chest in the living room, but they were all concerned with painting: order-forms and bills for materials, and articles she'd torn out of magazines. And she found the cupboard with the paintings in it.

She blinked and stepped back, not shocked but certainly surprised. It wasn't the sort of work she expected from a mother of two. Perhaps that was naive. Perhaps the very confines of her life made such escapism desirable. Except that desire was conspicuous by its absence.

"Ah," said Daniel, standing behind her. "You found them."

"You mean, you hid them?"

He shrugged, discomfited. For a man who was clearly tolerant and liberal-minded, he had an odd little prudish streak that amused Brodie every time she could bait him into demonstrating it. Almost everything Daniel knew – and he knew a great deal – he'd learned from books. He'd gone from school to university to school and his experience of the real world was correspondingly narrow. Sometimes it showed. "It's not my idea of art."

"If you'd found a Goya odalisque in the cupboard you'd have put it up."

He thought about that. Then he gave a rueful chuckle. "Do you know, I'm not sure I would?" One of the drawbacks with being fearlessly honest was that sometimes you had to admit to things you'd rather not. Sometimes it would be so easy, and so harmless, just to make the conventional response. Naked dead people art, naked live people pornography; "Waiting For Godot" an inspired allegory on the human condition; nuclear power dangerous, evil, bad. Once you started questioning the received wisdoms, and being honest about your conclusions, you raised your head above the parapet and it was only a matter of time before someone started shooting.

Brodie returned her gaze to the painting and pursed her lips. "So this is the boy she was seeing. The one it was all about."

Daniel nodded. "Nicky Speers. He works at the farm across the road. I'm not sure that what happened was about him, though. He just happened to be Serena's current project when the situation went critical."

"They weren't in love, then?"

Daniel regarded the canvas sombrely. "Do they *look* to be in love?"

Brodie had her mouth open to say one thing, then saw what he meant. "No. No, they really don't, do they? It looks as if she offered him just enough money that he couldn't refuse. That's not a portrait of the artist's lover. It's a painting of meat."

"The only use she had for him, so far as I can tell," Daniel said softly, "was to make her husband jealous."

They put the paintings away again. The air in the little cottage tasted more of sorrow than horror.

Brodie shook herself. "Across the road, you said?"

57

"Sorry?"

"Where Nicky Speers works."

Daniel had known Brodie Farrell long enough to know she didn't make casual conversation. His eyes were alarmed. "You can't possibly!"

She feigned innocence. "Can't possibly what?"

"Corner a nineteen-year-old labourer at his place of work and ask about his relationship with a married woman who's just been murdered by her husband! Even you have to draw the line somewhere."

Privately, Brodie liked being thought of as ruthless. "She may have said something to him about her sister. It won't hurt to ask."

"It'll hurt him!"

"You drop your kit and sprawl on a silver sheet so a married woman can humiliate her husband, it's a bit late in the day to come over all coy."

Daniel frowned pensively. "I don't claim to be an authority, but somehow I doubt they were talking about her sister."

Brodie laughed. "Daniel, you're such an innocent sometimes! Of course he doesn't know anything about her sister. It's an excuse to pay him a visit."

"But – why would you want to?"

She nodded negligently at the cupboard door. "I've seen the advert, now I want to examine the goods."

# Chapter Seven

Nine days into the murder inquiry, Detective Superintendent Deacon knew no more than he had two hours after he first went to Sparrow Hill. He hadn't found Robert Daws. He hadn't found anyone who had seen or heard from Daws since the death of his wife. He hadn't found his car, or anyone who had seen it after that day. His passport, credit cards and mobile phone were all missing but there was no record of any of them being used in the last nine days. The man seemed to have fled Sparrow Hill, leaving his wife bleeding on her studio floor, and disappeared into thin air.

Leaving his young daughters alone with their mother's body. Well, he panicked. He had to get away before the alarm was raised, and didn't think about the girls until it was too late. He'd know someone would take care of them. He might have guessed his brother would come home. But it had taken forty-eight hours for Hugo to arrive: forty-eight hours in which the only support those girls had was a rota of WPCs who stayed with them in the main house while Deacon's team busied themselves in the cottage.

It had been deeply unpleasant for the adults involved: who could guess how those two young girls had felt? If he hadn't known Hugo Daws was on his way Deacon would have had Social Services remove them from the scene, however tearful their protests. He had never been happier to see anyone than when the tall thin man got out on one side of the hired car and the broad black woman on the other, and he was able to transfer responsibility for the shocked and grief-stricken children to a blood relative.

Deacon was no good with children. His marriage had been brief and happily unblessed; since then he'd spent his time almost exclusively with criminals, other police officers and barmaids. It had not equipped him to deal with children of

59

any age or either sex. Treating them like other people – perhaps with a limited vocabulary although Deacon wasn't a man to use long words when pithy short ones would do – simply never occurred to him.

Detective Sergeant Voss put his head round his chief's door, carefully avoiding Deacon's gaze. "Superintendent Fuller says, would you please stop diverting your phonecalls to his office?"

Deacon grimaced. It was the promotion: he couldn't get used to it. When someone came on his phone and said "Superintendent" he'd transferred them before they could finish the sentence. He did it when the Assistant Chief Constable phoned to congratulate him. He also did it when Brodie phoned to congratulate him, with the result that she'd offered to bring the station's senior officer breakfast in bed before she realised what had happened. Superintendent Fuller was so flustered he accepted.

Now he'd done it again. "Who was it this time?"

"Dr Roy. Apparently he's found something odd."

"On Serena Daws?" The Forensic Medical Examiner undoubtedly had a full caseload, any of which could be currently perplexing him, but the only one Deacon was interested in was Serena. And it had been obvious from the start how she died, which was why he hadn't pressed for a full report before this.

"Apparently," said Voss. He was a young man with the freckles and look of permanent mild surprise that tend to go with red hair. "Don't call him back: he wants us to go round there. And take Exhibit A with us."

Exhibit A was a kitchen knife with a serrated blade a hundred and fifty millimetres long and twenty millimetres across the widest point. It had a stag-horn handle and a Sheffield steel blade, and it still had Serena Daws' blood on it. Deacon checked it out of the evidence cupboard – which was not a cupboard but a room, manned by a strong-minded constable who surrendered nothing, not even the time of

60

day, without the proper paperwork – and he and Voss headed for Dimmock General Hospital where Dr Hari Roy had his small, smelly domain in the basement.

He was a large young Asian man who wore good suits and flamboyant ties when he wasn't wearing scrubs, and he nodded approval at the evidence bag in DS Voss's hand. "You brought it."

Deacon frowned. "I don't understand. There can't be any question that this is the murder weapon. We found it on the floor beside her. That's her blood."

Dr Roy nodded. "I have no doubt Mrs Daws was stabbed with this knife. I have mapped the wounds and they match for depth, width and profile. This knife was plunged into Mrs Daws's body thirteen times, causing the injuries from which she died."

Deacon breathed heavily at him. "You've brought us across town to tell us this? You could have used the phone."

Hari Roy gave the slow, handsome smile that had nurses reaching for the *sal volatile* all over the hospital. "Curiously enough, Superintendent Deacon, every time I try to phone you I find myself transferred to Superintendent Fuller's office. You should have a word with your switchboard."

"I will," muttered Deacon, avoiding Voss's gaze. He was pretty sure Roy knew, but said nothing just in case.

"And anyway," continued the FME smoothly, "I *have* something for you to see. I'm afraid it means going into my office." He meant the mortuary.

He pulled a green plastic apron over his suit and led the way to the dissecting table.

None of the sights or smells associated with this place were unfamiliar to his visitors. Even the pungent formaldehyde unsettled them no more than it did him. It was the smell of an important job being done, of questions being answered, reassuring and hopeful rather than upsetting.

In the same way, there was nothing distressing about the body of the woman on the table. It was sad, because nine days and a loss of temper ago she'd been full of strength and vitality, and even knowing that her favourite way of working off excess energy was hurting those closest to her it was still a sorrowful thing to see her lying so quiet and waxy-pale, immune to the outrage of strangers' eyes on her. But there was nothing repellent about it. Her deep wounds no longer bled and death had smoothed the pain from her brow. She couldn't be hurt any more. But she could be satisfied, and that was the task of these three men. To establish beyond doubt what had happened to her, and to bring her killer to justice.

"It's a little hard to demonstrate." Dr Roy had a fine steel probe with a ball-tip. He used it two different ways: to emphasise his words, like a drum-majorette twirling a very small baton, and to map the extent and shape of incised wounds. Drawing aside the sheet that covered Serena Daws he slid it into a wound in her leg and pushed until it would go no further. He cast his visitors a significant look. "You see the problem?"

Deacon looked at the probe, at Roy, even at Voss in case he found some inspiration there. Then he shook his head. "No."

Roy sighed. He extracted the probe, marking the depth of the incision with his fingertips. "You have the knife?"

Voss held it up, still in its plastic bag. Roy held the probe against it. There was a discrepancy of perhaps three centimetres.

Deacon shrugged. "So the knife didn't go all the way in. He stabbed her thirteen times, I don't suppose he was paying that much attention to just how deeply."

"But it did go all the way in," said the FME. "See? The wound is the width of the knife at its widest point, close to the hilt end. If it had only gone in a hundred and sixteen millimetres it would have been narrower. Plus, there's something else." He put the probe into the same wound at a different angle and it buried itself in Serena Daws without resistance.

Deacon looked again at the knife but it was a perfectly normal shape. "How come?"

Having finished with his model, Dr Roy tucked the sheet round her again as if putting her to bed. Then he reached for a notepad and a pen, sketching what he could feel so that those with less educated fingers could picture it too. What he produced was the outline of the murder weapon but with a smaller appendix running off the lower aspect of the blade.

Deacon struggled with the implications. "You mean, all the other wounds were made with this knife, but this one was made with something else?"

"Yes," agreed Dr Roy, "and no. At its widest point this incision is half as wide again as the entry wound. An implement capable of inflicting this damage could not have entered the body through that wound."

Deacon was growing impatient. He knew Hari Roy was a clever man: there was no need for him to keep proving it. This was a murder investigation: the idea was to make matters clearer for him, not more obscure. "That isn't possible."

But Charlie Voss was a clever man too, even though he often found it politic to hide the fact, and he could see the ghost of an answer. "You mean, that injury wasn't made by one knife. It was made by two."

Dr Roy gave him a smile of approval. "Quite so. One hole, two weapons."

"Or the same weapon twice," hazarded Deacon. "Could he have pushed it in part way, partly withdrawn it and then driven it home at a different angle?"

"Good thinking, Superintendent," nodded the FME, "but no. What we shall call the secondary wound was created by a knife with a narrower tip than Exhibit A. It was a smaller knife."

"He was stabbing her with two different knives?" Deacon shook his head in angry confusion. "Why, for heaven's sake? He was doing a perfectly good job with one."

"Can you tell which knife he used first?" asked Voss.

If he impressed Dr Roy any more today he'd be handed a sweetie. The FME beamed. "No, I can't. You'll have to ask Mr Daws when you find him."

Voss was driving. He concentrated on the road and waited for Deacon to open the debate. He'd already put his head on the block by being a swot and a teacher's pet: he didn't need to annoy his chief any more by offering unsought opinions.

At first Deacon just muttered indignantly. "It's nonsense! What possible reason could the man have? He's got a nice big knife that he's skewering his wife with, and she's bleeding all over the place and weakening fast – so he goes back to the kitchen for another, *smaller* knife which he proceeds to stick into some of the holes he's already made? Like hell he does!"

"We didn't actually ask that," Voss remembered suddenly. "Whether there were any more double wounds. Sorry, sir, I should have done."

Deacon got Roy on the phone. The answer was inconclusive. "He didn't find any more, but that might be because of where she was stabbed. It might not have been apparent where the knives went into squishy bits: lungs, stomach, intestines. But where they went into the firm tissue of her thigh they left a footprint."

"He had two knives," mused Voss. "And he stabbed her thirteen times with the big one, and at least once with the little one. Then he fled, leaving Exhibit A at the scene. What happened to Exhibit B?"

"He must have taken it with him."

"Why? Why leave the one that did most of the damage and keep the other one?"

"He wasn't worried about incriminating himself," said Deacon. Now they were working the evidence he'd forgotten his bad temper, was only interested in teasing the truth out of this unexpected development, as troubling as bits left on the bench when you've finished reassembling your carburettor. "He knew we'd know who did it, so why try to hide what he did it with?"

Voss was trying to picture the scene. "The guy's in a panic. He's a quiet, mild-mannered man who's just murdered his wife: the last thing he's thinking about is disposing of the murder weapon. Weapons. He may have shoved the knife in his pocket without much idea what he was doing. It probably gave him a hell of a shock when he found it again."

It was entirely feasible. It's only in crime fiction that every action has a purpose. In crime things are messier, less well-ordered, not as well thought through. Panic could be the answer.

"But it doesn't explain why he used a second knife – at all, let alone in that way," said Deacon. "And he wasn't panicking then. He was steady enough to withdraw one blade from the wound and insert another so carefully that he didn't enlarge the incision. If he was calm enough to do that, *why* did he do it? It did nothing to hasten her end, and nothing to throw us off his scent. But it wasn't a random act. It meant *something* to him."

But neither man was able to hazard a guess at what.

# Chapter Eight

Brodie didn't like horses. They were big, unreliable at both ends, and mostly they moved too slowly but occasionally they moved too fast. In her experience, many of the same drawbacks applied to their owners.

There was a huge white one, about the size of a Transit van, leaving the farmyard as she drove in. It looked down its nose at her; so did the man on top. "Are you looking for someone? Can I help?"

He wasn't a nineteen-year-old farm labourer with the body of a Greek god so she doubted it. But she stopped the car and got out. "I'm looking for Nicky Speers."

The man nodded. "He's up in the woods doing a bit of path clearance. He'll be back before long, if you want to wait. In fact, I'll head up that way now and let him know you're here. Miss ... ?"

"Brodie Farrell," she said. "But the name won't mean anything to him."

"Then, can I tell him what it's about?"

"Probably better not."

"This is about Mrs Daws," the rider said quietly. Brodie rather suspected she'd misjudged him. He was certainly a big man, and he sat the horse without unnecessary movement, but in fact his broad intelligent face and whole demeanour spoke of reliability. "I thought the police had finished questioning him."

"I'm not from the police," said Brodie. "I'm trying to trace Mrs Daws's sister. To look after the girls. I'm hoping Nicky might know something helpful."

The man pursed his lips. "I'm not sure they talked much about their respective families."

Brodie tried not to smile. "I don't expect they did. Mr ... ?"

"Poole," he said. "Philip Poole." He reached down a hand.

With an uneasy glance at the horse she moved close enough to shake it briefly. "And this is Blossom." The mare regarded her solemnly with a dark liquid eye.

"As in Poole Lane?"

The man nodded. "The farm's been in the family since Tudor times."

"I know it's a long shot," said Brodie. "But it is urgent, and she just may have said something to Nicky that would put me on the right track."

Philip Poole nodded. "Of course. I'll head up to the wood and find him for you. Park by the house and tell my secretary to make you some tea. He'll be down in ten minutes." He clucked to the mountainous Blossom and they left the yard at a lumbering trot.

She did as he said, except she didn't ask for tea. She waited in the farm office while Poole's secretary answered phone-calls using words she didn't understand but Paddy, who thought the sun shone out of a tractor power-take-off, might have done. Then the throaty rumble of an engine outside her-alded a new arrival. "That's Nicky now," said the girl. "I can make myself scarce if you want to see him in here."

Brodie thought he'd be more at ease outside. "I'll catch him in the yard. We won't be five minutes."

Even with his clothes on she had no difficulty recognising Nicky Speers, and not for his fine physique or handsome young face so much as the look in his eyes which was exactly the one Serena Daws had captured on canvas. He looked at Brodie as he had looked at his artist lover: warily, uncertain of her motives, unsure what she would say or do next, vul-nerable in the face of her authority.

She had to put him at his ease if they were to make any progress. The way he was eyeing her, she doubted he could remember his own address let alone Constance Ward's. She chuckled. "Don't look so worried. This isn't official. I've been asked to find Serena's sister so I'm talking to everyone she knew. I'm sorry if this is a bit embarrassing but it's no secret that you spent time together. I thought she might have mentioned something about Constance's whereabouts."

"She didn't." In spite of his height – he overtopped Brodie by three inches – there remained the hint of a teenage whine in his voice.

"No?" Experience had taught her never to accept anyone's first offer as final. People who had no interest in lying, who had nothing to hide, still forgot vitally important details. If she kept them talking for a few minutes they started to remember. "You never met Constance then?"

"Never."

"Did Serena ever talk about her? I don't know – things they did when they were girls? Apparently they had ponies – did she talk about that?"

Nicky was looking increasingly uneasy. "No. I mean, you don't, do you? It wasn't a social thing. It wasn't us and the vicar and a plate of sandwiches. She wanted to paint me. Most of the time I was stood in her cottage with no kit on. And the rest of the time ... And we didn't talk much then, either. Not about her sister, and not about when she was a kid."

"I suppose not." Brodie went on regarding him amiably. Her lack of embarrassment only made his worse. "I don't suppose it's been easy for you. What happened. People blaming you."

"It wasn't my fault!" The wound was still raw, the nerves still jumped. He was still trying to convince himself. "I shouldn't have got involved, I know that. But I didn't make her do anything she didn't want to. And I didn't kill her."

"Of course not," said Brodie, so smoothly it meant nothing. "We know who stabbed her, don't we? Sooner or later the police will find him and then it'll be history. Except for the girls, of course. They'll live with the consequences for years – especially if I can't find Constance. Are you sure you can't tell me anything about her? Did Serena ever get letters or phone-calls from her? Did she never come here?"

The boy tried to remember. His brow furrowed, and Brodie thought that if he'd come up with anything he'd have told her. "I really don't think so. I'm sorry about the girls, but there's nothing I can tell you."

"OK." Brodie smiled brightly. "Well, thanks for your time. And would you thank Mr Poole for me, too?"

He nodded. Through the lank curtain of his fringe she could see the relief in his eyes that she was done. "I don't suppose he was much help either. He used to know them pretty well, but that's years ago."

Brodie froze in the act of reaching for her car door. "Philip Poole knew the Ward sisters?"

"Yes." The worry flooded back into his eyes. "Didn't he say?"

"I didn't think to ask." She frowned. "*How* did he know them? If Constance didn't visit."

"I'm talking years back, when they were kids. The Wards lived at Peyton Parvo, on the far side of Cheyne Wood. They all had horses. They used to hunt together."

In the privacy of her own mind Brodie kicked herself. She'd known the Wards were a local family, that Serena hadn't blown in from outside when she married Robert Daws – she should have asked Poole if he knew Constance. But he knew her reason for calling, so probably he'd have said if he knew where she was now. All the same, she thought she'd talk to him again. Experience had also taught her that if you ignore the little clues that chance throws in your path, one of them will turn out to be crucial. "Maybe I should wait for him. Do you know how long he'll be?"

Nicky shrugged. "Could be an hour or two. Once he gets up on the downs on the great white whale he goes for miles."

Brodie grinned. "I take it you're not a riding man yourself?"

"Sure I am." He waved a long arm at a gleaming black and silver motorbike propped beside the house and, in the place of the lusty young man whose rampant sex-drive had thrust

69

him into a situation he was ill-equipped to handle, Brodie saw an excited child on Christmas morning. "Seven-fifty cc," he confided with proprietorial pride. "Open it up and it sounds like a Spitfire."

When Brodie had gone Daniel summoned the girls to the school-room. He looked from one to the other of them, his pale grey eyes severe. "*That* was an unedifying spectacle."

They may not have known the word but they understood his meaning well enough. They glanced at one another and quickly away. Johnny made ringlets of her hair around one finger. Em stared so hard at the table-top that tears came to her eyes.

"Have you nothing to say for yourselves?"

Johnny cast him a brief rebel glance. "She's no business here. It's our house. We don't like strangers poking round. We're not a freak show."

For a moment Daniel breathed steadily, silenced by his own compassion. Then he sat on the edge of the table. "Nobody thinks you are. All these people getting under your feet are just trying to deal with the situation as best they can. Brodie is trying to help too. But even if she wasn't, she's my friend. I expect you to treat my friends with courtesy."

"She wasn't very courteous to me," grumbled Johnny.

"No," agreed Daniel, "she wasn't. Which is why I had a word with her before I came up here to have a word with you. While I'm staying here you're bound to bump into one another, and I don't want any repeat of that nonsense. You don't have to like one another. You do have to be polite."

There was a mutinous pause. Then Johnny said, "We will if she is."

Daniel nodded, satisfied. "That seems reasonable. OK. What do you want to learn today?"

Daniel had always known what he wanted to do. His first day in the classroom as a trainee teacher had been like coming home. It wasn't just his grasp of his subject – that's the easy part – more that he was good at teaching. Children liked him and responded to his enthusiasm. Mathematics is a hard subject to imbue with any glamour, but Daniel Hood – who had a certain homely charm but no glamour of his own – managed to share his own sense of wonder at the worlds it opened up. He took his students beyond the tedious remembering of formulae – which were, as he pointed out honestly, purely for passing exams: anyone using maths professionally has a slide-rule, a calculator and a stack of textbooks within reach – and out into a universe whose infinite possibilities could only be explored this way. He made them understand that maths wasn't a form of torture but a tool he was forging for them.

When the panic attacks that followed one long weekend – one infinitely long weekend – of mental and physical abuse meant he had to give up teaching, it was like a bereavement. He had no idea what else to do with his life. Salvation came in the form of a tearful thirteen-year-old who couldn't do long division to save her soul. Six months of maths with Mr Hood had given her the hope that one day she would master it: when he left she was distraught. She found out where he lived, and sat softly crying on his doorstep until he agreed to tutor her.

If their sessions together rescued her education, they saved his sanity. This he could do. If it wasn't teaching as he knew it, there were compensations. One of them was the freedom to tailor lessons to the pupils' interests and rate of progress. They had to acquire the knowledge in the way that a traveller has to reach his destination, but there was nothing to stop them taking the scenic route rather than the motorway.

To say they hadn't known him very long, the Daws girls were quickly getting Daniel's measure. Distress forgotten, Em eyed him slyly from under her bog-cotton fringe and said, "You could tell us about astro – astron ... "

"Astronomy," Daniel supplied automatically. Then he laughed. "Yeah, right. Em, that's the oldest trick in the book!

– get the teacher to talk about what interests him and he won't notice that you're reading *Pop Secrets* under the desk. Credit me with some intelligence."

"No, really," said Johnny, apparently sincere. "It's science, isn't it? – and that's education. And it's interesting. Mum – " She stopped dead, white-faced.

Em finished the sentence, diffidently. "Mummy didn't know a lot about science. We got it mostly out of books."

Daniel nodded slowly while his heart bled for them. But he recognised progress when he saw it. This was the first time they'd spoken to him of Serena. It was a huge, brave step. If he was careful now he could begin to help them; if he wasn't careful enough he could send them back into the bunker. "Everyone gets it mostly out of books. It's where most knowledge is kept. The clever part is knowing that, and taking the trouble to find it. I think your mother was a pretty good teacher."

Again that quick trade of glances. The sisters seemed able to convey whole sentences in a meeting of eyes. "She was," agreed Johnny quietly. "We learnt a lot. Anything she didn't know she found out. We went to libraries and museums and art galleries. We went to the places where history was made. We studied the Battle of Hastings sitting on the battlefield."

"It was a hot day," remembered Em. "An ant bit my bum." Johnny elbowed her in the ribs. "Well, it did," the younger girl muttered indignantly.

"That's a brilliant way to study," said Daniel. "I wish I could have done that with my classes. It's not practical with big numbers, but it'll have given you a feel for history – and geography, and science and the rest – that most kids never get.

"OK. Astronomy. Name me a star."

He wasn't catching them that easily. "The sun," said Johnny smugly.

"Good. Another." Blank silence. "Then name me a planet.

Other," he said, forestalling Johnny by an instant, "than the Earth."

They thought. "Venus," said Em. "Mars," said Johnny. "Jupiter." "Erm ... "

They were away. In the course of the next two hours they covered the components of the Solar System, including the Asteroid Belt and the Oort Cloud; the natures of the planets and their companion satellites; and how the size and distance of these remote bodies were established within fairly accurate limits from ancient times using only basic mathematics. They touched on the Greek myths, Galileo and the Inquisition, and Tycho Brahe's golden nose.

For the first time in nine days the monstrous shadows of what happened in the studio were banished from the girls' eyes. When Peris stuck her head through the school-room door to say lunch was ready she was astonished by their engagement. If Daniel achieved nothing more at Sparrow Hill she reckoned he'd already earned every penny they would pay him.

Unwilling to wait for Philip Poole, Brodie returned to her office to go through her trophies from Sparrow Hill.

There must have been fifty numbers in Serena's address book but none for Constance Ward. She kept a Christmas card list but her sister didn't feature on it. There was even a rough copy of her will, left in her desk after the formal draft was lodged with her solicitor, but Constance was not a beneficiary. Neither, Brodie noted, was Nicky Speers, or any of the handsome young men who preceded him. She left her estate divided between her husband and two daughters, for all the world as if they were a perfectly normal, happy family. Nothing in her papers hinted at what was happening or what was to come.

Brodie eyed the book with disfavour. Working her way through those fifty numbers was the hard way. She'd get unanswered phones, engaged tones and answering machines.

She'd get the wives, husbands, parents, siblings and small children of the people she was looking for. They'd take messages which they had no intentions of passing on. She'd be waiting for two days before it became obvious she'd have to call again. Even when she got talking to the right person, most of them – perhaps all of them – would have nothing to tell her.

She found herself looking at the photograph again. A lot of girls think ponies are the centre of the universe until they discover boys. But for some that first love endures and colours everything they do thereafter. They live on toast and Marmite so their horse can live in comfort. It puts them in hospital, and their prime concern is getting out in time for the Pony Club camp. They spend more on horse-shoes every eight weeks than they do on their own shoes every year. In spite of all this they think they're lucky. They think their life is infinitely preferable to those of their friends who have new cars and foreign holidays and smart clothes.

So it was possible that Constance Ward had continued riding though her sister had not. If so there were a number of organisations to which she might belong. A trawl of websites would provide her with contact numbers; conceivably the first she called would have the information she needed. With luck it would be quicker than working her way through Serena's address book.

The names, addresses and phone-numbers of people on membership lists is generally restricted, and people manning office phones will say they are unable to give it out. Brodie would never have made a career out of information if she hadn't found ways round this. Usually she thought up a little white lie, but this time the truth served better than anything she could concoct. Two little girls were going into care if she couldn't find their aunt. She told it straight and simple, with pauses in all the right places, and she'd have made stones weep. One after another these affected, helpful people called up their databases and scanned them for the name of Constance Ward.

74

And one after another they drew a blank. She was offered a Mrs Constance Ward, but if Constance had married her name would have changed. Which was part of the problem. The woman could be a member of every equestrian organisation in the country, but if she was now Constance Walking-Strangely there was no way either Brodie or the people she was talking to would know.

The last possibility exhausted, she put the phone down and glared at the address book. But she never thought she had a choice. She made herself a cup of tea, then she opened it at the letter A and began dialling.

# Chapter Nine

After lunch the girls disappeared upstairs. Daniel had set some homework and they gave him to understand that they intended to start immediately. Daniel didn't believe a word of it; and indeed, five minutes later the strains of pop music were crashing through the house.

Peris caught his eye and they traded a grin. "It's only a lie," said Daniel tolerantly, "if there's the remotest chance of misleading someone. Otherwise it's a fairy-story."

"And that's all right?"

"Certainly. The person hearing it without challenging its obvious shortcomings becomes a co-conspirator. Without the willing suspension of disbelief there could be no art."

Peris's face grew still. "Speaking of art – "

Daniel knew what she was going to say. "Safe for now. But before you leave this house you might want to dispose of them. I wouldn't like the girls to be sorting through a storage container in a few years' time and find themselves staring at the pictures that destroyed their family."

"They'll want to keep some of their mother's work."

"I'm sure they will. But not all the work she did should be preserved for posterity."

Peris agreed. She found herself agreeing with a lot that Daniel said. "No one can say those girls have had much luck. But I think they were lucky that Hugo found you."

"I hope so," Daniel said fervently. "I want to get this right, to help them. But it isn't always obvious what's for the best. You will tell me if you think I'm getting it wrong?"

"I doubt if there *is* a right and wrong," said Peris honestly. "I think there's just having your heart in the right place and doing your best. We can't change what happened. We can't protect them from it. We can only smooth the way a little. And remember that children are always tougher than we think. They have to be: growing up is an endurance test. Hell, just getting born involves being shoved through a mangle, having your oxygen cut off and being slapped till you cry! After that, anything's an improvement."

Daniel laughed out loud. Here was another of these strong, positive women who filled him with admiration. Confident and successful women like Brodie Farrell and Peris Daws seemed to him to know the secret of life, to get more out of it than anyone else. Where confident, successful men harnessed conflict, these women forged alliances. They drew their power up through roots deep in the earth itself, their strength was the strength of the planet, and they saw things clearly.

To Daniel the world seemed complex: a jigsaw without edges, poetry without rhymes, music without bars. He struggled to make sense of it, and often worried that this was because he was stupid. More than once Brodie had explained in words of one syllable that only clever people even try to understand. Most get along by refusing to lift their gaze above where the next meal, the next car, the next fortnight in Miami is coming from. Daniel tied himself in knots trying to comprehend things that didn't require his comprehension, that would continue their waltz to the music of time whether or not he knew the steps.

If he'd tried to explain any of this to Peris Daws she'd have sent for the men in white coats. Because he didn't, what she saw was not a bundle of uncertainties and contraditions but an intelligent, thoughtful, gentle man whose arrival in her family circle was the only positive thing to have happened in over a week. Difficult as the situation was, Peris could have been struggling with her nieces' moods alone. She understood why their behaviour was so erratic, but that didn't make them any easier to handle.

She sighed. "My problem is, I understand the theory of child-raising but haven't had the practice. My mother would have walked in here, boxed their ears, given them a hug and had them eating out of her hand before she'd got her coat off. But then she had six of her own to learn on. As the last, I never got any hands-on experience."

"You don't have children, then?"

She looked at him from under lowered eyebrows. "I can see you're short-sighted: are you colour-blind as well? Hugo and I have been together for twelve years; we've been married for two of them. Even now it's not easy. We moved down the road from Pretoria to Jo'burg because there's a difference between Afrikaans cities and English ones, but we still raise eyebrows, and hackles. We have the right to take what we want and pay the price for ourselves, but not to impose the consequences on babies."

Daniel had no right to argue with her. People had despised him for what he'd done, and for what they thought he'd done, but never for how he looked. "You could end up with children after all, unless Constance wants to keep the girls with her. How will you feel if she does?"

She cast him a hunted look. "Truly and honestly? Relieved. It's bad enough Hugo's colleagues treating me like his servant, I don't need it from his nieces as well. Which doesn't mean I won't do my best for them. I will, and there's no need for him or them ever to know how I feel. But if they do stay in England, it would be a lie to say I'll be upset."

She seemed to think Daniel would disapprove. She was wrong. "Then I hope things work out for you. You're here for them now when they need you most. It isn't selfish to hope that you won't have to give as much as you're prepared to."

The suspicion of a tear glistened in the corner of Peris's eye. Then in one fluid movement she leaned over the table and kissed him squarely on top of his yellow head.

Daniel stared at her in astonishment. She gave a deep throaty chuckle. "You're a nice man, Daniel Hood. How about we leave the girls here and adopt you instead?"

Less than halfway through Serena's address book Brodie's

dialling finger succumbed to repetitive stress injury. Twenty identical calls to twenty mildly concerned but wholly unhelpful strangers left her itching for a change.

She had other work to get on with, but nothing this urgent. She couldn't tell Hugo Daws that his nieces would have to go into care because her finger got sore and she went off to comb antique shops for a Meissen shepherdess for a dentist's wife who already had the shepherd.

She thought of Philip Poole. If he and Blossom were back by now, there was an outside chance that he could tell her something useful about Constance Ward. At least the drive would give her finger time out.

She didn't phone ahead to check that he was about and could see her. She generally preferred to turn up unheralded. She had some wasted journeys, but she got more out of people when they met face to face. If Poole was in the office when she called he'd take the phone and say no, sorry, he'd no idea where Constance Ward lived. But if she perched on a straw-bale and chatted to him while he did whatever farmers do – dusted the cows, vacuumed the sheep, polished the tractors – he would find himself feeding the conversation with snippets of memory or rumour, and one of them might prove more valuable than he had any reason to expect.

If not, the phone and the address book would be waiting when she returned.

Poole was tuberculin-testing the cattle. But he didn't send her away: he had his foreman take over and steered her into the pleasanter environs of the kitchen garden.

Once this walled half-acre would have fed the family and half a dozen farm labourers. But things change. Even farmers' children like spaghetti hoops sometimes, and may be more impressed by television advertising than the pedigree of a home-grown carrot. Today the garden was mostly in flowers, with the tail-end of a soft fruit crop against the wall.

If Poole didn't understand why Brodie was back he didn't complain. "I'd have told you if I knew where Connie was."

"I know," nodded Brodie. "But Nicky said you knew the Ward sisters as girls – that you rode together. It occurred to me that she might still ride and other local riders may have seen her about. Would it be a huge nuisance to ring some people and ask?"

He thought for a moment. "I'll call the hunt secretary, get him to make enquiries. The dealers get around too – if she's stopped hunting but still rides they're probably our best bet. Come inside for a coffee while I make a few calls."

It was that or go back to her own phone. Her finger spasmed in revolt. "Lovely."

As they sipped the coffee Brodie said, "You still hunt then, Mr Poole."

"Philip, please," he protested. "To everyone round here Mr Poole is still my father, and he's been dead for eight years. Hunt?" His lips twitched. "Yes and no. Yes, I go out with The Three Downs Foxhounds. Is there any hunting involved? – almost none. You've seen Blossom – well, she's the Three Downs' idea of a quality hunter. At fifteen years old she's considered a bit young and flighty. She has been known to gallop, and even jump, which is considered outrageous thrusting by the Three Downs. If we're not careful we find ourselves ahead of not only the Master but also the hounds.

"They're a bunch of geriatrics, too. We don't have a hunt kennels: some of us keep a brace at home. Mine are called Dozy and Grumpy, which probably gives you a idea of the pack as a whole. The only exercise they take is on hunting mornings, and even then they mostly sneak off home after the first point. Which consist of three old men on Clydesdales breaking into a trot and one of them falling off. It's the kind of hunting the League Against Cruel Sports loses no sleep over. The only chance of us harming a fox is if one ruptures itself laughing."

Brodie laughed too, but she wasn't entirely persuaded. "It's very odd," she said slyly. "People who hunt have lots of reasons why they ought to be allowed to continue, but they can never agree what they are. I've been told there are so many of you that rural employment would collapse without you, and so few you can't possibly do any harm. I've been told you offer a vital pest-control service to farmers, and now you tell me that you're quite incapable of making a kill. Hunts claim to be a force for conservation, genuine animal-lovers, the last bastion of Old England and the victims of urban ignorance. And I can't see how it can all be true."

Philip Poole was regarding her levelly. "What do you believe?"

Her eyebrows rose and fell in a kind of facial shrug. "I believe that money talks. I know what it costs to hunt, and I can't imagine you all spending that much selflessly on sup-porting rural employment or conserving nature. You're pay-ing for your pleasure. I think that, while hunting remains a legal occupation, you're entitled to pursue it – as long as you allow the same freedom of expression to those who oppose you. But there's something distasteful about bloodsports enthusiasts trying to capture the moral high ground."

His gaze never flickered. "You're right. I hunt because I enjoy it. I find it hard to be sentimental about an animal which, even if it's prettier, is vermin as much as mice and rats."

"There's nothing sentimental about it," argued Brodie. "Opposition to hunting is nothing to do with liking foxes. Taking pleasure in the pain and distress of a living creature is an ignoble thing. Some things, even things that have to be done, shouldn't be enjoyed."

A slow smile was spreading across Philip Poole's face. When he met Brodie Farrell earlier he'd noted the striking features, the taut figure and perfect drape of her stylish clothes, and filed her under T for Thinking Man's Crumpet. He saw now that he'd been wrong. She wasn't anyone's crumpet; she just might own the bakery. "My father would have despised every word you just said."

"But he'd defend to the death my right to say it?"

"Like hell he would," said Poole cheerfully.

They chuckled together like friends. Brodie said, "I take it he was a serious hunting man. Or was The Three Downs always a joke?"

"Lord no," he exclaimed. "It was a smart hunt when I first rode out with the Ward girls. Kennels, whippers-in, the lot. There were still men riding in top hats. There was a hunt button that you had to be invited to wear. And fast? The moment their feet touched grass they'd be off, and you'd have gone three fields before anybody took a pull. If you couldn't jump, either you learned fast or you fell off – and then you had to get out of the way pretty damn quick. Nobody waited for you. They didn't even check you were alive. Most casualties were found by foot-followers." Poole rolled his eyes. "I don't know how any of us survived. Lord knows what our parents were thinking of."

"I know what your father was thinking," said Brodie. "'Damned easy hunting these days – we went twice as fast when I was a boy.'"

Poole laughed out loud. "It was about then that skull-caps were coming in for cross-country riding. They're safer than the old velvet caps, but my father said he was damned if any son of his was riding out in public dressed like a jockey!"

"Parental affection like that makes you feel warm all over," commented Brodie. "So did you promptly fall off and crack your skull?"

"I've fallen off and cracked most things at one time or another," admitted Poole. "Most riders have. Connie Ward broke her ankle hunting when were about fifteen. That's when she came up with the idea of the Cheyne Phantom. The worst hunting injury I ever got was the thrashing my father gave me over that."

Brodie was intrigued. "Whatever did you do?"

"It's a local legend," said Poole, "the Phantom Rider of Cheyne Wood. Connie thought it would be fun if the ghost appeared more often. So we rigged something up with an old mirror. Every meet people came back white-faced and shaking, claiming the Cheyne Phantom had been galloping beside them. We kept the joke going for weeks – had half the hunt carrying rabbits' feet before we were found out. Someone saw Serena watching. She wanted to see the victim's face when the Phantom Rider appeared."

Brodie shook her head in wonder. "There aren't enough ways to die on a galloping horse in the middle of a wood without three brats trying to scare the living daylights out of you?"

"Different days," Poole sighed.

Brodie finished her coffee and thanked Poole for his help. He was sorry he hadn't got an answer for her yet but promised to keep asking.

She sensed there was something else he wanted to ask. As he walked her back to her car she nodded at the heavy machinery. "My daughter Paddy's a tractor buff. Other little girls have dolls and teddy bears. Mine has Massey Ferguson maintenance manuals."

Poole grinned but there was a hint of disappointment too. Without a word of a lie Brodie had gently readjusted his view of her. "How old is she?"

"Five. She wants a combine harvester for Christmas."

"Me too," said Poole fervently.

Unable to make sense of Dr Roy's discovery, Deacon returned to what he did best – asking questions and looking sceptical about the answers until people felt pressurised into elaborating. With no likelihood of finding new witnesses he went back to those he'd already interviewed and interviewed them again.

Because Robert Daws was a successful businessman, so were many of the people who knew him best. Deacon didn't like questioning important people, preferred a hardened criminal any day. You knew where you stood with people like that. You knew they'd lie to you for as long as they could get away with it but at least they didn't threaten you with their lawyers. Pillars of the community could lie with equal inventiveness and greater authority, and always knew someone who played golf with the Chief Constable.

In spite of which, Deacon didn't actually think he was being lied to about Robert Daws. He talked to suppliers, colleagues and competitors, and got the same story each time. Daws was respected and liked by everyone who had dealings with him. Many of them knew of his difficulties at home and sympathised. But they were universally shocked by what had happened. One after another they paraphrased the same sentiment: that Robert Daws was the last man on earth they would have expected to stab someone, even his wife. They would have been sorry but less surprised to hear that he'd killed himself.

And still, nine days after the event, none of them had any idea where he might be. Asking about company jets failed to provoke either confessions or discomfort. Those who had access to such facilities were able to produce log-books showing no discrepancies. A couple of them seemed quite flattered to be suspected. So far as Deacon could establish, for Robert Daws to have skipped the country he'd have had to turn into a swallow and fly south.

"All right," he said to Charlie Voss when they were alone again, "so he didn't leave the country. He's still around somewhere. Maybe he's still around Dimmock."

"Why?"

"Because ... " Deacon thought. "Because his daughters are?"

Voss found that plausible. "They're all he has left. Maybe he can't bring himself to head for Bolivia without them."

Deacon sniffed. "Maybe he's looking for a way to take them with him. Maybe ... maybe once they join their uncle in South Africa he'll reappear and whisk them off."

"But if that's what he has in mind, why risk staying?

84

He'd be better going to South Africa and waiting for them there."

"Maybe he waited too long." Deacon was thinking aloud. He thought Charlie Voss was a useful sounding-board because he could bounce ideas off him and they tended come back clearer and better than when they went out. "He failed to get clear during the first few hours before the ports and airports were on alert, and by the time he was ready to go it was too late. Now he's trapped. It isn't safe to stay here, but it's even more dangerous to move."

"What? You think he's staying in a B&B?"

"Using what for money? It's been nine days. Even if he had money on him it would be gone by now. Even a cheap B&B at the unfashionable end of Dimmock out of season doesn't operate as a charity. Every cup of tea, every newspaper, every night's rest he'd have to buy. He wouldn't be able to avoid using his bank account and we'd know. No. If he's still here, he's under someone's protection. Someone's putting him up and feeding him, or at least providing him with cash to feed himself. Someone knows where he is. A friend, a colleague, an old flame."

"I thought we'd talked to them all. Twice."

"You always miss someone, and one person is all it takes. We've been concentrating on businessmen. Maybe we should be looking for a nice understanding woman who let him kick his shoes off in front of her fire."

"I'll talk to his secretary again," said Voss.

Deacon had travelled to London to talk to Robert Daws' secretary. She wasn't his idea of a nice understanding woman. Now Daws was missing she was effectively running the firm. "Ms Steele?"

"I mean, if he had a girlfriend she'd know about it. But there is another possibility. We keep hearing it: people would have been less surprised to hear that he'd committed suicide. Well, maybe he did. Maybe the reason he isn't using his passport or his credit cards or his mobile phone is that he's outside the service area."

The superintendent stared at his sergeant. "And we haven't found his car because ... "

Voss nodded grimly. "Because he's still in it."

# Chapter Ten

Helpless, bound hand and foot by sleep, Daniel heard screaming.

This was not, per se, unusual. Still once a week, on average, he woke sweating, his own cries throbbing in his brain. But mostly, by the time he was bolt upright, kicking free of the jumbled duvet and groping for the light-switch, the echoes had died and he was aware that what had gone before was a phantasm, the after-glow of past horrors.

This time the screams did not fade with the dark. Nor were they his screams. He thought he could hear both girls, and Peris's voice raised above them. He couldn't make out words but he knew the sound of terror when he heard it. Cramming on his glasses, dragging his clothes over his pyjamas, he flung open the cottage door as the lights came on in Sparrow Hill.

His shoes crunched on glass and the back door was open. He crossed the kitchen at a run, emerged into the deep square hall, and two hysterical children in nightdresses hurled themselves at him, gripping him tightly. On the landing Peris Daws, stately in African print, leaned over the banister demanding imperiously, "What in hell is going on down there? *Daniel*? Is that you?"

"It is now," he said, breathless. "I heard screams and came running."

"There was someone here." A white-faced Johnny stared at him through shock-wide eyes. "A man. There was a man in the house."

Daniel threw Peris a fast glance, and she surged down the stairs like the launching of a royal barge. "*What*? What did you say? What did she say?"

"She said there was a man in the house," Daniel said briefly. He looked Johnny in the eyes. "You're sure? You're sure it wasn't me, just now?"

She shook her head vigorously, the chestnut hair flying and a dew-drop spinning off the end of her nose. "Something woke me. I came downstairs for a glass of milk. I bumped into him. Right here!"

"And that's when you yelled?" The girl nodded. "That wasn't me. All right. Peris, stay with them while I check the house."

Some stereotypes are difficult to escape. Any intruder would rather have met Daniel Hood in a dark corridor than Peris Daws, robed like a warrior queen and bearing down on him in furious indignation. Still Daniel knew the search was his responsibility. If it was successful he'd probably end up on his back with a bloody nose. But if he stayed with the women and waited for the police to arrive the shame would be worse. Daniel was not a man who worried overly what people thought of him, but he was a man and some obligations came with the testicles. One was evicting spiders, another was checking for intruders.

With Peris on the landing it seemed unlikely anyone had got upstairs. He started on the ground floor – living room, dining room, sitting room, scullery. He looked behind doors, under tables and in any cupboards big enough to hide in. He found nothing, but with every door he opened his heart-rate soared.

When he was sure there was no one downstairs he checked the bedrooms as well. Confident then that the four of them were alone in the house, he went back to the hall and sat the girls down on the stairs. "If there was someone here he's gone now. Can you tell me what happened – what you saw?"

Em was shaking uncontrollably, her little face pinched. Johnny was fighting to get a grip on herself. "I woke up. I don't know why. Maybe I heard something, maybe I just woke up. I wanted a glass of milk. I didn't put the light on. I came downstairs, and at the bottom I bumped into someone.

"We sort of bounced apart. I ended up sitting on the bottom step, and then I could see the shape of him against the window. He swore and groped round him. His hand brushed my hair and he grabbed hold. That's when I yelled."

Em nodded urgently and took up the story. Her teeth were chattering as she spoke. "I heard Johnny shout, and when she wasn't in her bed I came to look for her. I saw the man at the bottom of the stairs, and I screamed too."

"By now," said Peris, "I was out of bed and on my way. But by the time I found the landing light it was all over. Johnny and Em were hugging one another down here and there was no one else in sight. Then you arrived, and the rest you know."

"The pane in the kitchen door's broken," said Daniel. "That's how he got in. Broke it, reached through and turned the key."

"He," echoed Peris. "Who?"

Daniel shrugged. "A burglar?"

Peris did her old-fashioned look from under canted eyebrows. "A burglar? Just how unlucky can one family get?"

"Maybe he wasn't expecting to find anyone here."

"Of course he knew there was someone here! There's a car in the drive."

He wasn't sure what she was suggesting, or even if it was a suggestion. He turned back to the shivering girls. "This man. Did either of you get a proper look at him?"

The girls traded another of their significant looks. Em hugged herself, cheeks silver-streaked with tears.

Johnny said, "It was dark. And we were falling over one another. It was hard to see his face." She looked expectantly at her sister but Em had nothing to add.

"But you saw his outline against the window." She nodded. "Was he a big man, like Superintendent Deacon? Or a small man, like me?"

"Big," said Johnny. "Tall."

Daniel nodded encouragement. "And you heard his voice? When he swore. Did he sound familiar?"

She thought, biting her lips. "Maybe. I don't know."

"It's not easy, is it?" said Daniel. "When you're taken by surprise and you don't know what's going on. Did you have the feeling that you knew him?"

Peris was eyeing him oddly but Johnny didn't notice. "I'm not sure." Then she shook her head and would say no more.

"Well, try not to worry about it," said Daniel. "You scared him as much as he scared you, and when he realised he had two of you to deal with he turned and ran. He must have been going like a train or I'd have met him in the courtyard. Anyway, he's gone now and I can't see him coming back."

He straightened up. "Why don't you go back to bed, and I'll let the police know what's happened? Peris and I are going to have a cup of coffee, and it'll be coming light soon after that." The long-case clock in the hall was reporting four-fifteen, so there was actually time for a three-course meal before daybreak. But they weren't usually up at this time and didn't know. They trooped off upstairs without an argument.

Daniel followed Peris through to the kitchen. They left all the lights on and the doors open. Daniel looked at the broken glass. "I'll find something to nail over that."

"In the morning," said Peris, waving him to a kitchen chair. "I don't even know where they keep the hammer. Call the police, then come back in here."

He did as she said. The duty sergeant took the details, and said he'd have the area car call out immediately if there was any question that the intruder was still there. Daniel said that he'd gone and they'd be fine until Detective Superintendent Deacon got the message in the morning.

Peris was waiting for him with mugs and a quizzical expression. "Who do you think it was?"

Daniel tried to look blank. "I don't know who it was."

"No. But you have a suspicion. Haven't you?"

He couldn't lie. Even his face couldn't lie. "It might have been their father."

Peris stared at him. "Robert? He's in Venezuela by now!"

"We don't know that. Everything he cares about is here. Maybe he didn't want to leave it all behind. Maybe he wanted to see his home and his daughters again."

"So he broke in and scared them half to death?" Her voice climbed like a jet plane.

"He didn't break in. Look where the broken glass is – out in the yard. He let himself in with his front door key and left the same way. Otherwise I'd have seen him running away. He tried to make it look like a break-in."

Peris's broad face was perplexed but she was at least willing to consider it. "Robert was here? I've heard of people returning to the scene of a crime, but that would be madness."

"Not if everyone thinks he's in Venezuela. There was no reason to expect a trap. He thought he could see the girls, maybe apologise, maybe make plans to meet again, then he could leave the country. Ten days after the event it'll be easier to move around than it would have been earlier."

"But if he risked his liberty to see them, why stay just long enough to terrify them?"

"Because they'd raised the alarm before they realised who it was. Johnny took him by surprise, before he was ready, and yelled before he could reassure her. Then Em was screeching too, you were fumbling for the landing light and I was stumbling across the yard with my shoes half on. He could rely on the girls not to call the police, maybe he'd have tried to persuade you, but I was an unknown quantity. He got out while he could."

Peris chewed reflectively on the inside of her lip. "Do you suppose they know now who it was?"

"I hope not. If he daren't risk coming back, it's better the girls don't realise there was a chance to talk to their father but they scared him off."

Peris sipped her coffee, still thinking. "Would they have talked to him? Would they want to? He killed their mother and abandoned them. He might get a more sympathetic hearing from us than from them."

"He's the only parent they have left," said Daniel simply. "They may be willing to adjust their perception of what happened in order to leave the door open for him."

"Will you tell Superintendent Deacon what you suspect?"

Daniel considered for a moment. "Yes. But he won't believe it."

When Deacon found the message on his desk at eight in the morning, his first instinct was to find someone to shout at. As he couldn't see a way it could be DS Voss's fault he went to shout at the duty sergeant instead.

"A break-in at a house where I'm investigating a murder and nobody thinks to let me know? Worrying about the phone-bill, were you? Or is there a general consensus that I need my beauty-sleep?"

Sergeant McKinney had been stationed in Dimmock as long as Deacon had, and was about as easy to intimidate. He wore half-moon glasses for paperwork: now he lowered his head to stare over the top of them. The effect was of a bull buffalo lowering its head to charge. He rumbled, "If you wish to be informed of every event which could conceivably have a bearing on a case in which you're involved, Superintendent, I will make a note accordingly and ensure it happens. After ten days without sleep you won't know the difference between a clue and a cauliflower. If that isn't what you're aiming at you'll have to continue relying on my discretion. Let me know what you decide."

Now he was forty-seven and ostensibly a grown-up, Jack Deacon tried to avoid fist-fights. But enough proved unavoidable that he knew there were still very few people he couldn't take. His skill with the spoken word was less comprehensive. He lost arguments all the time: with Sergeant McKinney, Superintendent Fuller, Brodie, even Daniel Hood. In the depths of his soul where he tried to be fair he suspected he'd have lost them with his own sergeant if Voss hadn't been so adept at throwing in the towel at the last minute.

But no amount of practice would have made him a good loser. He curled his lip and sniffed. He growled, "You should have called me," and about-turned quickly enough to ensure that, if Sergeant McKinney had the last word, he wouldn't hear it.

Voss was coming in from the car-park as Deacon went out. He whistled him up like a sheep-dog. "There's been another incident at Sparrow Hill."

He found the household at breakfast in the kitchen: the two girls, the African woman and Daniel. "Mr Daws not here?"

For a moment the two adults were nonplussed, thinking he meant Robert. Then Peris realised he meant Hugo. "He flew home yesterday. He couldn't leave the business any longer."

The policeman nodded. "So what happened last night?"

Daniel listened carefully while the girls told the story again, waiting for some hint that they'd gone through the same thought process that he had and come to the same conclusion. There was none. They talked about a tall man in the dark hall who swore, grabbed Johnny and ran when Em started screaming.

"How did he get in?"

They showed him the broken pane in the kitchen door, the glass lying where it fell. Immediately Deacon saw what Daniel had seen. His eyes flicked across the kitchen and saw Daniel's drop. "Mm." He thought for a moment. "Sergeant Voss, perhaps the girls would give you a conducted tour of the house. Make sure that whoever was here really has left, and that he didn't drop any clues as he went."

When they had gone he sat down heavily in the chair opposite Daniel's. "You know there wasn't a break-in, don't you?"

Daniel pursed his lips. "I don't think anyone broke in through the kitchen door. I think there was someone here."

"Then how did he get in?"

"I think he had a key."

Deacon's eyes narrowed as he made the connection. "You think Robert Daws was here? Did anyone see him?"

"Only the girls, and they didn't recognise him. But it was dark and they were scared out of their wits."

"Then how did the glass get broken?"

"After he was inside," said Daniel. "To make it look like a break-in, I suppose. To stop you asking yourself who had a key. That's what woke Johnny."

Deacon nodded slowly. "So he returned to the house where, ten days ago, he was murdering his children's mother. And he let himself in quietly with his key, and then he smashed the glass in the back door loudly enough to wake people. That's what you reckon happened?"

If Daniel wasn't entirely happy with the explanation, he couldn't see a better one. "There wasn't time after he bumped into Johnny – I'd have seen him if he'd left that way."

"And you didn't. And" – his eyes switched to Peris – "you didn't. When the light came on he was gone. That's a stone floor in the hall: did you hear him running away? Or the front door?" Peris shook her head. "Did either of you hear a car?"

"No," said Daniel. "What are you saying – no one was here?"

"Think about it," said Deacon. "Those two girls have been through hell. If they're sleeping at all, they must be having nightmares. Suppose the older one was sleep-walking. The younger one heard her moving about and went to investigate. In the dark they bumped into each other. The older girl thought she was being attacked, and the younger one thought if she was screaming there must be something to scream about. They were struggling with one another."

Daniel stared at him in frank disbelief. "Then who broke the glass in the back door?"

"Maybe the girl who was sleep-walking," said Deacon. "And that woke the younger one."

"They have names," Daniel complained softly. "Juanita and Emerald; or Johnny and Em."

"Yeah, right," said Deacon heavily. "Well, I'll get the door dusted for prints but I don't think we'll find anything. I think *Juanita*" – he put an impolite degree of emphasis on the unusual name – "was sleep-walking in here and either tried to open the door or fell against it and that's how the glass got broken. Emerald heard the noise and came downstairs. They met in the hall, and for a few moments each thought they'd bumped into a burglar. Their yells woke you two, but by the time you could respond the drama was over."

Daniel's voice was incredulous. "You're saying they made it up."

"Actually, that's not what I said. Daniel, they're two deeply disturbed young girls who had a sort of waking nightmare, and they don't know exactly where the dream ended and reality began. I think they probably believe there was an intruder; but I don't believe that. Either a burglar, or their father come to bid them a fond farewell before heading for parts unknown. Why would he swear at them? He'd tell them who he was and they'd stop screaming. Even if Mrs Daws was awake by then, all he had to do was hide in the kitchen till everything quietened down again. The girls could have said they had a bad dream but they were going back to bed now, and half an hour later have come downstairs again."

"What you're suggesting doesn't make any sense. It would be a big risk for Robert to come back here, even if he's still in the area. If he was willing to take such a chance to see his daughters, he wouldn't just run away."

When he was wrestling with a dilemma Daniel's face twisted up as if it was trying to squeeze the answer from his brain. Deacon saw him grimace and knew what it meant. "You're not convinced."

"I don't know. Maybe. It would explain why neither Peris

nor I caught even a glimpse of this man, or heard him running away. But what if you're wrong?"

Deacon shrugged. "If I'm wrong and it was Robert Daws he may try again."

"Yes. Try what?"

The detective didn't understand. "To talk to his daughters, I suppose. To apologise? Tell them he loves them?"

Daniel nodded slowly. "Yes. Maybe. If that's all he has in mind there's nothing much to worry about."

Deacon always had problems in his dealings with Daniel Hood. It wasn't that the younger man meant to be difficult, more that he seemed to see things from a different angle. He was doing it again now. "So what might he have had in mind that *would* be something to worry about?"

Daniel flicked a glance into the hall but DS Voss and the girls were elsewhere. He glanced apologetically at Peris. "Robert Daws murdered his wife. Everyone says it was desperately out of character, that he wasn't a violent man. But he took a knife and stabbed Serena thirteen times – and smashed the phone so she couldn't call for help. If that wasn't an act of calculating evil, then it was insanity.

"Superintendent, if Robert Daws has genuinely lost his mind, we can't count on him behaving like a loving father. He may no longer be thinking of the girls as his daughters. He may be thinking of them as witnesses."

# Chapter Eleven

Deacon stared at him in astonishment. After a long minute he gave his head a bemused shake. "People reckon I have a nasty suspicious mind. But compared with you, Daniel, I'm an open book."

"Do you think so?" There wasn't a trace of irony in it: he was desperate for reassurance. "You think I'm letting my imagination run away with me?"

"Daniel," said Deacon patiently, "you're letting your imagination drive you off in an open-top sports car and book you into a Brighton hotel under the names of Mr and Mrs Imagination. I never heard anything so foolish in all my life."

"But is it? We know what he's capable of."

It might have been absurd but Daniel's concern was real. Deacon sighed and bridled his tongue. "He's their father. His wife was cheating on him, she taunted him about it and he stabbed her. There's no reason in the world to think he wants his children dead too."

But Daniel wasn't convinced. "Don't say it doesn't happen because it does. Every year some man somewhere murders his wife, then murders his children in their beds, because he can't face the break-up of his family. They use guns and knives and hammers and fire. And the neighbours say they never saw it coming. That he seemed a decent, hard-working man, a good husband and father. That a kind of madness must have got into him.

"Well, we know a kind of madness got into Robert Daws. And I don't think it's safe to assume it seeped away after Serena was dead. Some force he couldn't resist brought him back here, to the one place where people knew his face and knew what he'd done. Maybe it was just the longing to see his girls again. But if it was, why did he run so quickly, before they even knew it was him?

"Because he didn't want them to know it was him, that's why. Because he has unfinished business here, and once the alarm was raised he knew he wouldn't be able to complete it. If he ran, there'd be another chance. He'll make another chance."

"To kill them," said Deacon. "Let me get this right: that *is* what you're saying? That Robert Daws came here to kill his daughters."

"*Yes*," said Daniel, dipping his head. "At least, I don't know. But that's what I'm afraid of."

"Why? He killed Serena in a storm of passion, but that was ten days ago. He's had time to calm down, to think about what he's done and what he does next. The sort of killings you're talking about, they happen inside a few minutes, an hour at the most. Nobody disappears for ten days and then comes back to finish the job."

"But who knows what a man's going to do after he's taken leave of his senses? To kill Serena like that, to leave his daughters to find her, Robert Daws had become detached from reality. He was no longer the man everyone thought he was, the man he used to be. He'd lost all contact with who he was and what other people meant to him. And he can't reconnect because there's nothing left to reconnect to. He can't come home, his wife is dead, his children know he's a murderer. He's all alone. What he did cut him off from normal human relationships, even normal human feelings.

"He knows that what he did was unforgivable. He can't live with it and he can't find a way past it. He's stuck in the intolerable present with his guilt. And those girls know what he did – saw some of it and found the rest. I think maybe he can't bear them knowing. He can't undo it, but once everyone who was involved is dead it'll be almost as if it never happened."

Peris Daws was viewing him with horror. Jack Deacon felt a quiver in his gut that another man would have recognised as pity. Daniel's reading of the situation struck him as highly improbable, but it opened a window into his yellow head.

And it was a place full of violence and the fear of violence. Monsters lurked in its dark corners.

Deacon didn't suppose it was always so. But if you take a mild man and brutalise him, you rip the ground from under his feet. Daniel Hood had believed in order and social responsibility and basic human decency; and men who believed in none of these things had torn him apart in a quest for something he could never have given them.

Somehow he survived. But the scars on his body were only part of the damage he'd sustained. He no longer knew what to expect of people. There was no aberration so vile, no hurt so intense, no cruelty so calculated he felt it could safely be discounted. Deacon had thought Daniel's problem was an occasional panic attack. In fact his life had become one enduring panic attack which he struggled to master every waking minute.

The policeman found himself reaching out a hand to Daniel's narrow shoulder. His voice was low. "I'm sorry. I didn't understand."

Now Peris was viewing him with dismay. "You mean he's right? My brother-in-law came to kill his children? And he could come back?"

"No. No," said Deacon, taking back his hand and shaking his head. "I don't think so." He dragged his gaze away from Daniel's face to answer her. "Yes, people do bizarre things at times. But they don't go away for a fortnight then come back and do some more. Either the madness has passed by then or the ability to operate has. Genuine insanity is so disruptive that most sufferers can't get themselves dressed let alone plan, execute and get away with murder.

"I'm not convinced there was anyone here. But if there was, I'm pretty sure it wasn't Robert Daws."

"But he has killed once already," said Peris steadily. "Can anyone predict what a psychopath will do next?"

"Your brother-in-law isn't a psychopath," said Deacon shortly. "That's not something you can be driven to, by an unfaithful wife or anything else. It's a personality disorder, built in at a fundamental level. If Robert had been a psychopath, everyone who knew him would have known. Instead of expressing amazement at what happened, colleagues and acquaintances would be telling us they saw it coming. That they were always uneasy round him, knew instinctively what he was capable of.

"No one says that about Robert. The only way anyone can understand it is that Serena's behaviour, in general and particularly in those few minutes, made him lose control. That does happen, but it passes. If he'd hung around long enough for me to ask why he did it he'd have said he didn't know. That it was as if someone else was doing it while he watched. He'd have been in shock. But a psychopath would have explained calmly how Serena brought it on herself; and he'd have expected me to understand."

Peris was slowly shaking her head. "I don't know him that well, but Hugo does. He'd have known if there was always something wrong with him."

"Yes, he would," agreed Deacon. "Robert isn't a psychopath. He's a desperately sad individual who was unlucky enough to find himself in the same room as the woman he loved, a painting of the boy she betrayed him with, and a knife. It's not a complicated scenario. It's a very simple one."

As he listened intently to Deacon's argument Daniel's expression passed through understanding and relief and settled on faintly embarrassed. "I'm sorry," he said to Peris, "I didn't mean to frighten you. I was just ... so worried. But Superintendent Deacon's right. I put two and two together and came up with a hundred and eighty six."

Peris flicked him a weak grin. "I guess we're all a bit twitchy after last night. So can we mend the back door? We'd feel pretty silly if we really did get burgled tonight."

Deacon chuckled. "Yes, go ahead. The Scenes of Crime Officer has got everything he needs. I'll call a glazier, should I? He'll probably come quicker for me than he would for you."

Voss returned and Daniel saw them out. Again he felt the need to apologise. "I'm sorry for wasting your time. It seemed to make sense. I was frightened for them."

"I know," said Deacon. "But I don't think there's anything to worry about."

"Should I put it to them?" wondered Daniel. "When they've settled down a bit. That they may have had bad dreams and startled one another?"

"Why not? When they're feeling calmer the idea might occur to them, in which case they'll be glad that you know. Or they may always be convinced that someone broke in. Don't make a big deal of it, either way. It was an honest mistake."

Deacon remained on the steps while Voss walked to the car. It was as if he wanted to say something else.

"Superintendent?" said Daniel.

Deacon pursed his lips. "You know, it's probably not too late. I can find you a therapist. It might be helpful to talk it all through – shine some light in the dark corners, stop it festering. You wouldn't expect physical trauma to heal without medical intervention, so why should psychological damage? Even broken bones will knit in a fashion, eventually. But unless they're set well at the start they'll never be as strong and straight as they could be."

Daniel nodded pensively. "I've been considering that. It's not really my responsibility, but I'm sure Mrs Daws would agree if I said it was something we ought to arrange. You think it is, then? You don't think we should wait and see how they're coping in another week's time?"

Deacon was staring at him uncomprehendingly. Then he gave his head a weary shake. "I wasn't talking about the girls, Daniel. I was talking about you."

By mid afternoon Brodie had gone as far as she could with Serena's address-book. She'd called everyone in it, excepting only tradesmen, and called back everyone who was only there in the evenings, and now she'd called again to round up the last few stragglers.

No one had seen Constance Ward in fifteen years. No one remembered Serena talking about her. She hadn't been at the christenings of either of her nieces. The last positive sighting was at her mother's funeral, back in the eighties. After the Peyton Parvo house was sold it might have been expected that Constance would visit her sister from time to time, but if she did none of Serena's friends was aware of it.

No one was aware of a falling-out either. But Constance had vanished entirely from her sister's life, and even moving to Australia couldn't explain that. Hugo Daws, six thousand miles away in Johannesburg, had heard of the family's tragedy and arrived to take charge within forty-eight hours. Only a deliberate severing of contact seemed to explain the rift between Serena and her sister.

Brodie had had high hopes of that address book. She'd thought it would be tedious but expected it to pay off. When it failed to she threw it down on her desk and glared at it for a traitor.

Then she picked it up again. Her perfectly shaped eyebrows drew together in the faintest of frowns. She had no idea what it was, but something in there didn't add up. Nothing to do with Constance; nothing to do with Serena's friends. Then who, and what? The only other numbers in there were tradesmen, and Brodie doubted if the local plumber knew where Constance was.

But she'd seen something that didn't chime, something unusual ... She leafed through the despised book with mounting exasperation.

And then she had it. Serena Daws had two doctors. Well, it was mildly unusual but hardly suspicious. The Dimmock number was probably her GP, the other one a specialist of some kind. A gynaecologist maybe.

But it wasn't a dialling code Brodie recognised, so it wasn't the south coast and it wasn't London. She pulled out the phone-book to check. Then she sat back, wondering what use a woman living the south of England had for any kind of specialist who practised in the Midlands. A dull tingle at the back of her knees said this was significant. After a moment she rang the number.

Dr Spedlow was not a gynaecologist but the senior medical officer at a psychiatric hospital in Warwickshire. The secretary who answered the phone professed not to know why Serena Daws would have the number in her address book.

"She was never a patient of his, then?"

The woman's voice stiffened. She intoned, "Patient confidentiality – "

"Is only an issue," finished Brodie briskly, "if Mrs Daws was indeed Dr Spedlow's patient. So you're telling me she was?"

The woman stumbled, for once let down by her mantra. "Perhaps you should speak to Dr Spedlow yourself."

"Perhaps I should," agreed Brodie.

She was expecting a crusty middle-aged man's voice full of port, cigars and self-importance. Instead she found herself speaking to a woman, crisp and professional and probably not much older than herself. "Marion Spedlow," said the doctor. "How can I help you?"

Brodie introduced herself in return, steering a middle way between burdening the psychiatrist with extraneous information and leaving her unsure of her caller's motives. "I realise this is difficult for you so let's keep it simple. Whatever your connection with Mrs Daws, you ought to know that she's dead. She died as a result of domestic violence ten days ago. As her husband is missing I'm trying to reunite two little girls with their closest blood relative, Mrs Daws' sister Constance. If you can help in any way, you'll understand the importance of doing. This isn't a frivolous request."

There was a slight pause. Then Dr Spedlow said, "I *do* understand that, Mrs Farrell. And I know you understand that I cannot divulge information on my patients to third parties, however legitimate their interest.

"So let me see if I can help you without doing that. No, Mrs Daws was never a patient here. But I met her on a number of occasions when she visited the hospital. I'm terribly sorry to hear what's happened, and I'm sorry I can't give you the information you need to help her daughters. For what it's worth, it wouldn't solve your problem if I could."

For a few moments Brodie said nothing more, digesting what she had been told and what it meant beyond the immediately obvious. "I see," she said then, slowly. "Dr Spedlow, I think I've got this right, but since it is so important I wonder if I could just run it by you. I'm sure you'll tell me if I'm too far off the mark.

"You run a residental psychiatric hospital for people suffering from disabling mental conditions. Your duties bring you into contact not only with your patients but also with their relatives. Since most of your patients find it difficult to organise their own lives successfully, you probably couldn't recommend any of them as guardians for two vulnerable young girls. Is that about the size of it?"

She could hear the warmth of Dr Spedlow's smile. "That's exactly the size of it, Mrs Farrell."

"One more thing," said Brodie. "I imagine a lot of patients have been under your care for quite a while?"

"Oh yes," said Dr Spedlow softly. "Fifteen years, some of them. Some of them less, of course, and some more."

"I see. Well, thank you for your time."

"I'm sorry I wasn't able to answer your questions," said the doctor, her voice carefully expressionless.

"Never mind," said Brodie. "It would be awful if patients got the idea their personal information could be accessed by any Tom, Dick or Harriet."

# Chapter Twelve

Brodie called Jack Deacon. "Well, I've found Constance Ward. But she isn't going to be any help to anyone. She's in a psychiatric hospital outside Birmingham – has been for fifteen years. If she isn't capable of looking after herself she certainly can't look after the girls."

Deacon swore softly down the phone. "Then Social Services step in and place them somewhere. We'll just have to try and speed things up, get them cleared for South Africa as soon as we can."

"How long's that going to take? Weeks? Months?"

But he didn't know. "It's not a problem I've hit before. But you can't send somebody's children abroad without legal authority. I'll have a word with my tame magistrate, find out what the procedure is and get it under way. But I can't see it being completed in a couple of weeks."

"Still no sign of Robert?"

"Neither hide nor hair. We're beginning to wonder if he's driven deep into the woods somewhere and french-kissed his exhaust pipe."

It wasn't the crude levity an outsider might have taken it for. It was the gritty realism that got Jack Deacon and every other police officer through the scenes of horror and heartbreak that waited behind every taped-up door. To do the job they had to be able to consider the facts dispassionately; and if they couldn't always do that, at least to pretend that they could. They made grim little jokes not out of disrespect but necessity: some of the situations they encountered were too difficult even for professionals to confront head-on. Irreverence was a device to get them past the otherwise intolerable. Brodie knew this, had done even before she knew Deacon. It didn't trouble her. If a man has a dirty and dangerous job to do he needs protective clothing. A warped sense of humour was CID's answer to the Noddy-suit. Some things you have to laugh about because the only possible alternative is to cry.

"If he did, he went to a lot of trouble not to be found."

"People do," said Deacon resignedly. "People taking their own lives fixate on the oddest things. They take a hotel room for the night so they won't leave blood in their own bath. They wear their best clothes. They water the pot-plants. They're about to kill themselves, and they're afraid the FME will comment on their tired underwear and neglected begonias!"

Brodie shrugged. "They're tidying up loose ends. It's what suicide is very often about, anyway. Things have got messy, sorting it all out is going to take too much time and effort, it's easier just to call it a day. Not even despair so much as sheer exhaustion."

Deacon paused a moment, and afterwards Brodie wasn't sure if he'd changed the subject or not. "Daniel had me a little worried today."

He told her what had happened. What everyone agreed had happened, what he believed had actually happened, and what, for a time, Daniel thought had happened.

Brodie wasn't quite sure what it was he wanted her to know. "But you're satisfied he was wrong?"

"That Robert Daws returned under cover of darkness to murder his little girls? Yes," he said heavily, "I'm satisfied he was wrong. But doesn't it bother you that he even thought that? I've never understood what was going on in his head, Brodie, you know that. If that's an example, though, he's in more trouble than I ever guessed. He's hanging onto reality by his fingertips. If he was my friend and I had an ounce of influence with him, I'd get him an appointment with a psychiatrist."

Two things astounded Brodie: his assessment of Daniel's mental state, based it seemed to her on very little evidence, and the extent to which he seemed to care. She was resigned to the fact that the two men in her life were so diametrically different that neither would ever see what she liked in the other. She was used to Daniel looking nervous when Deacon was mentioned, and Deacon looking exasperated when Daniel was.

She was familiar with his habit of deriding what he didn't comprehend, and on a couple of occasions she'd cut him off in mid-tirade when he overstepped the bounds of what she was prepared to hear about someone else she cared for. But he had never said, or so far as she knew thought, anything like this before. She stared at the phone. "Jack – what are you saying? That Daniel's losing his mind?"

"I think he's under a lot of strain," said Deacon forcibly. "Even more than we knew or should have suspected. I think he's having trouble separating reality from fear. It's no bloody wonder, given what's happened to him in the last six months, but if he doesn't get himself looked at soon I'm afraid the damage may be past repair. I know he's your friend, Brodie, that's why I'm saying this to you. If you can't or won't make him get help, I doubt if anyone else can."

When the girls reappeared for tea they had something to say. Daniel too had things he wanted to talk about but thought he'd let them go first. Then he realised he wouldn't need the list of tactful questions he'd been preparing for the last hour.

Johnny began. She glanced at Peris but spoke to Daniel. "We've been talking. Upstairs. About what happened. There really was someone, you know."

"Yes?" said Daniel encouragingly.

"That policeman thinks we made it up."

"I'm sure he doesn't. He may think you made a mistake. A lot of people tell the police things which they believe to be the truth but which turn out to be wrong."

"He grabbed me," said Johnny stubbornly. "I didn't imagine it. He grabbed me and pushed me down, and pulled my hair. I didn't see his face, but I know he was real."

Daniel nodded. "What about you, Em? Did you see him?"

Em looked up from the table, eyes bright in her pinched little face, and said, "Yes."

The adults exchanged a glance. Peris said, "There wasn't much light in the hall. Not till I found the switch."

"No," Johnny said coldly, "but there was some. The moon must have been out – there was light coming in at the windows and through the kitchen door. If there hadn't been I'd have had to switch on the light to go downstairs."

"The moon's just about full," Daniel confirmed softly. "And it was a clear night."

"All right," said Peris. "So what did you see?"

Still Em smiled her brittle smile round the table. Her sister poked her in the leg with the toe of her shoe. "Go on, tell them. Tell them what you told me."

"I know who it was," said Emerald.

"Who?" It was Peris. Both girls looked at her for a long moment, and then looked away in a manner so dismissive it must have been a deliberate insult. Daniel saw the woman's jaw clench, and felt himself blush with shame. It was intolerable how these two young girls treated her. For their sake and no other reason she'd crossed the world to keep house in a chilly English town. Perhaps she hadn't stayed when Hugo left for the thanks it would earn her, but common courtesy was the least she was entitled to. Instead they treated her like a servant.

While for some reason they regarded Daniel, who was in their family's employ, with the kind of adulation most young girls reserve for the lead singer with a boy-band. No one in his entire life had ever mistaken Daniel for a pop-singer. He'd had friends but never fans before. But he wasn't flattered so much as deeply uneasy. If the information they were waiting, shiny-eyed, to present him with had been less important he'd have made it wait while he spelled out the minimum standards of behaviour he was prepared to accept from them.

But it was important, and he didn't want them to clam up with resentment before they had shared their knowledge. He hoped Peris would understand that this was justice delayed rather than denied. He said quietly, "Your aunt asked who it was that you saw."

He thought Em was going to say it was her father. He thought he'd been right all along and Jack Deacon had been wrong. That they weren't prepared to tell the police but wanted him to know seemed like confirmation.

A very small feather moving on a very light breeze would have floored him when Em said, "It was the man in the paintings."

He stared at her until the little girl started to cringe and look to her sister for support. "Johnny ... !"

"I'm ... I'm sorry," stammered Daniel. He passed a hand across his mouth. "But are you *sure*?"

"She should be," said Johnny acidly, "she's seen him often enough. We both have."

Daniel hardly knew what to say. He looked at Peris, mainly to check that his ears weren't deceiving him, but all the reply she could manage was a helpless shrug.

He leaned forward and made Em look at him. "That's a serious thing to say about anyone. *How* sure are you? Do you mean, he reminded you of the man in the paintings? He was a tall man, a young man, it could have been the man in the paintings? Or are you telling me in all honesty that you saw his face well enough to say that was him?"

"I did," the child insisted. "He looked up when I screamed and I saw his face. It was all silvery in the moonlight but I know who it was."

"Nicky Speers," said Daniel. He didn't want there to be any doubt about who she meant. "The labourer from the farm across the road? Your mother's friend."

"Her toy-boy," Johnny said disparagingly. "We know who he is."

"What, to see? In the flesh?" He realised he could have put that better and winced. "I mean, you don't just know him from the pictures – you've seen him in person?"

"All the time," shrugged Johnny negligently. "She'd send us to do something in the house, but if we kept an eye on the studio we'd see him sneaking in. Then sneaking out again half an hour later and, hey, maybe what we'd been sent to do wasn't half done but suddenly it was done well enough and it was time to come downstairs again. Like we were stupid. Like we didn't know what the two of them were doing."

Daniel breathed lightly. "You know, kids aren't the only ones who behave badly sometimes. Adults do too. And it can matter more."

"You can say that again," said Johnny bitterly. "She fancies a bit of rough, and we end up in a scene from 'Uncle Tom's Cabin'!"

Peris's capable hands hit the table so hard it, and all around it, jumped. She wasn't exactly shouting. She was actually whispering very loud. "I have had just about *enough* of this."

"So have I," said Daniel with absolute certainty. "Johnny, you apologise right now. Your Aunt Peris is the only thing standing between you and a children's home. She's left her own home, her family and her country six thousand miles away to help you through a difficult time; and if the best you can do is snipe and sling insults at her, I can't imagine why she'd stay. And you needn't think I'll take her place. If she leaves, so will I. Think about that. But don't think about it very long."

Em caught her sister in a panicky look. "Johnny ... !" she whined again.

Even Johnny seemed aware that she'd overstepped the bounds of what tolerant people who felt sorry for her would take. A dull flush travelled up her cheek and her fierce gaze dropped. She kept her eyes on the tablecloth. "I'm sorry."

But having finally been roused to anger, Peris wasn't ready to be mollified. "I'm sorry too, but it's not enough. If you have problems with the colour of my skin, until you can find someone white to look after you you'd better keep them to yourself. I'm not your servant, and I'm sure as hell not your slave. I've tried to behave like family to you. If you resent me so much, maybe I should go home. Maybe you'd sooner live in an orphanage. And maybe I don't much care what you'd prefer."

Em started to cry, little sobs that flooded the button-bright eyes, stole her breath and bounced her up and down on her chair. "John-n-n-ny ... !" she wailed. If she hadn't a huge conversational repertoire, she could at least wring the maximum number of meanings from one word.

For a second the older girl seemed determined to hold out. Then she sucked in a deep, unsteady breath and turned hot eyes on the angry woman beside her. "I'm sorry," she said again. "Really. I don't know why I keep saying such horrible things. I don't know where they come from. Please don't leave us. We can't manage alone ... "

For a second Peris was torn between the entirely human temptation to push her advantage for all it was worth and a sudden unexpected welling of almost maternal sympathy. Then she shook her head in despair, threw a plump arm round each of them, and groaned, "Why would I do that? When we're having such fun together?"

When the girls had left the table, with little diffident smiles she found almost as hard to deal with as the sniping, Peris spread her palms flat on the tablecloth and looked over them at Daniel. "Nicky Speers. I never saw that coming. I suppose we believe them?"

Daniel was as taken aback as she was. "We can't afford not to. They could be mistaken, but they seem pretty sure. They could be lying but I don't know why they would."

"Because they blame a lot of what's happened on Nicky Speers?" suggested Peris. "They've lost their mother, to all intents and purposes they've lost their father, they're going to lose their home, and the most obvious cause is a farm-boy who couldn't keep his trousers on in the presence of another man's wife. You can't blame them for hating him. And they're two young girls who do a thorough job of hating. I can imagine them trying to make trouble for him."

Daniel puffed out his cheeks like a bemused chipmunk. "Well, it's not something we can deal with. I'll call Superintendent Deacon, see what he makes of it. I just hope ... " His voice petered out.

"What?"

"I just hope they're not making more trouble for themselves than, even in the circumstances, they can expect to be forgiven for."

Rather to Daniel's surprise, Deacon took the girls' accusation seriously. Partly because he felt it wasn't safe to do anything else. But also because some of the things that hadn't quite fitted might be explained if Nicky Speers was the intruder. He was a regular visitor to Sparrow Hill, and while he seemed mostly to have met Serena in the cottage it was entirely possible that he had acquired a key to the house. She may have given it to him or he may have pocketed it, tempted to see if he could share in the wealth of the Daws family.

The policeman interviewed both girls again, one at a time, in the presence of their aunt. They each told him exactly what they'd told her and Daniel. Johnny was unable to identify the intruder, although she could give a physical description that matched Nicky Speers. Em still insisted that she'd seen his face well enough to recognise him.

"Why didn't you tell me this when we were talking earlier?"

Em's eyes dropped to the bony knees under her pinafore. "Don't know."

"Maybe you weren't sure then," suggested Deacon, surprising not only Peris but himself with his patience. "Maybe it was only when you were talking to your sister later on that it struck you who it could have been."

But Em shook her head, the pale floss of hair bouncing. "I knew who it was. I didn't think anybody'd believe me."

"Why wouldn't we believe you?"

"I'm eleven," she said with devastating logic. "Nobody believes you when you're eleven."

He grinned at her and she ventured a shy grin back. "Em, being eleven doesn't make you less trustworthy than somebody older. But people of all ages make mistakes, and it can matter tons if they say that somebody did something bad when he didn't. I'm not saying you're mistaken about Nicky Speers. But I want you to think really hard before you say you're sure. Was it Nicky? Or could it have been someone who just looked very much like him?"

She did as he asked and gave it more thought. Then she nodded. "It was him. Really it was." And then, as the obvious way of confirming it occurred to her: "Why don't you ask him?"

"Don't worry," said Jack Deacon, nodding earnestly. "I intend to."

# Chapter Thirteen

Deacon went straight to the farm but Nicky Speers had finished for the day. Philip Poole directed him to a cottage a mile up the road where the peeling front door was answered by a middle-aged woman with bad teeth.

"Are you Mrs Speers?"

"'s." She didn't ask who he was or why he wanted to know.

Deacon produced his warrant card anyway. "I need a word with your son Nicky. Is he home?"

This time he didn't get even a single consonant in reply. She turned from the open door, and taking this as an invitation he followed her up rickety stairs to a room in the eaves. She didn't knock but pushed the door open and left him standing there, unannounced and unexplained. Deacon sighed and got out his warrant card again.

Nicky Speers, sprawled on his unmade bed in unconscious echo of Serena's painting, surrounded by posters of motorcycles, looked puzzled and then, when he realised who his visitor was, afraid. But Deacon had been a detective too long to think that a fear of the police was the prerogative of the criminal classes. Mostly it worked the other way round. Career criminals dealt with the police all the time, knew how to conduct themselves, knew it was easier to know who was responsible for a particular occurrence than to prove it. It was the law-abiding majority who tended to panic at the sight of a police-car in the drive.

Speers gave a statement to DS Voss the day after the murder but this was the first time he and Deacon had met. He got up from the bed, unfolding under the low ceiling like a stick-insect emerging from a chrysalis, and kept wary eyes on the policeman as if there was a prospect of violence. "What do you want?"

"I want to talk to you. About events at Sparrow Hill."

The boy drew an unsteady breath. "It wasn't my fault. I didn't make her do anything. She ... made the running."

Deacon snorted with malicious humour. "What – she jumped your bones?"

"Yes! Well, sort of. I mean ... "

"I'm not sure what you mean," said Deacon heavily. "I take it you're not accusing her of rape?"

"No. 'Course not."

"Of course not," agreed Deacon. "Then you were consenting adults and the responsibility was shared between you. I suppose you could argue that she was the one with a family to betray, but do you know, I doubt if those little girls see it like that?"

Nicky stared at his feet and mumbled, "Suppose not."

"So." Deacon turned slowly on the spot, looking at the posters. "Motorbikes, hm? Is that yours at the gate?" Nicky nodded. "Nice. Expensive. A lot of bike for a farm labourer to be knocking round on."

"I saved up," said the boy defensively.

"Yeah, right," said Deacon ironically. "Nicky, if you started saving your pocket-money when you were ten years old you still wouldn't have the deposit for a bike like that. She helped you, didn't she? Mrs Daws."

He shrugged, six feet of barely adult awkwardness. "So? I helped her."

Sheer astonishment made Deacon laugh out loud. "Nicky, you got her killed! You messed around with a married woman until her husband was so angry he stabbed her. Thirteen times. Then he jumped up and down on the phone so she couldn't call an ambulance, then he left her body for her little girls to find. Just exactly how does that count as helping her?"

Nicky Speers was blushing furiously. "That's not what I meant! She wanted to paint me. I ... you know ... posed for her. She wanted to pay me. For my time. She paid the deposit on the bike."

Deacon nodded and sniffed. "I see. Well, I suppose it's nice to have a memento of her. Something else that's out of your league to take for a ride."

Jack Deacon was not a famously articulate man. It was perhaps his tragedy that he found it easier to find the right words when they were hurtful than when a little kindness was called for. Because of this he had almost no friends. People will forgive a man who can never think of the right thing to say, but not one who hits the nail on the head only when the point is lodged in someone's flesh.

There aren't many careers in which there would be any up-side to this, so perhaps it was fortunate that Deacon had found one. Occasionally his spikes nailed to the wall someone even nastier than he was, and then people who normally tried to avoid being in the elevator with him were full of slightly appalled admiration. Deacon himself, in those rare moments when he engaged in introspection, recognised it as both a strength and a weakness, but it never occurred to him it was something he could change. Be a bit slower with the poison darts and quicker to praise. If challenged, which he never was, he'd have said he spoke as he found and people could take him or leave him. Practically, though, it's hard to ignore a six-foot-two, fifteen stone Detective Superintendent with the power to lock you up without your shoelaces.

Nicky Speers, at the tender age of not-quite-twenty, had taken a fair bit of stick over his relationship with Mrs Daws. When friends or workmates goaded him he gave as good as he got. But he had no way of dealing with the invective of a senior police officer, so he stood there and took it. His lips trembled and tears spilled onto his hollow cheeks.

"For pity's sake," grunted Deacon disgustedly – some of his disgust was possibly for himself – "if you've got the morals of a ferret you'd better develop a hide to match." Unaccountably this didn't seem to make the boy feel any better. Deacon shrugged and moved on. "Where were you last night?"

"*Last* night?" Nicky had thought they were talking about the murder. "Here, at home."

"From what time?"

"About eleven."

"Until?"

"Until I left for work at five to eight." He wiped his sleeve across his face. "Why?"

"Because I want to know," said Deacon shortly. "Was anyone else here?"

"My mam."

"What time did she go to bed?"

If a lie would have served he'd have lied. But Cissie Speers hadn't been a nighthawk when she was her son's age: now she was mostly tucked up with a mug of cocoa half way through the evening. "About nine o'clock."

"So you can't actually prove you were here at, say, four o'clock this morning?"

Nicky stared at him blankly. "Can anyone?"

Deacon bristled. "Don't get smart with me, sonny. Not when I've got witnesses who put you somewhere else. Somewhere you'd no business being, at four o'clock this morning or any other time."

"Where?"

It was a natural enough question, Deacon supposed, though to someone who had genuinely been in his own bed it should have been immaterial where anyone else thought they'd seen him. "Sparrow Hill."

If the boy's eyes opened any wider they'd pop out. "I haven't been near Sparrow Hill. Why would I, now – you know? Last *night*? I was here last night. Why would I go to Sparrow Hill?"

Deacon didn't answer. "Do you have a key?"

"Not to the house."

"Do you have one to the cottage?"

Nicky hesitated and his gaze flickered. "I did have."

"Where is it now?"

"I threw it away. After – " Again, the gap left for the unsayable.

"So you could have had a key to the big house too, and thrown it away at the same time."

"I didn't!"

"But you could have."

"Serena gave me a key to the cottage because that's where we met. Why would she give me a key to her house?" His voice vibrated with the need to be believed.

"Maybe she didn't. Maybe you took one."

"*Why*?"

Deacon gave him a cynical look. "Robert Daws is a wealthy man. There are valuable things in his house. Now, I don't suppose you expected Serena to leave him and come and live with you and your mother in a labourer's cottage, so at some point you knew she was going to get bored and show you the door. If you had a key to the house you could come back and help yourself to a retirement package."

"I'm not a *thief*!" exclaimed Nicky Speers indignantly.

"Jesus, Nicky," growled Deacon, "this whole thing happened because you couldn't keep your hands off another man's property."

The boy's brow furrowed as he tried to make sense of it. "Is that what they're saying? That I went to the house last night – this morning – to steal things? That somebody saw me?"

Deacon nodded. "Pretty much."

"It isn't true."

"My witnesses are lying?"

"Yes! What was taken?"

The policeman pursed his lips. "They're still looking round." It wasn't *exactly* a lie; anyway, he didn't mind lying.

Nicky spread gangling arms. "Do you want to search my room? You can do. If you can find anything that belongs at Sparrow Hill you can arrest me here and now."

"Actually," grunted Deacon, "I could do that anyway. But

since you offer ... " He lifted the eiderdown and looked under the bed. Then he straightened, shuddering. "Do you know there's half a pizza under there?"

"Is there?" From his tone Deacon suspected he'd haul it out and eat it when he was alone.

He didn't expect to find anything in Nicky's room and he didn't. "Shall we have a look downstairs now?"

He ended up checking every room in the house, and then the garden shed. He found no goods which looked to have come from Sparrow Hill. Of course, none had been reported missing. It was just too good an opportunity to miss: a suspect inviting a policeman to inspect his property.

They were finished in the shed and Deacon was about to turn off his torch when a tiny glint caught his eye. He shone the beam into the dark corner to see what it was. Then he took a plastic bag out of his pocket and carefully, deliberately, picked the thing up through it.

"You want to tell me what this is?"

Nicky blinked. It was, after all, fairly obvious. "It's a knife."

"In fact, it's a kitchen knife." Deacon's voice was expressionless. "What's it doing in your garden shed?"

"Somebody must have dropped it."

"You?"

"I don't think so. I've never seen it before."

Deacon considered. "Is there a lot of passing traffic through your garden shed?"

"My dad used to come in here. My mum does. Look, it's an old kitchen knife. Somebody was using it in here and dropped it. What's the big deal? You're not telling me that was stolen from Sparrow Hill last night?"

Deacon shook his head. "Not last night, no. But I've seen something like it before, Nicky. Do you know where? In a little drawing the Forensic Medical Examiner made for me after he'd done the autopsy on Serena Daws. She wasn't stabbed with one knife, Nicky, she was stabbed with two. One of them we found at the scene, one we didn't. It was smaller – about this size. And narrower – about this shape.

"Nicky, let's go and get your coat, and tell your mum that you're coming into town with me. I want us to talk some more at the police station. I want you to explain to me how a knife that corresponds with some of the wounds in Serena Daws' body came to be dropped in your garden shed."

Peris Daws knocked diffidently on the cottage door. Inside Daniel's voice said, "It's open." She glanced back at the kitchen door of Sparrow Hill, resplendent with its new glass, and the two girls hovering on the doorstep waved encouragement. So she did as he said.

Once inside it was clear why he hadn't come to the door. He had a star-chart as big as a rug spread across his knees, with open books located strategically within reach.

Peris frowned and shook her head. "Whatever ... ?"

Daniel waved an apologetic hand, and one of the three small books he was holding in it like playing-cards slid onto his knee. "Sorry about the mess. I can't work out what it is I'm seeing. In Cassiopeia, just south of Shedir. It's not its companion: I know what that looks like, and this is brighter than ninth magnitude. I'm thinking, comet? Rogue asteroid? Nova? The Milky Way runs through Cassiopeia, it could be a major event on the far side of the galaxy.

"And then I'm thinking, certainly. None of the observatories have reported it, none of the big comet-hunters have picked it up, but I've spotted it with a second-hand telescope cobbled together out of garden canes and old spectacles."

About then he realised he was boldly going entirely alone. With a wry grin he put aside the books and papers that covered him like leaf-mould and gave her his full attention.

Peris was still frowning. "I have no idea what you just said."

He took her to the terrace where the telescope was pointing at the sky. Of course, the sky had moved while he was inside with the star-charts: he adjusted the alignment and showed her. "That white spot, just to the left of the reddish star?"

"Fly-speck?" she hazarded.

"It wouldn't be the first time an amateur astronomer has tried to give his name to a bit of dust on his mirror," admitted Daniel. "What can I do for you?"

They went back inside. Peris glanced around the living room. Packing away Serena's belongings had lightened the oppressive mood of the cottage. "You're quite comfortable in here, aren't you?"

Daniel nodded, wondering what was coming.

Peris wasn't good at subterfuge. She gave a gusty sigh. "I've been sent with a message – though it's only fair to add I'm not happy myself. After what happened last night – whatever it was – and with Hugo away, we're three poor defenceless women alone in a big spooky house with night coming on. We wondered if we could persuade you to move into the main house. We've got a guest-room ready, and we'll help you shift your stuff, and ... "

"And?"

"And if you don't, we're going to move in here with you."

When Brodie arrived at Sparrow Hill to deliver the bad news about Constance, sounds like a party in progress greeted her through the sitting-room window. She identified the voices of two adults and two children, playing some sort of word game. From the speed of play and the level of excitement she judged the scores were pretty even.

The game, she knew, would be Daniel's idea – he had a huge repertoire of the things kept in reserve for last-days-of-term – but he wasn't good at any of them. If whoever had drawn him as a partner thought she'd got the inside track, by now she'd be feeling rather disappointed. He thought too much instead of firing from the hip. When they did this at her flat Brodie always beat him. So, actually, did Paddy.

121

She rang the front door bell. Peris answered it, standing in the block of light escaping from the hall. "Mrs Farrell? Oh – have you some news for us? Come in, we're through here."

"Can we talk privately for a moment? You may want to think about what you're going to tell the girls."

Puzzled, Peris pursed her lips and glanced back at the sitting-room door. And then it was too late, because the door opened and Emerald bounced into the hall with her sister a couple of strides behind.

Johnny said, "It's your turn, Peris," and Em said, "It's Daniel's friend." Then Daniel came out into the hall as well and she had the full set.

She nodded to him over the top of the girls' heads. "I got somewhere with that job I was working on." Then she said, "I'm parched. Does anyone mind if I make a cup of tea?"

"I'll make it," Peris said significantly, leading the way into the kitchen. Brodie followed.

Daniel steered the girls back into the sitting-room. "I'd better see what she wants. You play for me, Em, and Johnny can play for Peris. And no cheating. And no words you wouldn't use in front of us."

They beamed and went back inside, and he shut the door and followed the women to the kitchen.

"I've found Constance," said Brodie. "But she won't be able to help. She's been in a mental institution for fifteen years."

Peris put a hand to her mouth. "Damn!" Then, suddenly embarrassed, "I mean – "

But Brodie wasn't shocked. The two women had never met, Constance's condition was the misfortune of a stranger, but its implications for Peris and her charges were profound. No wonder her own problems weighed heaviest in her mind. "Damn's putting it mildly. I sat and swore for five minutes after I got off the phone."

"How did you find her?" asked Daniel. She told them

about the two doctors in the address-book, and the carefully choreographed discussion she had with the second one.

Daniel sighed. "There doesn't seem much doubt, then."

Brodie shook her head. "I'm sorry, Mrs Daws. There was always the risk that, when I found Constance, she wouldn't be able to help."

Peris was pulling herself together by sheer strength of will. "Of course there was," she said briskly. "You've done all we asked, Mrs Farrell, and sooner than we hoped. At least now we know we're on our own. I'll call Hugo, decide what we do next."

"Are you going to tell the girls?" wondered Brodie.

"I don't know." Peris looked to Daniel. "What do you think?"

His narrow shoulders lifted in a helpless shrug. "Maybe we should. They know Brodie's here, they know she was looking for Constance, when they think about it they'll guess it's not good news or we'd in there sharing it with them. I think if they work it out for themselves they'll to be more scared than if we come clean. I don't want them thinking they can't trust us."

Peris nodded slowly. "It's better that we're honest. Even if they're upset, even if they get angry. Daniel ... "

He knew what she was going to say. "Do you want me to tell them?"

Her eyes were grateful. "They'll ask me questions I can't answer, at least until I've spoken to Hugo. Tell them I'll stay as long as I can. Tell them we'll take them home as soon as we can."

"Tell them Jack'll expedite things as much as he can," added Brodie. "He couldn't say how long it would take but he's already onto it. Tell them they'll be all right, wherever they end up. It won't be for long, and you and I will still be around. We'll make sure they're OK."

Daniel nodded and reached for the kitchen door. "If you hear the sound of flying furniture, come and rescue me."

He paused outside the sitting-room. It wasn't going to be easy to bring them up to date without scaring them. But he didn't believe in secrets. He thought sometimes children needed a simpler version of the truth than adults, but the truth itself was a kind of basic human right, that no one had the right to deny to anyone else.

He could hear their voices inside, still playing the game. There was more animation in them, more enjoyment, than at any time since they first met. His smile was edged with regret. They'd made a start on the road back, and already someone was ready to knock them into the gutter; and it was *him*.

When he'd told them Em looked at Johnny, seeking a cue as to how serious it was. Johnny got up from the sofa and stalked over to the uncurtained window, head down, fists deep in the pockets of her denim skirt. "Of course," she muttered bitterly. "Why would we expect anything different? Our mother's dead, our father's missing and our aunt is shovelling cornflakes into her ear in a lunatic asylum. Isn't that what they mean by 'par for the course'?"

"You've had some rotten luck," Daniel acknowledged quietly. "But it's not all doom and gloom. Hugo and Peris want you to go and live with them. It'll take a little time to organise but then you'll have an exciting new country to get to know."

Johnny turned and stared at him in astonishment. "We're not going to live in South Africa! This is our home – why on earth would we want to go to South Africa?"

This was being harder than he'd expected. "You're too young to live alone. Until you're old enough to take responsibility for Em you have to be in the charge of an adult."

The girl shrugged. "Peris is an adult."

"Peris can't stay forever! She has her own life to get back to. She'd be good to you, you know. As you get to know one another better, learn to respect one another, it'd get easier."

Johnny was frowning. "We don't need her forever. We don't *want* her forever. We only need her to stay until my father gets back and sorts things out."

If she'd hit him in the face with a cricket bat Daniel could hardly have been more stunned. He'd known their understanding was incomplete, their emotions in turmoil. He hadn't realised that the basic facts of what had happened had somehow passed them by. He hadn't asked if they realised that their father had killed their mother, and neither had anyone else.

He dropped into the deep armchair, his knees suddenly gone to string, with the eyes of both girls expectant on him. "Oh dear God," he whispered, sufficiently disturbed to forget for the moment that he was an atheist. "You think he'll come back, and then everything'll be how it was?"

"Hardly," sniffed Johnny. "Our mother's dead. Murdered. She wasn't the easiest woman in the world to live with, but it's a bit harsh to suggest she won't be missed."

Daniel's brain was tripping over itself in the effort to catch up. "Who-o-o – ?" He swallowed and tried again. "Who do you think killed her?"

The girls traded a fast look. "We don't know," Johnny said firmly, "we didn't see. But Daddy went after him. When he gets back he'll be able to tell us."

# Chapter Fourteen

A nineteen-year-old male is a mass of contradictions. He has the body of a man. Sexually he's at his peak. Physically his strength-to-weight ratio is as good as it will ever be – he may gain in strength over the next few years but he'll have more mass to move around as well. He's fast on his feet, his reactions are superb, and he can go all day on chips and the odd can of lager.

The reason that even men whose careers hang on their physique don't reach their maximum potential for another ten years is that most nineteen-year-olds are emotionally still boys. They're old enough to fight and die for their country, to marry and have children, to vote for their government and drive a car, but emotionally they are not yet men. Few of them are genuinely independent, psychologically or financially. Few of them are ready to take full responsibility for themselves much less anyone else. More of them than would admit it are still constrained in their actions by what their mothers would think.

In addition, their experience of the world is severely limited. As athletes progress through their twenties, their thirties and even sometimes their forties, their fund of experience coupled with their greater maturity offsets their declining physical prowess. Their minds work faster and better. They may have less energy but they also waste less. The confidence that comes from having overcome most challenges is worth more to them than the naked strength of the younger man.

Nineteen is therefore a bad age to be accused of murder. Nicky Speers sat in the interview room at Dimmock Police Station, with Detective Superintendent Deacon eyeing him across a table that was nowhere near wide enough, and trembled with the adrenalin flooding his muscles because his still-immature brain thought this was a situation that could be resolved by fight or flight. It wasn't. Even Nicky knew it wasn't. But his head was full of cotton-wool while his hands itched for action. He knew if he left them to their own devices they'd rip the tape-recorder off the wall and toss it at someone's head, and that would be as good as a signed confession. He was concentrating so hard on controlling them that he genuinely didn't understand half of what Deacon was saying to him.

The superintendent sighed. "It's a simple enough question, Nicky. Where did the knife come from? Did you buy it? What did you buy it for?"

"I've never seen it before!" insisted the boy, a whine in his voice that wasn't far from a sob.

"Yet it was in your shed. What are you suggesting – that shortly before you and I went out there, Robert Daws decided your shed would be a good place to dispose of one of the knives he stabbed his wife with? That he sneaked past your cottage so quietly that neither you, me nor your mother noticed, then sneaked away again after he'd left it where it could be found? Is that how you read it?"

By and large – there are exceptions – farmers don't do irony. The sense of humour on agricultural premises inclines to the broad. A working farm is the last place in the civilised world where nailing someone's wellingtons to the floor is considered the height of wit. Nicky had no experience of repartee. He thought Deacon was looking for a rational explanation. "You can get in over the back wall ... "

"The back wall!" exclaimed Deacon, leaning back in his chair, his eyebrows arching in admiration. "I never thought of that. Tell me, how high is your back wall?"

Nicky shrugged. "I can see over it. I can climb over it."

"Five foot?" suggested Deacon. "Six?"

"Maybe five foot."

"And you can climb over it. Of course, you're nineteen. Robert Daws is forty-six. And he's a fat man, so I'm told, and

127

a grocer. OK, a big nationwide sort of grocer, but still a grocer. Do you know, I can't see a fat forty-six-year old grocer scrambling over your five-foot back wall even if he wanted to. And I can't for the life of me see why he'd want to."

That at least seemed pretty obvious. "To shift suspicion onto me!"

Deacon nodded pensively. "Well, yes, he might want to do that. Only, if a man runs away from a murder scene and lies low for ten days, it's a bit late to try to persuade people it was all a misunderstanding, it was actually someone else holding the knife. You know? And this is an intelligent man, Nicky, a man who makes big money out of guessing right. I can't see him staking everything on a wild card like that."

"Fine," snapped Nicky, his patience and his voice wearing thin. "It wasn't Daws, it was someone else. But it's not my knife, and I didn't know it was there. You spotted it because you were looking for something suspicious. All I'm looking for when I go in the shed is a saw, or a hammer, or some oil for a squeaky hinge. I find it and go. I don't spend a lot of time poking round on the floor!"

"You're saying it could have been there for a while and nobody noticed it?"

"Yes!" exclaimed Nicky, relieved finally to be making some progress.

"So it could have been there since the day of the murder."

Too late Nicky saw the pit yawn for him. Even back-pedalling for all he was worth he felt himself sliding into it. "How would *I* know? I never saw it before. It isn't my knife!"

"It's a kitchen knife," said Deacon. "You buy them in sets, four different sizes."

"So maybe you should ask my mam."

"You think it might have come from your kitchen?"

"It might have."

"You think she might have the other three?"

"She might have. Ask her!"

Deacon pursed his lips. "What if she's only got two?"

128

Again the sensation of the ground crumbling under the boy's feet. "What?"

"Well, we assumed the weapon she was killed with came from the kitchen in Serena Daws' cottage. Now you're telling me it could have come from yours. If the two knives she was stabbed with match, and match other knives in *your* kitchen, and one of them was found at the scene of the crime, you have to admit that won't look good."

He couldn't remember admitting anything. He couldn't remember saying that either knife came from his house, let alone both of them. He gritted his teeth to stop them chattering. "I didn't kill Serena. I never hurt Serena. I never would have."

"So why were you in her house last night?"

Nicky stared at him, aghast. "I wasn't *in* her house last night!"

"Nicky, you were seen! Give me a reason. Tell me you dropped your dear old dad's watch last time you were there, or you wrote her some love-letters you wanted to recover, or even that you wanted one of her paintings as a keepsake. Make something up if you have to, but don't tell me my witnesses imagined bumping into you in their hall in the middle of the night!"

"They did!" he exclaimed, his young voice soaring. "Who did?"

"For pity's sake," growled Deacon, exasperated, "the whole bloody household was there. If you weren't returning to the scene of your crime, what were you doing?"

Nicky's eyes, white-rimmed with panic, flicked round the room as if seeking a way out, as if he was about to make a run for it. He wouldn't, of course, have got three paces. Deacon would have stopped him before he reached the door; if by any chance he managed to evade the superintendent, his sergeant would have given chase; and if he made the corridor he didn't know the way out. It was absurd. It was a measure of his desperation that he even considered it.

He didn't know what else he could say. He'd denied everything he'd been accused of, and he hadn't been believed. He said thickly, "She wasn't killed in the house. She was killed in the cottage."

The way Deacon looked at him, that was a mistake. "So she was," he said gravely, "so she was. How did you know?"

"*Everybody* knows!" yelled the anxious youth. "It was in the goddamned papers! Mr Poole found her there and called the police. Everyone in Dimmock knows she was killed in the cottage!"

There are two kinds of police interrogation. One is handled like a scalpel, delicately, precisely, teasing out information, dissecting down through the layers of deceit to the kernel of the truth. The other is more like a bludgeon, swung with more strength than accuracy, hitting hard enough to lift the suspect off his feet. In this kind of interview the quality of the questions is less important than the number and the way they just keep coming, from a variety of angles and too quickly for the suspect to know which are relevant, which should be answered with particular care. The purpose is to unsettle him, to get him angry, to make him say and do things he wouldn't if he were calm.

Jack Deacon was an expert in the latter type of interrogation. Not because he couldn't use a scalpel but because he enjoyed hitting the table hard enough to see the pots fly. "But everyone in Dimmock wasn't seen prowling late at night in the home of his murdered ex-lover!"

Charlie Voss knew what Deacon was doing. He knew he hadn't made a single claim that couldn't be brushed aside by anyone calm enough to analyse it. But Nicky Speers wasn't calm. He thought he was in a trap, and he was too spooked by Deacon's confidence to appreciate the paucity of his argument. He thought he was going to be charged with murder, and after that the trial was a mere formality. He thought Deacon had the power to lock him up until he was an old, old man.

He came to his feet with a rush, with a sound that was half a roar and half a wail, that made the hair stand up on the back of Voss's neck, and his long arms flailed about him more as if he were swatting flies than fighting policemen. His eyes rolled wildly in the sweaty pallor of his face, and he looked as if he'd try to dig his way out through the wall if he couldn't reach the door.

In a way this was what Deacon had been aiming at. He wanted to break the boy's nerve, to strip away his defences and leave him naked, without a lie to cover him. He should, thought Voss, have looked happier at his success. Instead, still sitting, he pushed his chair back from the table and said gruffly, "Calm down."

But it was too late. Nicky no longer had control of either his mind or his limbs. He threw his fists about like a shadow-boxer, then turned and slammed himself against the wall. "I can't stay here," he cried desolately into the dingy beige plaster. "You can't keep me. Let me go."

Afraid he might hurt himself, Voss moved to restrain him. But Nicky threw him off with enough force to spill the sergeant onto the table. More surprised than hurt, Voss picked himself up for another go. But Deacon waved him back with a hand the size of a Sunday roast.

"Sir?" Voss wasn't sure what he intended, but he knew Deacon was physically capable of ripping the hysterical youth off the wall and bouncing him off the ceiling if he thought it necessary. He'd never seen Deacon use violence on a suspect who hadn't started the fight himself, but there was that about the big man that suggested that one day, with enough provocation, he might. The aura of threat was more valuable to him than a truncheon; but it only worked while it seemed credible. If even Voss didn't know for sure, it was certainly that.

"Stand aside, sergeant," Deacon said distinctly. "You don't want to have to explain a black eye to Superintendent Fuller, do you?"

Nicky saw him coming and thought he was going to be hurt. He was literally crying with fear. At the end of his long arms the clenched fists swung out of control, easy to dodge. Deacon ducked under them and his own hands shot out, powerful and precise. Voss winced and wondered again if he should try to intervene.

But they'd both misunderstood. Deacon grabbed the boy by the shoulders, pinning his arms to his sides. Still his fists flailed, desperate and unco-ordinated, and his nose ran and his lips trembled and tears flooded down his ashy cheeks.

With an abrupt movement Deacon turned the boy in the ambit of his arms, and closed his hands over Nicky's fists, holding him still against his broad chest. "Steady," he said quietly into the boy's ear. "It's all right. Nobody's going to hurt you. Calm down."

Voss watched in amazement and respect as the man known throughout Dimmock Police Station as The Grizzly went on holding the terrified boy, and talking quietly to him, until the rigor of absolute panic passed, his long body relaxed and his wild eyes stilled and then closed.

In the corridor outside Deacon, unaware that he'd managed to surprise his sergeant yet again, shook his head irritably. "He didn't kill her. And I don't think he was in the house."

"What about the knife?" asked Voss.

The big man shrugged. "Maybe it *is* a coincidence. Maybe his mum dropped it after tying up her tomatoes."

"Dr Roy will be able to tell us that."

"Call him," said Deacon, "ask if he has anything for us yet."

When Voss came back five minutes later, Deacon knew the answer from his expression. "Nicky's knife matches exactly the unexplained wound in Serena Daws' thigh. And there are traces of her blood still on it."

# Chapter Fifteen

Brodie stared at her friend in dismay. "They don't know. Everyone's assumed that, because it was obvious to us ... But they don't *know!*"

Shock had knocked all expression out of Peris's face and voice. "Should we tell them?"

Daniel had no idea. Either way those two young girls had a whole lot more grief waiting for them. The only question was whether they would be better facing it now, or waiting till their father was found and charged, or waiting for understanding to dawn on them gradually. And for once Daniel couldn't see what was the right thing to do. "I don't know."

Brodie had a qualification neither of the others possessed: she was a parent. She found their eyes settling on her. "God damn it, don't look at me like that! Yes, I've got a little girl of my own. But I've never had to decide whether or not to tell her that her father murdered her mother! Daniel, you've had hundreds of children in your care, you must have had to break bad news before now."

"Yes," he nodded slowly, remembering. "But only when there was no choice."

"*Do* we have a choice?" asked Peris.

"Actually, we do," said Brodie. "We're talking as if we *know* Robert is a murderer, and the girls are the only ones who don't. In fact, none of us knows. We have a pretty good idea, we'll be astonished if he proves us wrong, but it's still conjecture. Maybe, if it comforts them to hold onto an illusion, it's too soon for us to take it away."

"It'll get easier?" asked Peris dubiously.

"It'll never be easy," said Daniel. "But Brodie's right: until we can tell them there's no doubt we have nothing to tell them. They're as entitled to their view as anyone else."

That Peris could accept. "We'll have to remember, though. We'll have to be careful what we say around them."

"Like walking on eggshells," nodded Brodie.

"Eggshells with landmines under them," said Daniel weakly.

Deacon spent another hour with Nicky Speers, an hour entirely wasted. All the questions had already been asked and answered. Everyone present was too tired to think up new ones.

In a way, finding the knife changed little. The Speers' garden shed was not a secure private place in the way that a house or even a garage might be: anyone could have planted the knife there. Even if Robert Daws wasn't up to scaling high walls, he could have sneaked up the garden path any time in the last ten days to avenge himself on his rival.

Deacon was uncomfortably aware that, if someone was jerking his strings, he was responding exactly as required. But what choice had he? The knife he found in Nicky's shed was previously in the body of Serena Daws. If its presence on his property didn't prove the boy's guilt, it certainly put him up there on the list of suspects. And it was a very short list.

On the other hand, there was no evidence that Nicky had ever handled the knife. It had been both wiped and washed so that all remained was a few grains of dried blood between blade and handle. Voss had returned to the cottage to speak to Mrs Speers but discovered nothing helpful. She said she didn't recognise the knife, but then she would. She didn't have two others like it, but she did have a drawer full of assorted kitchen implements collected over a lifetime. There was no way of knowing if the two knives now in the possession of the police had been among them or not.

Unless – It was a long shot but he got SOCO out to take samples of the dust and fluff gathered at the back of the kitchen drawer. If there were traces of corresponding gunge on the knives, that would connect them physically to the inside of locked premises occupied solely by the Speers family and Nicky would go to prison because his mother was a slattern.

Meanwhile time was passing, the clock ticking away the hours Nicky could be held for questioning. Already Deacon was up against the law of diminishing returns. At midnight he phoned Superintendent Fuller. "I'm going to send him home. The time is more valuable than anything I'm doing with it."

There was a silence in which he could feel Fuller blinking owlishly at the phone. "But you have physical evidence connecting him to the crime."

"It's tenuous," said Deacon, shaking his head as if someone could see him. "We have nothing tying *him* to the knife. He's right, it could have been put there by someone wanting to incriminate him. I can't show that it wasn't. It makes no sense to go on holding him at this time. He might as well sleep in his own bed, and leave me with extra hours to question him if I turn up something to shake his story."

"You don't think he'll do a runner?"

Deacon shrugged. "I doubt he knows many people with private planes. He has a motorbike so he could hit the road. He could, even without it. But I don't think he will."

"Why not?"

"Three reasons. If he runs he makes it pretty plain he has something to hide. If he doesn't get far enough he's in a worse position than he is right now. And ... "

"And?"

"And actually, sir, I don't think he did it. I think we know who did it: Robert Daws, who hasn't been seen since his daughters saw him slashing his wife's paintings a few minutes before she was stabbed to death. Unless we believe in a conspiracy between her husband and the boy she was bedding, I don't see any *room* in this for Nicky Speers. He didn't need her dead, and as far as I can make out he didn't want her dead. If it was all getting too heavy for him he could just walk away. He'd got his bike by then, he had nothing to stay for – and he certainly wasn't going to get any more out of her after she was dead. She wasn't likely to have mentioned him in her will."

Fuller thought about it, the phone silent but for a soft rasping sound Deacon finally identified as Mrs Fuller asleep beside him. "All right," Dimmock's senior police officer said then. "Let him go. But keep an eye on him. If he tries to run, we charge him."

Deacon thought, "With what?" but didn't say it aloud. It had taken him a while but he'd finally learned that, once you've won the argument, you stop arguing. "Yes, sir."

Compared with the Post Office, the bush telegraph that operates in rural areas is efficient and cheap. It's also quick, but it isn't instantaneous. So news of Nicky's arrest didn't reach Poole Farm until hours after he had in fact been freed without charge. It took a little longer again to cross Poole Lane and arrive at Sparrow Hill. It was Saturday morning: with no lessons the girls were playing in the lane when they heard the tidings. They tumbled into the kitchen like excited puppies, hardly able to get the words out.

Peris listened without comment, then went to the foot of the stairs and called to Daniel. He was in the schoolroom, preparing the next week's work. "Can you come down here for a minute?"

When he arrived Peris said to the girls, "Tell Daniel what you just told me."

They both wanted the honour; unable to reach a compromise they only succeeded in drowning one another out. Finally Johnny claimed the privilege of the first-born. "Nicky Speers is in prison," she announced proudly. "That policeman interrogated him all last night, and in the end he confessed!"

"To breaking in here?" Daniel sounded perplexed.

"Oh, that too," said Johnny dismissively. "But mostly, to murder. To killing my mother!"

Em had been left with very little of the story to add, but

she wasn't going to be excluded like that. "*Our* mother," she muttered rebelliously.

Daniel felt his jaw drop unstoppably. He knew from the burning sensation that it was time he blinked and couldn't seem to do that either. He looked at Peris, and she too appeared to have been hit behind the ear with a sock full of wet sand. Her lips were pursed as if there was a question on its way but she couldn't decide which one.

Finally Daniel got his brain in gear enough to ask, "Where did you hear this?"

"They were talking about it across the road," said Johnny, chattering in her excitement.

"They stopped when they saw us," said Em honestly, "but we'd heard enough by then."

Daniel folded his hands before his mouth and breathed lightly into the arch of them. "Well – maybe. No, listen," he added, seeing their delight turn to indignation, "I don't mean you've got it wrong. But the men on the farm might have got it wrong."

"And they might not," insisted Johnny, her colour rising, ready to fight for a version of events that chimed so perfectly with her needs. "Did you think she stabbed herself? He ruined her, he broke our family, then he killed her. It's so obvious I can't think why it's taken eleven days to arrest him!"

Daniel wasn't sure if she genuinely believed that or if she wanted to believe. If he'd seen it as part of his job to disabuse her he could have asked where, in that case, did she suppose her father was? If he raced off in pursuit of Serena's killer, why had Nicky been around since the tragedy while Daws was still missing? But Daniel saw no justification for poking holes in a frightened girl's parachute. He said quietly, "Shall I phone Superintendent Deacon? Then we'll know the facts."

Johnny tossed her hair haughtily. "If you want to." So far as he could judge she had no reservations about what she'd overheard.

He knew, when he returned from talking to Deacon, that

the truth would provoke a fury that would fall largely on his own head. But they had to be told. "The police found a knife in Nicky's shed. They've linked it to the murder, but they can't actually link it to him. Nicky says he never saw it before. He says he didn't stab your mother and he didn't break in here. Mr Deacon believes him. He doesn't think it adds up. He thinks the knife was planted."

For a few seconds there was silence. Then, characteristically, Em began to cry and Johnny to shout. "Believe him? Believe a dirty thieving *animal* like that? He's got the *knife*. He found it in Nicky Speers's shed. And he *still* doesn't think he did it? Who *does* he think did it? Us? Daddy?"

Neither of them was quick enough with an answer. Almost any answer would have done; just telling her to mind her language might have distracted her long enough. Instead they froze, and sought the reassurance of one another's eyes, and avoided Johnny's. The last word she'd said hung in the air like an accusation.

Her face changed as she realised what the silence meant. Her eyes and her mouth opened wide; the colour blazing in her cheeks drained so suddenly she looked she was going to faint. She actually staggered and one hand went to the back of a kitchen chair to steady herself. Her voice was a ghost, a stunned whisper. "That's what you think? That my daddy stabbed my mother, and that's why he hasn't come back?"

Daniel found a voice, and tried to find something to say with it that wouldn't make matters worse. "It's what the police think, Johnny ... "

"The police!" she spat, chestnut hair flying as she turned on him. "What do they know? They had the killer and they let him go!"

"That isn't the end of it," Daniel said quietly. "They only have so long to question someone. They may be saving some of that time for when they know more. They could pick him up again tomorrow."

"What are they going to know tomorrow that they don't

know today?" yelled the infuriated girl, all control gone. "Who are they going to question that they haven't already questioned?"

Her rage had taken him by surprise. Daniel tried not to flinch before it. "They haven't questioned your father yet. They think he killed your mother, you think he saw someone else do it. Either way, it's vitally important they talk to him."

Emerald was softly crying. Peris eased an arm round her. But the child seemed to find no comfort in it, went on sobbing in quiet desolation, chin on her chest, as if she were alone in the room. Peris looked at Daniel in despair, but he was fully occupied with the elder sister. He felt as if she was drifting beyond his grasp. He was afraid that by the time she was willing to take his hand she wouldn't be able to reach it.

But she was running on fear and outrage, unaware of the danger. His mild acceptance only angered her more. "For the love of God," she screamed, "what more do they want? They know what he is. *Everybody* knows what he is – a dirty animal who couldn't keep his hands off somebody else's wife. He took her money, he broke my daddy's heart, he broke up our family, he killed her – and then he came back to her house to see what else he could take! How can anyone believe he's innocent?"

She didn't really want an answer, and Daniel didn't offer one. He just wanted to make contact with her. He thought the storm in her breast would go on building until something earthed it. He reached out a hesitant hand to her heaving shoulder. "Johnny – "

But she didn't want his hand or the comfort he offered: she threw it off with a roar of anger and a mighty shudder like disgust. And then, as if afraid she hadn't hurt him enough, she lunged at his face.

Johnny was as tall as Daniel and possibly as strong, and she was very, very angry. Peris saw his eyes widen in surprise, then his glasses flew off and he gave a little grunt and his head turned under the blow. He stumbled against the table and went down on one knee, his left hand pressed to his cheek.

Em blinked and the tears stopped on her face. Peris held her breath. Even Johnny froze, her right hand raised, astonished at what she'd done, waiting for the sky to fall. The only sound in the kitchen was Daniel softly panting.

As his breath steadied he straightened up, one hand on the table for support. Peris said faintly, "Daniel ... " There was blood on his face, three deep parallel scratches that filled until the blood dripped from his jaw. Johnny hadn't just slapped him, she'd clawed him.

Peris dragged in a deep breath and took control. She indicated first Emerald, then Juanita. "You: sitting-room. You: the school-room. Don't stick your head out until I come. Daniel, sit down while I see what there is in the bathroom cabinet. I'll be back in a minute." Before she went, though, she bent and passed him his glasses.

Johnny, who'd fled upstairs ahead of her, heard her coming and opened the door a crack. Peris yanked it shut. "I'm not ready to deal with you just yet. There's a good man bleeding on the kitchen floor who takes priority. By the time I've dealt with him I may have calmed down a little. It's in your interests to hope so." She stalked downstairs with an armful of salves, plasters, disinfectant and enough bandages to wrap a small mummy.

Daniel had wadded kitchen towel against his cheek and the bleeding had all but stopped. He looked sheepishly at Peris as she spread her booty on the table. "That could have gone better ... "

"I don't know what to say," she said flatly. "From the moment you arrived you've done your best to help and comfort them. And all the thanks you get is one of them trying to rip your face off."

He sighed, a little shakily. "It's not as bad as that."

"She could have had your eye out!" snapped Peris. "She could have blinded you, Daniel. It's only dumb luck that she didn't. You could be on your way to hospital right now, and she could be behind bars. And maybe that's where she belongs!"

"Peris." He took one of her hands in his own, halting her angry busyness and making her look at him. "It's all right. There's no harm done. It's only skin, it'll heal soon enough."

"But she *attacked* you! You're her teacher, and she attacked you."

"She's a frightened, unhappy fourteen-year-old girl," said Daniel patiently. "She's still struggling to come to terms with what happened. Her emotions are out of control, but she's not to blame for that. Maybe if I'd handled the situation better she wouldn't have got that upset."

"How can you *say* that?" Peris snatched her hand away to dash antiseptic into a bowl. He thought she was embarrassed, as if it was she who had lost her temper and done something unforgivable. "You've treated those girls with more kindness and understanding than what's left of their own family. But for you I'd have gone home and they'd be in care. Maybe that's where they should be. Maybe people trained to look after disturbed children would know when they've tried hard enough and it's happy-pill time. Maybe we should hand them over to the experts. Say the word, Daniel, and I'll make the call."

"Because of this?" His smile went impish around the corners. "You want me to admit to the world that I got beaten up by a little girl? Honestly, it's not that important. Worse things than that happen in schools every week. I've had kids pull knives in class, I've had them throw chairs. With much less excuse. Please, Peris, let's deal with it ourselves. They've lost their mother and their father. Hugo had to leave. If they lose you and me too, they're going to think that nobody in the world cares about them."

She stared at him, the capable hands falling still. "And that wouldn't be true, would it? Because you do."

He nodded. "Yes, I do. Partly because it's my job to – it's what you're paying me for. And partly because – "

She waited but he didn't finish. "Well?"

He darted her a fugitive glance. "Because things have happened to me that only make sense if they were a kind of preparation. If they were to help me help them through this."

She went on regarding him, both angry and deeply touched, until she felt tears prick her eyes. Then she tore off a chunk of cotton-wool and tilted his head roughly towards the light. "Keep still."

He yelped as the antiseptic hit raw flesh. "Isn't there any of the stuff that doesn't hurt?"

She banged the bottle down in front of him. "This *is* the stuff that doesn't hurt! Keep *still*."

# Chapter Sixteen

Persuading Peris that it was his job to talk to Johnny, not hers, took time but confirmed in Daniel's head the certainty that he was right. The woman was too angry, there was too much potential for things to be said which could never be forgiven. If these people were to see one another as family that had to be avoided. Daniel, on the other hand, could walk away any time he felt he was causing more problems than he was solving. That was his strength. Also, he was the calmest of the three of them.

Before he went upstairs he went into the sitting-room. Em was huddled on the hearth-rug, hugging a cushion. She looked up at the sound of the door like a startled forest creature, ready to run.

Daniel gave her an amiable grin. "You OK?"

She nodded wordlessly, eyes like saucers on his cheek.

"Me too," he said. "I'm going upstairs to make sure your sister is. But Peris is a bit upset. I don't think she's used to people losing their tempers. It'd be nice if you went back in the kitchen and gave her a hand with the washing up, and told her everything's going to be all right."

For a moment she stayed where she was, crouching by the fire. Then she threw the cushion aside and rocked to her feet with the unthinking agility of the very young, and ran to the door. As she passed Daniel she paused just long enough to give him a hug. Then she was gone. Cheered, he proceeded upstairs.

Johnny was seated at the school-room table, watching the door. As it opened she sprang to her feet, retreating towards the window. When she saw who it was she seemed first surprised, then shocked. She couldn't tear her eyes off his raked face. Her voice trembled like a reed. "Oh God! Daniel ... I'm *sorry* ... !"

He closed the door and took the nearest chair. "Come and sit down." After a moment she did. They faced one another across the sturdy table.

"This," he said carefully, "is not the end of the world. It matters, but not as much as you think and possibly not for the reasons you think. Can you tell me why it happened?"

She was still having trouble believing that it *had* happened. Her eyes were raw. "I don't know. I don't know! Oh God, your face!" Her fingers ventured tentatively towards him, as if a gentle touch could repair the damage they had done, before she snatched them back, fisting her hands tightly on the table-top.

"Do you resent me? Do you want me to leave?"

"No!" He thought she meant it. As if to leave no doubt she said it again. "No. Please."

"Did you want to hurt me?"

"No," she said again; and then, reviewing that with an honesty that impressed him, "Actually, yes. For a moment. I don't know why. I don't know what I'm doing!" Panic thickened her voice.

He wanted to take her clenched hands, to hold her, to tell her he understood and it was all right. But it had been drummed into him in his earliest days of teacher training that male teachers are vulnerable to the overcharged emotions of pubescent girls, and anything that could be misconstrued must be avoided. He probably shouldn't be alone here with her; he certainly shouldn't be alone here with her behind a shut door; if he gave her the hug she so desperately needed he could probably wave the remnants of his career goodbye.

It wasn't right. Being *in loco parentis* should mean exactly that, and a father who wouldn't hold his daughter at a time like this was unworthy of the name. But he'd followed the rules for too long to feel comfortable ignoring them now. Also, he couldn't risk confusing her any more. He stayed where he was and kept his hands on his side of the table, and hoped she knew he felt for her.

"You're trying to deal with an horrendous situation that you didn't create and which you don't have the power to resolve," he said quietly. "If the strain overwhelms you sometimes and you strike out at someone who isn't to blame but who is handy, that's neither surprising nor dreadfully wicked.

"All the same, I meant it when I said that what you did matters. Not because of this" – he made a negligent gesture towards his face – "but because it shows what's going on inside you. And it's scary. You need to regain control. There's a lot that's out of your hands, but that only makes it more important to stay on top of things where you can. None of what's happened is your fault, but it may start feeling like it if you give yourself reasons to feel guilty. Self-respect requires self-control. Lashing out feels great for a split-second, but after that you feel like trash."

She nodded mutely, choked by tears.

"And you're not," Daniel insisted. "The world is full of people who'd struggle to cope with what you're facing. I'm one of them. I wish I could help you more. Maybe you don't need a tutor so much as a counsellor. If you like I'll find you one. If you'd find it easier to talk to a professional, maybe a woman – anyway, someone other than me – "

"No!" From the speed of her response, the way her head jerked up and her eyes flared, she meant it. "Daniel, there's no one I'd rather talk to than you. If you weren't here I really would go mad. Like – " Her eyes dropped, guilt-stricken.

"Like?" And then he knew. "Like Constance?"

She dared to meet his gaze. "She is mad, isn't she?"

"She's ill," said Daniel quietly.

"She's been locked up for fifteen years, and she can't be let out even to take care of us," said Johnny flatly. "Whatever you want to call it, that's mad."

He didn't argue with her. There was more than words at

stake. "Johnny – are you afraid you're going to end up the same way? Because you lost your temper once?"

She shrugged in mounting agitation. "I've lost my temper lots of times. That doesn't scare me. Hurting you: that scares me."

"It really isn't that big a leap from shouting and banging the table to slapping someone's face. You're reading too much into it."

"But I hurt you!" Unable to sit still any longer, she jerked to her feet and went pacing about the room. "I hurt you. For no reason. Maybe that's how it starts."

"Maybe it is," said Daniel, "for some people. But for most people it's just an isolated, mildly embarrassing episode. Johnny, most of us have hurt someone at some time in our lives. And mostly it's people we care about. Take it as a warning. Learn to recognise when your temper's getting out of hand and have a strategy for controlling it. Count to ten, or leave the room and go for a walk round the garden, or tell people what's happening and let them help. But do something. Emotions are our strength. But they make better servants than masters."

"And if I can't? If I try to stop it and can't? That's when we make a block-booking at the lunatic asylum?"

Daniel laughed out loud. "Johnny, as long as you can make jokes about it there's no need to worry. Yes, your aunt Constance obviously has a problem with her mental health. That doesn't mean she goes round hurting people. People with psychiatric illness are much more likely to hurt themselves than anyone else; and most people who come before the courts accused of violence are not mentally ill. It's come as a bit of a shock, I know, and I wish either you'd known about it sooner or it hadn't come out at all. But there's no reason to suppose that whatever Constance's problem is will ever affect you."

"Things run in families," she insisted. "Mummy and Aunt Constance were known as the Wild Wards. Now one of them's in a lunatic asylum and the other was murdered by – I don't care what you say! – by a dirty farmboy she brought to the house. And now it's Em and me, and Em's crying all the time, and I hurt people who try to help me! I think we're all Wild Wards, all cursed. It's history repeating itself."

He no longer cared about the rules. He got up from the table and had his arms round her before she could put in another frantic lap of the room. Her body was rigid with despair.

"No," he said firmly, "it's not. Constance is ill. Your mother was unlucky – what happened to her is incredibly rare. People have affairs all the time, it doesn't cost them their lives. Sometimes it costs them their marriage, usually it just costs them their dignity. I'm desperately sorry that your family was the exception, but I'm sure there's no kind of curse at work. You and Em are two different people to your mother and her sister. Nothing that happened to them will happen to you."

Her voice was tiny, buried in his shoulder. "Promise?"

If he'd been another man, who didn't hold the truth in the kind of reverence usually reserved for gods, he'd have promised and she'd have been comforted. Daniel had to find another way. "I can give you the mathematical probability. It's rather less than winning the National Lottery. Maybe about the same as being eaten by an alligator."

She snuffled against his shirt. It might have been a chuckle. "An alligator?"

"A one-eyed alligator," he elaborated, "answering to the name of Sidney. That's pretty long odds."

He put her back in her chair, returned to his own. "Johnny, you're the last person in the world who should worry about turning into someone else. I've never known anyone with such a distinctive individuality. Yes, you have your mother's genes. You also have your father's. But the sum of them is you and you alone, and I can't imagine a force powerful enough to tug you away from the core of your own being.

147

You're not a copy or a reflection of anyone. You're your own person. You're strong. You'll get through this. You'll be happy again."

But she didn't believe him. Her lip trembled. "I want my daddy."

His heart cracked. "I know."

They sat in ashy silence for a while. Then they went down-stairs together.

Deacon had been increasingly of the opinion that Robert Daws was dead. That he died by the same hand that killed his wife and not long afterwards. That he found himself some quiet spot where he could be sure of being undisturbed, and remained undisturbed yet.

The more days that passed without any sight of him, the more confident Deacon grew. He sent patrols to check local woodlands, quarries and lakes. He asked for a police helicopter to do an aerial search. Talk about the south coast and people think of Brighton on a Bank Holiday. But there were great wild tracts of the Three Downs where a small army could escape notice for weeks on end, where a body in a car might not be found for a year. Deacon wanted this wrapped up before then.

Finding the knife made him reassess everything. One of his assumptions was wrong. If Robert Daws was dead then Nicky Speers was not the confused innocent he appeared. But if the knife was planted to make him look guilty, then Daws was alive and still in the neighbourhood.

Which meant Deacon had to think again about Daniel's flight of fantasy: that the intruder at Sparrow Hill was in fact its owner. Deacon still didn't believe he was there to silence his daughters, but Daws may have had another purpose. The missing knife only turned up after the excitement at Sparrow Hill: could he conceivably have left it behind after the murder, not in the studio with the other one but in the main house? And have returned to recover it so he could plant it where it would implicate the boy he blamed for his predicament?

Deacon wasn't convinced. But he'd known intelligent men do stupider things, and he wasn't ready to dismiss the possibility until he had something better to replace it with. At the end of another day he had nothing new.

Soon after midnight his phone rang, waking Deacon and annoying his cat. It was Charlie Voss. "I'm at the hospital, sir. Nicky Speers has just been brought in. He rode his motorbike into a stone wall."

By the time Deacon reached the hospital he'd had time to consider the options. He found Voss in A&E, sipping stewed coffee from a polystyrene cup, and greeted him with a single word. "Suicide?"

Voss ignored the curious glances of the night's other casualties and reminded himself that, even if an easy mastery of the social niceties wasn't one of them, Deacon had some admirable qualities. "Not yet, sir. They're still working on him."

"But it was a suicide attempt?"

Voss didn't like giving an opinion when he didn't have all the facts but there didn't seem to be much doubt. "As far as we can tell, no other vehicle was involved. It's not a straight road at that point, but there are no sharp corners. There was no reason for him to leave the road."

"Where did it happen?"

"About a quarter of a mile from his cottage."

"On Poole Lane?"

"Yes."

"On the road that he drives from home to work and from work to home most every day?"

"Yes, sir. He must know it like the back of his hand."

Deacon nodded pensively. "Do we know what speed he was doing?"

"The speedo on the bike was stuck at just over fifty. Which

is a pretty good speed for even a sweeping bend on Poole Lane."

"Which way was he heading?"

"Towards home. He hit the stone wall on his off-side."

"Brake-marks?"

"There's a small skid-mark on the nearside where he turned. And he braked just before he hit, but it was too late to do him any good."

Deacon nodded again, picturing the scene. "Damage to the bike?"

"Comprehensive, but all from the wall. Nothing else hit him."

"Who found him?"

"Philip Poole. He was coming the other way, heading home after visiting friends. He saw the bike in pieces and Nicky lying in the road. He called it in at eleven-forty. The ambulance was there in ten minutes and they had him here in twenty. He was still alive when he went into theatre."

Absent-mindedly Deacon took the cup off his sergeant and drank the coffee. "Am I wrong, Charlie? Did he do this? Did he stab Serena Daws – because she was getting difficult and demanding, or because he was scared of her? Did he go back to Sparrow Hill looking for the missing knife, not realising he'd dropped it in his own shed? And when he realised he was in the frame, did he know that sooner or later we were going to get enough to make it stick and decide to take the emergency exit?"

Voss shrugged apologetically. "That's how it looks."

"Where had he been? Dimmock?"

"Probably. There was alcohol on his breath, though we don't know yet if he was over the limit."

"Even if he was, if he was capable of riding the bike at all, why would he suddenly turn it into a wall? Unless he meant to."

But Voss didn't have an answer. He thought that *was* the answer.

Deacon button-holed a passing doctor. "Nicky Speers, RTA. I need to know how he's doing."

The woman looked down her nose at him. "He hit a stone wall at fifty miles an hour. He's not very well."

The detective bristled. "He's not very well as in he'll be in here for a week? Or, he's not very well as in I'd better spot-clean my black tie?"

He was saved from shocking the waiting-room further by the arrival of one of the theatre team. "Superintendent? You'll be looking for an update on Nicky Speers."

"*Yes*," said Deacon heavily.

They walked down the corridor. Deacon, finishing the coffee, gave the cup back to Voss.

"We've got him stable," said the surgeon. "I think he'll be all right. He's got multiple injuries, internal as well as fractures, but I think we've done all the repairs necessary. There doesn't seem to be anything that won't heal.

"What we won't know, possibly for some days, is how much brain damage he's sustained. There's severe concussion but no skull fracture. He owes his life to his helmet. Even so, until he's awake and lucid we won't know how badly he's been affected. He might remember everything or nothing. He might not know his own name. He might not know which way is up. At this point I don't know and can't guess."

"Try," suggested Deacon.

"The first thing they teach you about head injuries," said the doctor, "is that none is so trivial it may be discounted and none so serious it should be despaired of. The difference between leaving a neurological ward to return to work and leaving it in a persistent vegetative state may be just millimetres. Which bit of the brain was damaged. How deep the damage went.

"You want my best guess, it's that he'll wake up some time tomorrow – today, rather – with a thumping headache, and no recollection of what he's doing here, but no lasting disability. And if I'm wrong ... "

"Yes?"

He shrugged. "It won't be the first time."

Deacon's lips tightened. "If you're right, how long will he be in here?"

"Weeks, anyway. He's going to be pretty immobile to start with."

"When can I talk to him?"

"Not today. Maybe tomorrow. If I'm happy about it."

Deacon frowned. "You do know the situation? He's a suspect in a murder inquiry, and this crash may not have been an accident. I'd be grateful if you'd prevent him from committing suicide, at least until he's signed a confession."

The doctor turned to him and smiled. "Superintendent, he won't be able to sign anything until he has the use of his arms again. But as luck would have it, he also won't be able to cut his throat. Don't worry, he's safe with us."

Deacon returned home, evicted Dempsey from the warm spot in the bed and went back to sleep. The alarm went at eight, and before he dressed he phoned the hospital. Nicky Speers was still stable, still unconscious.

Insofar as he reckoned on taking a day off, Sunday was it. But not when he was up to his ears in a case. He phoned again from the office at nine, from his car at eleven, and from the little French restaurant where he and Brodie were having lunch at one. This time the news was better. Nicky had woken up, taken a sip of orange juice and gone back to sleep.

"How much does he remember?"

"He remembered which hole the orange juice goes in," said the doctor coldly.

"I'm on my way," said Deacon.

"He's a sick boy. I'm not waking him up for you to bully him."

"I'm not *going* to bully him! I just need to know what happened."

When he'd put the phone back in his pocket Brodie said mildly, "Wash your mouth out."

He didn't understand. "What?"

"Jack, you bully everybody. As a matter of course. I don't think you even know you're doing it any more."

"I do not!" exclaimed Deacon, apparently quite shocked. "I don't bully you."

"No, you don't," she admitted. "Only because you can't get away with it."

"Who, then? Who do I bully?"

"Jack – *everybody*! That doctor, you were trying to bully him. You bully Charlie Voss. You can't see Daniel across a crowded room without trying to bully him. Now you want to bully a nineteen-year-old boy who's just woken up plastered rigid in a hospital bed. That's cup-winners' cup bullying, that is."

Deacon was genuinely taken aback. "I don't know where you've got this idea from. Asking questions is my job. That's not the same as bullying."

"When it's you it's exactly the same," she said firmly. "Are you really going to interrogate a boy who's still hovering on the edge of consciousness?"

"I have to," he said. "I have to know why he drove into that wall. He's more likely to tell the truth now, while he's still shaken, than when he's had time to think about it."

"All right," she said, collecting her bag and signalling for the bill, "I'll come with you."

He stared at her in astonishment. "You'll ... ?"

"Certainly. You tell me you can question a groggy, badly injured teenager in his hospital bed without bullying him. Well, let's see you do it."

It was a measure of his surprise that he couldn't think of a single reason why not.

Almost their first experience of one another had been in circumstances identical to this: in a hospital room, sniping at one another over the battered body of a young man. Then it was Daniel, now it was Nicky Speers. The memory was uncomfortable for both of them.

Brodie concentrated on the boy to avoid meeting Deacon's eyes. The doctor hadn't exaggerated: he really was immobile, the perfect demonstration model for serious First-Aiders. And he was sleeping again. His face was bruised and swollen, his eyelids the colour of storm-clouds, and his broken lips moved in a muttered commentary of which only the odd word was clear.

Brodie turned towards the door. "We've no business here. Not yet."

Her voice seemed to reach the boy. His eyes flickered open, bloodshot. A ghost of a smile bent his scabbed lips. "Hello." He hadn't seen Deacon.

Brodie sighed and turned back, stitching an answering smile in place. "Hi. How are you feeling?"

"Pretty crappy." Which was unsurprising. It was reassuring in that it was the appropriate answer for the circumstances. There might yet be gaps in his memory but his mind was functioning.

Brodie looked at Deacon, assuming he'd want to step into Nicky's limited field of vision now and start his questioning in a positively non-bullying fashion. But she was wrong. He nodded to her to continue. More for Nicky's sake than Deacon's, she complied.

"You came off your bike. Last night. Do you remember?"

"Mm." She wasn't sure if it was a yes or a no. "What's the damage?"

"I'm not a doctor. There's a lot of plaster, if that's anything to go by."

It's hard to deliver a withering look with two black eyes but Nicky Speers managed it. "Not me. The bike."

"I haven't seen it," admitted Brodie. "But I don't think hitting a stone wall is ever good for them."

His head jerked and he sucked in an unsteady breath. "I hit the wall? I don't remember."

Out of sight, Deacon scowled.

"You were nearly home," Brodie prompted him. "Then for no apparent reason you crossed the road and hit the wall at fifty miles an hour."

"No reason," he echoed. The effort of keeping his eyes open proved too much and he let them slide shut. But after a moment they flickered again. "No reason?"

"The police don't think there was any other vehicle involved. And you had been drinking."

"*One* drink," said Nicky positively. "I had *one* drink. What do you mean, no other vehicle?"

Deacon shot into his vision as if rocket-propelled. "You mean there was another vehicle?"

Nicky started. It was about the only movement he was capable of. "You? Then, who ... ?" He looked uncertainly at Brodie.

"My name's Brodie Farrell. We met at the farm, remember? I just wondered how you were doing."

"Tell me about the other vehicle," said Deacon.

"I can't, I never saw it. But I know there was one."

"What do you mean, you never saw it?"

"It was dark, all I saw were headlights. I came round the bend and it was on my side of the road. I swerved but he hit me."

Deacon shook his head. "The only thing that hit you was the wall."

"He was coming right at me." Nicky's voice began to climb with the memory of it, the terror.

Brodie laid a cool hand on the only bit of his arm she could reach. "It's all right. You're safe now. It's all over."

"Try to tell us what happened," said Deacon. "You say he was coming right at you?"

Nicky managed a fractional, painful nod. "I mean, *right* at me. I swerved to the other side of the road and he kept coming. He was trying to kill me. He must have thought he had done."

"Who?"

"*I* don't know!" exclaimed the youth impatiently. "If I didn't see the vehicle I sure as hell didn't see the driver. But I know what he did. I know I could have avoided him if he hadn't switched lanes to make sure. Maybe I did hit the wall, but only because he left me nowhere else to go. I'm telling you, he tried to kill me!"

# Chapter Seventeen

When Deacon returned to his office Brodie headed for Sparrow Hill. She knew the bush telegraph would have beaten her with the basic facts, but she had details no one else could have yet. She was anxious to share them with Daniel, wanted to know what he made of them. If he came to the same conclusion she had.

She hadn't taken his concerns much more seriously than Deacon had. She'd always thought that the likeliest explanation for the intruder alert at four o'clock on Friday morning was the girls bumping into one another in the dark. Latest events cast doubt on that. If someone really had tried to kill Nicky Speers, there was one obvious candidate. He probably wasn't top of anyone's Christmas list about now, but this wasn't a nuisance phonecall or someone letting his tyres down, it was an attempt on his life. Only Robert Daws hated Nicky that much.

Brodie got no answer at the cottage door, but Peris saw her from the kitchen window and waved her over. "I think he's in the school-room."

Brodie blinked. "On a Sunday afternoon?"

"The girls have gone out. Daniel's planning next week's lessons. He takes this very seriously, doesn't he?"

Brodie bridled slightly. "Of course he does. This is what he does – his job. Did you think he wouldn't go to much trouble for a class of two?"

"I'm sorry," said Peris, chastened, "I didn't mean it as a criticism. I suppose I'm just so grateful to have him here that actually teaching the children seems like a bonus. Go on up. It's the first door on the right at the top of the stairs."

Brodie was aware she'd over-reacted. "No, I'm sorry. I tend to jump to Daniel's defence, whether he needs it or not.

As if he was a child. As if he was *my* child. It's absurd. I make a fool of myself and embarrass him."

Peris smiled, plump cheeks dimpling. "Don't apologise. He has the same effect on me. It's being little that does it, I think. And the glasses, of course. You kind of want to pat his head, like he was a spaniel."

Brodie laughed too; and then, remembering why she was here, grew suddenly sober. "Listen, what I came to tell him – I think you should hear it too." Puzzled, Peris followed her upstairs.

Daniel looked up at the sound of the door. With leaning over the table his glasses had slid to the end of his nose. The two women studiously avoided looking at one another.

Then Brodie saw his face. She knew what it looked like, couldn't imagine how it had happened. Not to Daniel. "What happened to you?"

He wouldn't dignify the matter with undue significance by refusing to answer. "When I told the girls Jack had questioned Nicky and released him, Johnny lost it."

"And *clawed* you?"

"It was over in a second," said Daniel evenly. "And now it's been dealt with, and I'd rather you didn't mention it again. Why are you here?"

Brodie frowned. But it was his business, if he thought a teenage pupil scratching his face merely an occupational hazard she wasn't going to argue with him. Not just now, anyway. She said, "I've just come from the hospital. Have you heard about Nicky Speers?"

"What about him?"

So she repeated all she knew. About the crash, and how Nicky said it happened. She watched Daniel's eyes, waiting for the synapses behind them to fire.

Peris wasn't doing calculations. She was thinking about the boy in the hospital. None of them would have been here but for him. Still ... "How is he?"

"He's pretty beat up, but he'll be all right. Eventually."

"Good." The woman gave a wry little shrug. "I know he hasn't behaved very well, but he's only nineteen. He couldn't have known what he was getting into, what it would lead to." She looked away. "And there's enough people wishing him ill without me joining in."

"The girls?"

"When we heard yesterday that Mr Deacon had let him go ... well, I was glad neither of them has access to a shotgun."

"It's understandable, of course," said Daniel. "If Nicky's young enough to get a fool's pardon, so are the girls. Of course they blame him. The only alternative would be to lay the responsibility where most of it properly belongs, and that's asking too much of them."

"Their father."

His gaze flickered. "Actually I was thinking of their mother. But yes, Robert too."

He still hadn't made the connection. Brodie spelled it out, carefully. "Nicky says someone put him into that wall. Deliberately. It wasn't an accident, it wasn't suicide, it was attempted murder. I could only think of one likely suspect."

Daniel's eyes flew wide, appalled behind the thick lenses. Then the shock turned to alarm and he hurried to the window. "Where are the girls? In the house?"

"They went out on their bikes," said Peris, who hadn't yet caught up. "Why, what's – ?" Then she had it. Her eyes saucered white in her face. "*Robert*? You think *Robert* ran Nicky off the road?"

"We really don't know," Brodie told her. "But if it really wasn't an accident, it's a possibility. I thought you ought to know right away. So you can keep an eye on the girls – for your own peace of mind as much as their safety."

Daniel's peace of mind had flown out of the window soon after Brodie came in by the door. He knew that in all likelihood everything was fine: the girls were cycling in Poole Lane as they often did and would be back for tea. But he couldn't just wait and see. In the cauldron of his mind Robert Daws was out there somewhere, tying up loose ends. He might stop with Nicky. He might not.

"I'm going to look for them," he mumbled. "Brodie, can we take your car? We'll cover the ground quicker that way."

"You two go one way," said Peris, "I'll go the other. Meet back here in fifteen minutes: if we haven't found them by then they'll probably have made their own way home."

In the event it didn't take fifteen minutes. The girls came in at the gate before the search party reached the cars. They stopped in surprise at the gathered adults, grit spitting from the bicycle wheels. "What's the matter?"

Brodie recovered first. "Nothing. Daniel and Peris were just seeing me to my car."

"Where did you get to?" asked Daniel.

"Up the lane a bit." Johnny had changed into jeans and a thick sweater since he saw her last, with a baseball cap over her chestnut hair. Playing-out clothes, with green patches on the knees and elbows.

Daniel's eyes narrowed. "Which way?"

Johnny pointed left, Em pointed right. Johnny rolled her eyes and gave a gusty sigh. "All *right*! We wanted to see where it happened."

"Where what happened?" asked Daniel, deadpan.

"Where that dirty farmboy smashed his head against the wall!" declared Em triumphantly. "We heard Mr Poole talking about it. We wanted to see if there was any blood."

"Emerald!" exclaimed Peris in dismay.

"If you want us to," said Johnny loftily, "we could apologise. But it wouldn't alter anything. That's where we've been, and that's why we went."

"And was there?" asked Daniel quietly. "Any blood?"

"Couldn't see any," said Johnny. She swung her back-pack off her shoulder and hugged it thoughtfully. "There was a lot of oil. And bits of metal and stone. He must have hit pretty damned hard."

160

He ignored her language. "He did. He's badly hurt, he's going to be in hospital for a while."

"Good," said Johnny unfeelingly. She pushed her bike down the drive with Em, in pink dungarees, tucking into line behind her.

"Look on the bright side," said Brodie. "They're safe."

"That's the bright side?" said Peris.

In the middle of the night Brodie found herself wide awake and listening. She thought at first something had disturbed her, and got out of bed and padded across the hall to Paddy's room. The little girl was fast asleep, thumb in her mouth, wrapped around a somewhat threadbare green dragon. Dragons had been her first love, even before tractors. This one was called Howard.

Brodie tucked the quilt closer around both of them, not because it had slipped but because you can't love someone that much without wanting to make them warmer, happier, more comfortable. The child mooed, and Brodie dropped a featherweight kiss on top of her head and left her to sleep.

Still thinking she'd heard something she checked the rest of the flat, but everything was fine so she returned to bed. But she didn't sleep, and soon she realised what it was that had woken her. Not an external event but the chinking of mental gears, the fizz of synapses, signs that her brain was up to something that it wasn't letting her in on just yet.

It might be ignoring her but she couldn't ignore it. She sat up with the quilt draped round her, hugging a pillow in unconscious imitation of her child, and tried to puzzle it out. This consisted of re-running everything she'd said, heard or thought about in the last twenty-four hours until she heard a beep. Then she surveyed another line until she heard the beep. At some point the beeps would reach a kind of critical mass and a nuclear reaction would begin, blasting the answer to the front of her consciousness.

But though she sat there for an hour, thinking about what

Deacon had said and what Daniel had said and what Nicky Speers in his hospital bed had said, fission never occurred. The sparks fizzled out, leaving her cold and tired. She lay down. No sooner was she asleep again than the alarm went off.

She woke Paddy, said good morning to Howard – if she forgot he would certainly be presented for a proper greeting when she was putting her make-up on – and dragged herself to the bathroom.

A hot shower pummelled some life back into her but didn't improve her mood. She glared at herself in the mirror and, not for the first time, considered the advantages of an Eton crop over dragging a brush through a frizz of dense black curls every morning. She hadn't succumbed to the temptation yet. That didn't mean she wouldn't one day.

She found herself peering critically into the steamy depths of the mirror. Not a pleasant sight, she thought – Jack Deacon would have disagreed – but she always looked like this first thing in the morning. The next ten minutes would do much to mend the damage. So what was she looking for? She frowned and tried moving her head around. Nothing had fallen off in the night, nothing undesirable had grown. Whatever was she doing, staring at her reflection in a mirror?

And then she knew. Not quite as a revelation, more a cascade – one fragment of comprehension triggering another bumping off a third and fourth. She stood in front of the smeared glass, the brush snared in her thick hair, and watched understanding grow in her own face. Then she dived for the phone.

Paddy and Howard came through the living-room on their way to the kitchen. "Mummy's got *no clothes* on," Paddy remarked disapprovingly, and Howard averted his gaze.

The nurses were reluctant to put Nicky Speers on the phone. He'd had a good night, they said, but was still very weak, and anyway they were in the middle of breakfasts. Brodie appreciated that it was a bad time but offered them a straight choice. If she could talk to Nicky she'd be done in a couple of minutes. If not she'd have to talk to the police, and Detective Superintendent Deacon would turn up in the middle of doctors' rounds and take a great deal longer than two minutes.

There was a muttered discussion in the background. Then someone asked her to hold, and the next voice she heard was Nicky's.

She reminded him who she was. "How are you feeling this morning?"

"Sore," he said briefly.

"I bet. How's the head?"

"Not bad. Why?"

"I want to ask you about what you saw. Unless thinking hurts too much."

"No," he said wearily, "I think about it all the time. I *can't* do much else *but* think about it."

"All right," said Brodie. "So you were coming round the bend on Poole Lane, about quarter of a mile from your cottage, heading for home – yes? And as you came round the bend there was a vehicle heading straight for you, on your side of the road. Is that right?"

"That's right." He grunted in discomfort. All he had to do was hold the phone to his ear and it was causing him pain. She was sorry, but not enough to absolve him of helping resolve a situation he'd been instrumental in bringing about.

"And you didn't see what kind of a vehicle for the glare of the headlights."

"No."

"Could it have been another motorbike?"

He was silent. She could almost hear him thinking. "Maybe. Yes, could have been. There was a lot of glare – if there were two headlights they were pretty close together. It could have been a bike. And then ... "

"What?"

"The way it moved. Cut across the road the same time I

did. A car would have trouble doing thaat. Maybe that's why he didn't run over me on the ground – he was narrow enough to get past. I wondered about that. It's only a minor road: with me sprawled across half of it I couldn't see how he'd managed to avoid me. But if he was a bike ... " She heard him frown. "How did *you* know it was another bike?"

"I didn't think it was," she said cryptically. "And I still don't." She rang off, unkindly leaving him puzzled.

As soon as she'd taken Paddy to school Brodie drove to Poole Lane. She knew what she was looking for, recognised it as soon as she found it. Three quarters of a mile past Sparrow Hill the lane made a sweeping bend to the right. There were high stone walls on either side, the boughs of trees overhanging them. She slowed to a crawl, and then she could see the bright scars along the right-hand wall where something had impacted hard and sent stone-chips flying in a killing hail.

Leaving the car in a gateway she walked back. The girls were right: there was no blood, and now even the bits of bike were gone. Only the scarred wall told where Nicky Speers hit it at fifty miles an hour. It could have killed him. It was *meant* to kill him.

She kept walking, past the scene of the crash, back to the bend where Nicky first saw the on-coming vehicle. The only skid-marks were his: the other party hadn't tried to stop or even swerve. But when Nicky in desperation crossed to the wrong side of the road the other followed. Then Nicky lost control and hit the wall, and knew no more. He assumed the other rider had threaded the wreckage and vanished into the night.

And to this extent Brodie thought he was right: that when Nicky lost consciousness his Nemesis did indeed disappear.

She combed the road and both verges without finding what she was looking for. So perhaps she was looking for the wrong thing. She headed back to Poole Farm.

Philip Poole was still having breakfast. He insisted that she join him for toast and marmalade, and since she hadn't eaten she was glad to. Only when she had a cup of coffee in her hand and a plate in front of her was he willing to answer more questions.

Twenty-five years is a lot of time, though, and some of the details eluded him. And he was puzzled why, with Serena dead, Robert missing and Nicky Speers in hospital, Brodie was concerning herself with an ancient practical joke.

"Because I know what ran Nicky off the road," said Brodie. "He's right: it was a deliberate attempt on his life. What he saw when he came round that bend at fifty miles an hour, filling his side of a narrow lane lined on both sides by high walls, was the Cheyne Wood Phantom."

# Chapter Eighteen

Philip Poole's expression turned slowly, defensively, blank, as he considered the possibility he was giving breakfast to a dangerous lunatic. After a moment he moistened his lips with the tip of his tongue and said carefully, "I thought you understood. That was a trick we played."

Brodie gave an impatient flick of her marmalade knife. "Of course I understand. That's what I mean. That's what Nicky saw. A mirror. He came round a fast sweeping bend, and as his headlights came back to the road they hit a mirror. It was a dark, narrow lane, and it looked like another vehicle coming at him. He swerved, so did the lights ahead. He hit a stone wall at fifty miles an hour trying to avoid his own reflection."

Now he'd caught up with her, if anything Poole was looking more worried than before. "You don't think ... You're not accusing *me* – ?"

She stared at him in amazement. "Whatever makes you think that?"

He cleared his throat, slightly reassured. "Well, three of us were involved. And now one of us is dead, one's in a psychiatric hospital, and hey, here's me, living less than a mile from where the crash happened and employing the victim."

"It never occurred to me it could be you," Brodie said briskly, and moved on before he could decide if that was a compliment or not. And before she could ask herself if she should at least have wondered. "Other people knew what you'd done. The rest of the hunt, of course, but also anyone any of the three of you had talked to. You told me about it the first day we met. I imagine, in sixteen years of marriage, Serena told Robert."

"*Robert*? You think Robert tried to kill Nicky?"

"I can't think of anyone with a better reason," Brodie said

frankly. "If you hadn't come along when you did he'd have succeeded – the boy would have died at the scene. Finding no trace of another vehicle, and particularly since Nicky'd been drinking, the police would have assumed that he either lost control on the bend or drove into the wall deliberately. They might have put it down to guilt, inferred that he played a bigger part in Serena's death than they'd thought. If Robert turns up at a later date it would have been a useful argument in his defence – either man could have stabbed Serena but one of them head-butted a wall when the police started showing an interest in him."

"You think Robert tried to kill Nicky so he could use him as a scapegoat." The farmer thought the way God's mills grind: not swiftly but thoroughly.

Brodie helped herself to more toast. "That's what I think, yes. Everyone assumed he'd done a runner after the murder. I don't think he did: I think he's been here or hereabouts ever since. I think he's been back to Sparrow Hill. They thought they had an intruder there a few nights ago. Daniel wondered if it was Robert and we all laughed at him. But maybe he was right. About who if not why.

"I think he needed something from the house, and between Daniel, Peris and the girls the place was never empty. So he let himself in at four in the morning. It was just rotten luck that Johnny was restless and heard him."

God's mills had got left behind again. "Needed what from the house?"

"The *mirror!*" exclaimed Brodie. "Oh Philip, do try to keep up. Either the one you used twenty-five years ago, if Serena still had it, or one they had at Sparrow Hill that would do as well. That's what I came here to ask. Do you know what happened to the mirror after the Phantom's cover was blown?"

He shook his head. "No."

"Where did it come from?"

He thought back. "The girls found it in an outhouse at

their place. It was a cheval mirror, except that it had lost its stand. I know it was a heavy damned thing – it took all three of us to shift it."

"Victorian? Ornate wooden frame, that kind of thing? About six foot high?"

"Probably. But it was rather the worse for wear then, I doubt if it's still around today."

"Possibly not," agreed Brodie. "But what one big mirror will do another will do. It was the idea that was the clever part."

Poole shuddered and pushed away the remains of his breakfast. "Nicky could have died. When I found him I thought he *was* dead. Because of a stupid practical joke we played as kids quarter of a century ago."

"You can't blame yourself," said Brodie. "If Robert hadn't heard about the Phantom he'd have found some other way to get at Nicky. Less clever but maybe more certain. Perhaps the Cheyne Wood Phantom is the reason Nicky Speers is alive today."

Poole managed a weak grin. "Thank you. You're very kind."

Brodie considered that but dismissed it. "No, I'm not. No one who's known me long goes on thinking that."

He chuckled. "So what now?"

"Now we find the mirror."

His eyes flickered, alternating between hope and alarm. "You don't think that's a job for the police?"

"Actually," she said diplomatically, "I meant me and the police."

Jack Deacon caught on quicker than Philip Poole. He was shouting instructions to Charlie Voss before Brodie had finished explaining. Twenty minutes later he had search parties combing the woods either side of Poole Lane.

For once he'd been able to describe what they were looking for in some detail. This was a rare luxury – usually all the guidance they got was: "You'll know it when you see it."

"It's a mirror. A big mirror, probably about six foot long. What they call a cheval mirror, which means it's big enough for someone to see what a prat he looks on his horse. It might be an old one, in which case it could be very battered, or it could be a modern copy. Or it could just be something that would do the same job – a sheet of polished steel, for instance. But it would have to be big to maintain the illusion of another bike coming at him long enough to put the kid off the road."

While he was briefing the searchers, back up the road Brodie was briefing Daniel.

"So Robert *was* here?"

"It looks a bit like it," she nodded. "I know: you said so all along, we should have believed you."

But told-you-so wasn't Daniel's style. "How could he hope to move something that big without waking the house? In fact, if it took three teenagers to shift it, how did he hope to move it at all?"

"He's a big man," Brodie reminded him. "Just because he mostly works with his brain doesn't mean his muscles have atrophied. If he wanted it moved, he'd move it. Though it may not have been the Victorian original he used. Maybe there was another mirror in the house, still big but lighter."

"If there's a big mirror missing from here the girls should know. They're the only ones who will. Neither Peris nor I are familiar enough with the house."

"Have they said anything?"

"No. But then, I haven't asked. Maybe I should."

They were in the school-room, poring over a hefty volume in apparent fascination. They looked up as Daniel returned. "Is it all right if Brodie joins us for a minute?" he asked – because it was their school-room before it was his.

Almost they were trying too hard to mind their manners. Em nodded with an enthusiasm she couldn't possibly feel, and Johnny said carefully, "Of course. Shall I bring another chair?"

Brodie suspected irony but saw no traces of it. "No, thanks. I won't stay – I mustn't interrupt your work. What are you reading?"

"*Henry the Fifth*," said Johnny.

Brodie looked at Daniel in surprise. "I didn't know anybody still taught Shakespeare."

He shrugged. "I'm not an English teacher, how would I know what they teach? OK. Brodie has a theory about our intruder. Do you know if there's a mirror missing from the house?"

The girls regarded their visitor with studious vacancy. Johnny said, "A mirror?"

"Yes. A big one, big enough to see your whole self all at once. It might have been on the wall, it might have been on a stand on the floor, it might have been in a storeroom. And now it isn't." She paused, looking from one expressionless young face to the other. "Is this ringing *any* bells with you?"

Johnny said with restraint, "I don't think so, Mrs Farrell."

Daniel hid a grin. "Have a look round, see if anything occurs to you."

They rose obediently and headed for the stairs. At the door Johnny hesitated and looked back, wanting to be sure she'd got this right. "You want us to look for a mirror that isn't there any more?"

"Yes, please," said Daniel.

When they'd gone he chuckled and sat down on the table. "And another theory bites the dust."

"Not necessarily," protested Brodie. "It may still be why he came. But he was disturbed, so he fled and found something else he could use."

"In which case there should be a big mirror in the house here somewhere, since he was disturbed before he could remove it. And if there was the girls would know."

She had no answer to that. She scowled at him. "That's how it was done. I *know* that's how it was done. He got hold

170

of a mirror, set it up in the road and waited for Nicky to come home."

"It's possible," conceded Daniel. "I don't know how you'd prove it."

"If Jack finds a six-foot mirror in the woods, I'll slap anyone who mentions the word 'coincidence'!"

The search party found nothing in the woods. Not a six-foot mirror; not the shattered remains of a six-foot mirror that proved unequal to abseiling over a five-foot stone wall; not the drag-marks in the chalky soil where something heavy had been hauled away. There was no sign that Robert Daws or anyone else had been in these woods in the recent past.

When the search had expanded to quarter of a mile from where Nicky Speers hit the wall Deacon called a halt. "If he brought it this far it wasn't in order to leave it – he had something else in mind. But I don't think he did. If he'd been here, manhandling a large heavy object on his own, I think we'd have found signs of it by now."

"Mrs Farrell's going to be disappointed," said Charlie Voss. "She was convinced she'd cracked the case." Deacon looked round quickly but his open expression was innocent of mischief. All the same, Deacon was beginning to suspect that there was more to his sergeant than was printed on the label.

"Yes, well," he growled. "Brodie's always had the idea she could do my job better than me. It'll do her good to see that for every ounce of inspiration it takes a pint of perspiration." Jack Deacon would be the last man in England to go metric.

"Are you going to call her?"

Deacon looked at his watch. Then he did a quick head-count. "That's eleven of us been down here since ten o'clock. That's ... thirty-three man-hours down the tube thanks to her. I reckon she owes me" – he did mental calculations that twisted his face like wringing out a dish-cloth – "lunch. I'll see you back at the madhouse at two."

Brodie wasn't so much disappointed that he'd failed to find any physical evidence to support her theory as annoyed. She thought he hadn't looked properly. There had to be some sign that a big man had brought a heavy mirror here, from Sparrow Hill or elsewhere, and set it up at a time and place when he confidently expected Nicky Speers to come along on his motorcycle, and after the broken bike and the broken boy had come to rest in the road had lugged the mirror away and disposed of it.

"Did you look at the road surface?" she asked. "It's a country lane, it doesn't get a lot of traffic, it doesn't see a road-sweeper every day – there must have been some marks on it."

"Oh, there were," said Deacon sardonically, cutting his steak as if he held a grudge against it. "Tyre-marks: lots of different tyre-marks. One set was yours. One was Philip Poole's Land Rover. There's some from a digger, some from a tractor, and two skinny ones from a pair of bicycles. That's all we could separate. It's thirty-six hours since Daws was there – *if* he was there. No marks he left in the road would still be visible."

Brodie's eyebrows rose indignantly. "It's not *my* fault thirty-six hours passed before someone worked out what happened. You're the detective: how come you didn't get there sooner?"

He breathed ominously at her. "Gee, I don't know, Brodie. Maybe it's because I never read the Nancy Drew Mysteries and have to rely on twenty-five years as a policeman instead. It slows you up. I keep telling Division, what we need is a more imaginative approach. Never mind evidence and witnesses and all that crap: what we should be looking at is creative dreaming ..."

"I didn't dream it," Brodie snapped back. "I was mulling it over while I was asleep: it's not at all the same thing. And if it was such a stupid idea, why did you keep eleven men and women working on it for three hours? It's not me that has to explain that to the Sub-Divisional Commander, it's you."

"Don't remind me," he grunted. "Well, I'll tell him it was a valid theory that explained how Nicky could have been hurt even if we're not sure it's how he was hurt. That it was important to look for anything that would cast light on the movements of the prime suspect in a murder case. And that failure to find the mirror thirty-six hours after the event doesn't prove that it wasn't there are the critical moment. Absence of evidence is not evidence of absence."

She leaned forward over the table litter and kissed him. Reddening, Deacon looked around guiltily, half afraid that someone would have noticed and half hoping that they had.

"You're a good man, Jack Deacon," said Brodie. "You're not always a nice man, and you're not right nearly as often as you think you are, but you're a good man and a good copper. It's a pity you'd make such a terrible husband."

And after that they could have brought him creme brulee for dessert or hundreds-and-thousands sprinkled on a kipper: he wouldn't have known the difference. He had not, for one second of their acquaintance, even when his body was exploring the infinite possibilities of hers, considered proposing to Brodie Farrell. Now she'd dismissed the notion out of hand he could think of nothing else.

# Chapter Nineteen

Brodie left the restaurant feeling obscurely pleased with herself. She knew she'd rocked Deacon to his foundations, which was cause enough for satisfaction. She also suspected she'd planted an idea that would never of its own accord have occurred to him. It wasn't that she was waiting for him to propose. She wouldn't even have welcomed it: she liked things as they were. Liked being able to neglect him for days at a time if she was busy, confident that he'd still be there when she wanted him. On the other hand, she didn't want him feeling that complacent about her. It was good to keep him on his toes.

She went back to her office, put in an hour's work on matters unrelated to Sparrow Hill. Or almost unrelated: among the invoices she prepared was one for Hugo Daws. It wasn't her problem that when she found Constance Ward the woman was unable to help.

With the paperwork updated she lingered over a cup of tea, enjoying the peace and quiet. Brodie was a woman who got a buzz from things happening around her, from making them happen and dealing with their consequences; but sometimes it was pleasant just to sit in the empty office and think.

Losing her husband to another woman after six years of marriage, after putting a home together and making a child, had come as a devastating shock. Probably more, she now suspected, than it should have done. She knew that only about half of marriages succeed. But she'd been so content with her life that it hadn't occurred to her that John wasn't. When he finally confessed that he'd met someone who made him feel the way he made her feel, safe and comfortable and happy, it seemed to Brodie that not just her marriage but her entire existence had crumbled about her ears. As if she'd gone to the doctor with hives and come away with cancer. The shock was like six inches of roof insulation wrapped around her: binding her limbs, muffling her cries, suffocating her. She thought she was dying.

And it was not too fanciful to say that Mrs John Farrell did die then. The woman who took her place – who used her divorce settlement to buy a flat and start a business, who was raising her daughter to be a stronger person than she herself was raised, who had friends and lovers that would have been denied to Mrs John Farrell – was a quite different person. So different Brodie herself was surprised. She no longer had regrets about the past. She liked her life. She liked being at the centre of her own existence instead of orbiting it at a polite distance. She liked knowing that she'd earned everything she had. She had liked being loved, but it was also good to be respected.

At half-past three, with no clients hammering urgently on the door and no work demanding her attention, she thought she'd reap one of the benefits of self-employment and finish early. One of the drawbacks, of course, is that if you don't work you don't get paid, but she reckoned that if she was prepared to work late when the need arose she was entitled to leave early when she had the chance. She thought maybe she and Paddy could have a girls' night out: find an amusement arcade, throw quoits for tacky prizes and stuff their faces with candy-floss, and get home tired and sticky at about half-past eight.

Poole Lane was not on her way home; it wasn't even the scenic route. Still she found herself driving up the Guildford Road and turning right, as she had done a number of times in the last week and as Nicky Speers had done on his way home from Dimmock on Saturday night. He'd passed Poole Farm and Sparrow Hill, and as the last bend opened up he probably picked up speed. Brodie did the same thing.

And then, right here, just past the apex of the bend, everything had gone pear-shaped. He saw oncoming lights and tore the bike out of their path; and when they followed him had nowhere left to go but the stone wall looming over him. In the fraction of a second left for thought, he must have thought he was dead.

Brodie parked again in the gateway and walked back. If it was a mirror he saw it must have been – she looked up and down the road, calculating – about here. Not on the bend or he'd have seen it too soon, had time to realise what it was. After the bend, then, where the road straightened out.

How had Daws known his trap would catch Nicky Speers and not some other motorist? Well, because he knew how little traffic used the road late at night. Poole's tractors would be safely locked up in his yard, no one from Sparrow Hill would turn this way, the only house ahead was the Speers cottage. Mrs Speers would be at home that late.

But Nicky had set off on his motorbike during the evening, after a bad day with the police, and it took no clairvoyant to guess he was heading for the pub. That he'd be coming back after closing time, slightly lubricated if not well oiled. That, unless Daws got seriously unlucky, his bike would be the only traffic on the road at that hour.

Brodie stood still and listened. After a moment she picked up the throaty rumble of heavy machinery at Poole Farm. Daws would have done the same: listened for the distinctive growl of a motorcycle. When he heard it he pushed the mirror out into the road.

So he was there when Nicky hit the wall. When his bike smashed into a hundred pieces, and his bones broke and his lungs filled with blood. Standing watching. He didn't just want to punish the boy, didn't just want to hurt him. He wanted to kill him, and to watch him die. Daniel was right: the man had lost all sense of propriety, of civilised behaviour. He wanted to watch a nineteen-year-old boy choke up his life alone in a gutter because he hadn't the wit to stay away from a manipulative woman.

Then he heard another vehicle coming: Philip Poole's Land

Rover. He grabbed his mirror and got it and himself out of sight. He didn't wait any longer, thought his job was done.

But if he didn't throw the mirror over the wall, what did he do with it? He must have put it back in his car so he could dispose of it where it would never be found, or at least where no connection with Nicky's crash would ever be suspected. But he hadn't much time. The Land Rover was already close enough to be heard: Daws couldn't risk being seen. And still he was wrestling a six-foot mirror into the back of his car? And somehow he managed to get it loaded and drive away without Poole seeing him? Brodie thought it was just about possible. But you could try a dozen times before you pulled it off.

She was missing something. Something that made it easier, faster. She looked around again. Nothing about the road, the stone walls, the over-hanging trees could have been other than they were, which left Daws, his car and the mirror. Still she was left with the image of a stout middle-aged man wrestling with a mirror as big as himself as red-handed discovery bore down on him at thirty miles an hour. It didn't work. Something didn't add up.

The problem was weight. A mirror big enough to do the job would be heavy: too heavy to set up and take down in the moments available, too big to be disposed of discreetly after its purpose was accomplished.

She was still standing in the middle of the road, eyes uplifted for inspiration, when the yellow digger came round the bend. It wasn't doing fifty miles an hour, or more than about fifteen, so it had no trouble stopping. But Philip Poole swung out onto the step with an troubled expression, clearly worried that her condition had deteriorated further since last he saw her. "Is everything all right?"

Brodie flashed him an apologetic grin. "Yes. I'm just thinking. Am I in your way?"

He climbed down to the ground. "There's no rush. I admire thinking, I try never to interrupt anyone who's doing some. What were you thinking?"

"I'm still trying to work out what it was that Nicky saw. It couldn't have been a real mirror – it would have been too cumbersome, one man would have had difficulty both getting it here and then disposing of it, and I don't believe he could do it without leaving marks somewhere. So what's big enough to give a reflection of the whole road but light enough to chuck in the back of a car?" She tossed her head in exasperation. "And the answer is, absolutely n– "

She didn't get as far as the vowel. Her voice stopped as her body froze. She was looking at the branches overhead.

Then she looked at the digger. At the digger bucket. "Philip," she said, and now her voice was quietly odd, "can you lift me up in that thing?"

He stared at her. "I could. I can't imagine why I would."

"Because I'm asking nicely?" But batting eyelids were no substitute for an explanation. "I can see something. It may not be significant but I'd like a closer look."

He stood beside her and peered up where the trees leaned over the road. "Where are you looking?"

She pointed at a projecting branch. "There's something tied round it. It may have been there for years, in which case it's no help. But I want to take a look."

Poole went on peering a moment, then shook his head. "Your eyes are better than mine. All right, I'll get you up there. But" – he was looking at her clothes – "the last thing I had in the bucket was cow-shit."

Her heart sank. But everything she had on was washable, all she had to do was grit her teeth and disrobe in the shower as soon as she got home. She took off her shoes and her jacket and put them on the wall. "Let's do it."

It could have been worse. Poole found a plastic fertiliser bag on the floor of the digger, and split it with his knife to make a mat. She clambered into the bucket, resolutely ignoring the squelch underfoot, and Poole lifted her carefully into the branches above the road.

She was right: there was something tied round the branch.

And it hadn't been there for years: there was none of the discolouration that results from even a brief contact with trees. All the same, Brodie couldn't see how it was relevant. Even given a suitable branch, you couldn't hang a six-foot mirror from it with kitchen string.

But something had been hung from it, and it must have been about six feet long because now she was up here she could see a second piece of string tied around the bough a couple of metres from the first. She hadn't spotted it before because it wasn't hanging down but had blown up into the leaves.

She gestured to Poole and he moved the digger closer to the wall. She felt among the twigs for the loose end and pulled it free.

It hadn't broken under the weight hung from it. When Daws had finished he'd pulled it down by the part he could reach from the road. One of the lengths of string had broken and been left dangling, but the other had torn away a piece of material. It was unlikely Daws even noticed. It had done its job as well as he had any right to hope, and he'd never need it again. He bundled it up and took it with him only so no one would guess how it had been done.

Brodie had been right, and she'd been wrong. Right about the Phantom of Cheyne Wood: that was clearly where he got the idea. Wrong about the mirror: he hadn't burdened himself with two metres of wood and glass, either Victorian or a modern copy. Right about the fact that Nicky Speers saw himself, his own headlights, speeding towards him as he came round the bend. Wrong about the time it would have taken to tidy up afterwards. A few seconds was enough, and then the assassin was on his way.

Half-hypnotised, Brodie stared at the little wedge of fabric. Daws had been clever, but he hadn't been clever enough. Here was the evidence not only of how he did it but of who did it. She'd never seen the stuff before but she knew it came from Sparrow Hill and this corner would prove it whether or not the rest was ever found.

Her first instinct was to cut it down and take it with her. Common sense intervened. Deacon would want to see it in situ. She replaced it among the leaves as she'd found it and waved to Poole that she was finished. "Ground floor, please."

He helped her out of the bucket, feeling the thrill of discovery like an electric current passing through her body. "You found something."

"Yes. Nicky's right: somebody tried to kill him. I can show how, and I think I can show who."

Poole's round face was at once fascinated and appalled. "So – who?"

Brodie smiled apologetically. "I have to talk to the police first. When I've done that I'll bring you up to speed. All right?"

He hadn't much option. "All right."

She couldn't get a reply on Deacon's mobile so she tried his office. But he wasn't there, and neither was Sergeant Voss. The switchboard wasn't sure when they'd return: would she like to speak to someone else?

Brodie decided against. What she had discovered was more important than urgent, it would be easier to explain to Deacon than to someone not involved in the inquiry, and he had it coming. He'd taken all the set-backs in this case, he was entitled to the break-through. "I'll try again in an hour. If you hear from him before that, ask him to meet me at Sparrow Hill."

She considered guarding her discovery until she could pass it on to Deacon. She could keep an eye on it from her car. Or she could ask Poole to: she thought he would do whatever she requested. But really there was no need. The thing was safe up there among the branches: if it hadn't been disturbed in two days it was unlikely to suffer much harm in the next couple of hours. And if she couldn't share her triumph with Deacon, and bask in his grudging admiration, she wanted to share it with Daniel.

In retrospect, though, that was a mistake. She should have

made herself comfortable in her car, turned on the heater, turned on the radio and waited for Deacon to reappear from wherever he and Voss had gone and get in touch. And not because the evidence would have been safer.

Improbably enough, at that very moment Detective Superintendent Deacon and Detective Sergeant Voss were holding hands in a Lovers' Lane in the heart of the Three Downs while the autumn sun set over the pale expanse of Frick Lake.

Admittedly, they were holding hands because a surfeit of lovers, or actually of cows, had reduced the lane to a quagmire and Deacon had just fallen to his knees. But it was a genuine beauty-spot and notorious rendezvous, even if the council knew it more prosaically as Pond Lane.

Neither man was interested in either the view or the romantic possibilities. They were hurrying towards the lake where a police inflatable and two divers, black and shiny, were already visible. There was also a police Land Rover, which had wisely taken the longer way across adjacent farmland. A mobile crane trundled down the field towards them as they arrived.

Deacon came directly to the point. "What have you got?"

"A dark red Mercedes saloon," said one of the divers, "with a body in the driver's seat."

"Numberplate?"

The diver nodded. "It's his all right."

When the crane was ready they went down again to secure the straps. The boom reached out over the water.

Voss was making notes. "What's that – about ten metres out?"

Deacon scowled at him. "Nearer thirty feet, I'd have said."

Voss was careful not to react. "He's come down the bank at speed. There's no tide to carry him out, he must have given it some welly or he'd just have sat there in the shallows until he got bored and went home."

Deacon nodded. "That's how it looks. We'll see when they get the car out – it'll still be in gear."

It was a deep lake in a fold of the downs: even ten metres from the shore there were fathoms of water. The crane took the strain, the hawser jerked straight and thrummed, but it was another moment before the water started to bubble white where something was coming to the surface. The aerial came first; then the roof above the rear windscreen; finally the whole thing was hanging in its straps and pouring water from every orifice.

The crane swung and lowered it gently onto the bank. It was muddy and there was a green film on the glass: it wasn't immediately obvious who or what was inside.

When the streaming water slowed to a trickle Voss tried the driver's door. It was unlocked and opened easier than he was expecting. The last of the lake-water ran out over his shoes.

Every so often a murder inquiry has to be stopped when it becomes apparent that the perpetrator is also dead, and has been for hundreds or thousands of years. Rates of decomposition vary enormously depending on conditions which can be extremely localised. Occasionally people come out of the ground after centuries looking as well as they did when they went into it. Or some suspicious bastard like Jack Deacon gets a bad feeling about a recent death and exhumes what should still be a body, to find only bones and what's known in the trade as "yucky stuff".

It was impossible to say by looking at the drowned body of Robert Daws when he died. But since Deacon had a fair idea what he was up to as recently as two nights ago he was unlikely to have been in the lake for forty-eight hours. He may have come straight here, convinced that his work was done, and kept his foot down on the accelerator until the car filled with water and, thirty seconds after that, his lungs did. Or he may have driven round for hours, trying to see an alternative – wondering if a good lawyer could get him off, wondering if he could snatch the girls and some realisable assets and be out of the country before the police net closed in.

Voss was reading his thoughts again. "He must have thought we were closer to him than we were."

"The old dragnet wasn't doing a great job, was it?" said Deacon pensively. "Great holes, plenty of them; not enough string."

"If he'd made a run for it he might have got away."

"And left everything behind? His home, his children, his business? I guess he decided it wasn't worth it. That he no longer had a life worth living."

Voss was a young man: he couldn't imagine death ever looking more attractive than life. "He could have done his time. He'd have come out eventually."

"Sure he would," said Deacon. "Old, broken in health, homeless, disowned by his family, deserted by his business contacts. On the other hand, if he went into the lake he might never be found. And he will never be convicted: we might know what he did but legally he remains a murder suspect. If they choose to, the girls can refuse to believe that he killed their mother. That just may have mattered to him."

"Or else he couldn't live with what he'd done."

As a young man, Charlie Voss was also a romantic. Deacon, who'd been trying to teach him better, breathed heavily. "There's no evidence that he felt guilty. What looked like a frenzied attack on his wife was actually fairly calculating – he didn't stick two knives into the same hole by sheer luck. After he was finished he smashed the phone to deny her any chance of help. Then he planted the second knife in Nicky Speers' shed, and set a trap to make the boy's murder look like suicide. Guilt doesn't come into it. He just felt he'd achieved everything he needed to."

Voss frowned. "I still don't understand the business with the knives. Why he needed two. And why he left one at the scene if he was going to plant the other on Nicky Speers."

"Me neither," said Deacon honestly. "And now he's dead I don't expect we ever will. I doubt if it matters very much. He isn't going to hurt anyone else. If that isn't the perfect ending, it'll do."

Voss frowned. "I thought you didn't believe he was a threat to the girls."

"I didn't. I don't." He shuffled crossly inside his raincoat. "Look, maybe Daniel was right and maybe he wasn't, but now we know for sure that Robert Daws isn't going to hurt his daughters. The kids will get his money and can go off and join their aunt and uncle in South Africa. We can close the file on Serena Daws. If that isn't exactly a triumph of police detection, at least it's tidy."

Voss found himself looking at the way the body slumped in its seatbelt. Like all corpses it didn't look like a dead person so much as something that had never been alive. But Voss was obscurely touched that a man intending to kill himself by driving into deep water had put his seat-belt on first. Because it was the law, and apart from murdering his wife and attempting to murder her lover Robert Daws had been a law-abiding man.

Deacon followed his gaze but not his thought processes. "Stupid sod," he sniffed. "Now, will somebody turn that Land Rover round and give me a lift back to my car?"

# Chapter Twenty

"I know how he did it," said Brodie. She was breathless, as if she'd run from the crash scene on Poole Lane. "Robert Daws. Like I said, it was all done by mirrors. Just not the one we were looking for."

She'd lost Daniel. But whatever her revelation, he wanted to hear it himself before the girls did. He glanced round but the kitchen and hall were empty. He thought the girls were upstairs. Peris, he knew, was shopping in Dimmock. "Come in," he said, "and tell me what this is all about."

But she didn't want to come in. She wanted him to come to the studio with her. He asked why but she refused to explain. "Easier to show you than tell you." Daniel took the key off its nail by the kitchen door and followed her across the court-yard.

He opened the cottage door and put the lights on – it was dark now. Brodie made a bee-line for the cupboard where Serena's art-work had been tidied away. She pulled out canvases until she found what she was looking for.

"The picture Robert slashed – Jack has the remains as evidence?"

Daniel nodded, waiting patiently to understand.

"But give or take a few details – Nicky standing up, Nicky lying down, Nicky – " She looked at the last canvas and blinked. "Yes, well. But apart from those details, these are the same?"

"I think so," said Daniel. "I never saw the one they fought over, but I gather it was the same sort of thing."

"What's he lying on?"

With just a hint of distaste Daniel looked closer. "Some sort of silvery fabric? It could be baking foil for all I know."

"It could indeed," agreed Brodie. "Or one of those foil blankets the emergency services wrap you in after accidents.

Hill-walkers carry them too, you can get them at any outdoor pursuits shop."

Daniel didn't doubt it though he'd never had the occasion to ask. He wasn't really an outdoor pursuits sort of person, except in so far as astronomy is mostly pursued out of doors. "So?"

She breathed heavily at him, although she'd have been annoyed if he'd made the connection quicker than she had. "Heat-reflective, yes?"

"Yes."

"And what will reflect heat ... "

Now he had it. His eyes shot wide and he gave a startled gasp. "... Will reflect light. The mirror!"

"Exactly," said Brodie, satisfied. "A mirror light enough for one man to move around quickly and easily – put it up where it can do its job, pull it down once it has. The back of his car? He could have shoved it up the back of his jumper."

Daniel hadn't seen what she had seen. "But it wouldn't stand up. How would he – ?"

"Hung with string from a branch sticking out over the road. Then he tugged it down, but the strings are still there. There's even a corner of foil tied up in one of them."

Daniel ran the sequence of events through his head in the light of this new information. His eyes flared again behind the round glasses. *"That's* what he was doing here! He'd seen the pictures, knew Serena had a foil sheet that she used as a backdrop. He knew I was in the cottage so he thought he'd check the house first. Either that or he knew where she kept it."

*"Yes,"* said Brodie. "He could hardly nip into *Camp Followers* in town, could he? At four o'clock in the morning he thought he could search every drawer and cupboard in the kitchen and scullery and never be challenged."

"So it was Robert," said Daniel softly. "Not Nicky."

"No. Emerald was wrong. She saw what she expected, even wanted, to see. To her Nicky is the archetypal intruder: if he'd stayed away from her house she'd still have a family."

Daniel was nodding slowly. "I hope – " He didn't finish the sentence.

Brodie didn't like mysteries. "What?"

"I hope that's all it was. An honest mistake. I hope she wasn't trying to punish him."

"For the damage he did here?"

"It's natural enough that she'd want to. We know the girls don't believe Robert stabbed Serena, that they were waiting for the police to arrest Nicky. When they let him go, maybe the girls thought they needed a prod in the right direction."

"So when they bumped into their father in the hall they lied – to shift suspicion away from him and onto Nicky?" Brodie gave a little grimace. "It's possible. There was time to think it through – it wasn't till later that Emerald claimed to have recognised the intruder. Oh but Daniel, they're two young girls! It's pretty sophisticated thinking for two young girls."

"Is it? Girls their age can be highly manipulative. I've known teachers suspended because pubescent girls came up with entirely fictional but plausible allegations against them. Anger a boy of the same age and he might take a swing at you, he might even pull a knife. But anger a girl and she can nurse the grudge until she finds a way of hurting you that doesn't put her in danger. Even if she isn't believed, her claims may be impossible to disprove. The idea stays at the back of people's minds that they could be doing her an injustice, that there was something in what she said. That's the situation we're in now. We don't think Emerald saw what she says she saw. But we'd rather think that she was mistaken than lying."

"All right," said Brodie, "so maybe she was lying. So what? In a way she's right – a lot of this *was* Nicky's fault. Maybe she thought she was just making that clear to everyone. In the circumstances, can you find it in your heart to blame her?"

187

"For accusing someone of a crime she knew he didn't commit?" His voice was quiet, his tone adamant. "Oh yes."

Brodie shrugged. "Well, we'll never know for sure. She could have been mistaken. For everyone's sake I think you should leave it at that."

Daniel thought so too. "I'm not going to accuse her of something I can't prove. She'll deny it, and where do we go from there? All the same ... "

"What?"

"Doesn't it bother you? Knowing what they're prepared to do to get what they want? Doesn't it make you wonder what they'll do next time someone crosses them?"

Brodie's smile was affectionate but also concerned. "Daniel, you've got too close to this. I warned you about that. Now you're seeing conspiracies where there are just two unhappy little girls. They've had a hard time, and it isn't over yet. OK, maybe they don't always behave perfectly. Name me someone, adult or child, who – in the same circumstances – would."

He thought she was probably right and he was being unreasonable. He thought she was probably right and he'd become too deeply mired in the tragedy at Sparrow Hill. He thought it was because he wasn't up to his job – or no, that wasn't fair: his job was tutoring, he'd taken on himself the rôle of counsellor and guide – that he was seeing danger where none existed.

"So what's happening? Is Jack meeting you here?"

"When he gets my message," said Brodie. "He and Voss were out on a call."

"Stay for tea," suggested Daniel. "Peris is going to be late back, I said I'd run something up. Or do you have to feed Paddy?"

"No, Marta's got her. Neither of them will miss me. What are you making?"

Spending time in Peris Daws' company was having its effect on Daniel. He said with a hint of pride, "Mushroom risotto."

"Count me in," said Brodie.

The risotto was ready and still Deacon hadn't called. The girls came downstairs and Daniel served.

At first the conversation was stilted. There was only one thing in Brodie's mind but she knew better than to make any reference to it in front of the man's daughters. There was only one thing in Daniel's mind, and he didn't see how he could raise it without provoking a furious argument he couldn't win.

Relief came from an unlikely source. "Daniel says you've got a daughter, Mrs Farrell," said Johnny, scrupulously attentive. "How old is she?"

Brodie smiled. "Paddy. She's five now. She's heavily into dragons and tractors."

Both girls laughed. "I don't think we've got a tractor," said Em. "Have we, Johnny?"

"I've never seen one. Unless there's one upstairs. This was Daddy's house when he was a little boy," she explained. "Daddy's and Uncle Hugo's. Most of the toys in the attic were theirs. Our things are mostly in our bedrooms. Except for the things we had when were were little," she added with the nonchalence of the recently teenaged.

"There's a rocking-horse," volunteered Em. "And a puppet theatre. We found it when we were showing the policeman around. I don't remember seeing it before."

"I do," said Johnny. "It was put away when you were small. You didn't like the crocodile."

"I love rocking-horses," said Brodie. "We never had one at home, but a cousin of mine had one. I always meant to get one for Paddy, but I haven't really the room for it."

"You should bring her up to have a ride on ours," said Johnny.

Brodie was touched. Four days ago these girls could barely tolerate her presence. "I'd love to. Is it very old, do you know?"

Johnny shrugged. "It's big, I know that much. And

dapple-grey. The tail's a bit threadbare. That's how we used to make him go faster – whoever wasn't riding would stand behind pulling the tail."

"He had a name," Em remembered suddenly. "What was it, Johnny? What did we call him?"

"Dapple?"

"Yes," said Em slowly, "but that wasn't all. He had a proper name. It was on a label on the saddle."

Johnny's beam lit her face like sunshine. "I'd forgotten! It was the maker's name, but when we were little we thought it was what the horse was called. Gregory Birkinshaw."

It was the first unshadowed laughter the house had heard in a fortnight; perhaps for longer than that. "I have *got* to meet Gregory Birkinshaw," said Brodie.

Daniel's culinary efforts done proper credit, they trooped upstairs. Their feet echoed like gunfire on the last, uncarpeted flight. Johnny turned on the landing light and led the way into the first of the attic rooms.

Gregory, dappled and dusty, stood in the middle of the floor, a splendid Victorian steed caparisoned in red leather and mounted on a great bow-shaped rocker. Perhaps his long white tail was a little thin; perhaps his flanks were scratched by generations of children who thought kicking would make him go faster; perhaps the fire in his eye was dulled by cataracts woven of cobwebs. Brodie didn't care. He was the most perfect rocking-horse she'd ever seen. She wouldn't have thanked Philip Poole for the gift of Blossom, but this fabrication of wood and paint and scraps of leather filled her with longing. She let out a gasp of sheer delight.

Daniel watched in private amusement as she walked round stroking it, patting its insensitive rump, holding her hand under its bared teeth as if it might take a sugar-lump – if she'd had a sugar-lump. Most of the time she intimidated him with her sophistication. She was intelligent, confident, elegant, admired and respected: a successful professional, a genuine grown-up. But show her a dusty old rocking-horse

190

and twenty years fell away and the cloud of dark hair gravitated towards plaits.

"Oh, go on," he said with a grin, "take it for a trot."

Brodie shook her head emphatically. "Don't be absurd!" But she didn't walk away.

"Oh, do!" said Em, dancing up and down and clapping her small hands in encouragement.

"I think you should," said Johnny, straight-faced. "You want to make sure he's not too fresh for Paddy to ride."

Brodie waved an admonitory hand at them. "Oh, hush."

But they took her hands and positioned them on Gregory's withers and the back of his saddle. "Left foot in the stirrup," said Johnny, "and *up* you go." Before she could protest further Brodie found herself atop the padded saddle with the arch of Gregory's neck capped with its flowing mane rising to his sharp ears before her.

For five minutes she was a child again. But not the child she had been, pretty and neat and circumspect, playing with dolls until she was judged responsible enough to have a kitten. No, the child she should have been – the child who'd have grown into the Brodie Farrell she was now, Daniel Hood's friend, Jack Deacon's lover, brave and strong and sure of heart and mind. She rode like a natural – like a Wild Ward – spurring on whenever the great bows seemed to flag, the wind of her passage tearing through her hair and making the blood sing in her cheeks.

When she finally dismounted she felt obscurely bereft. As if she'd had a glimpse of something wonderful and then someone had drawn the curtain.

"Are you all right?" Daniel's face was briefly anxious as he searched hers.

Brodie nodded. "Dizzy." She clung to his arm, and his eyes cleared and he laughed.

The girls were thrilled with Gregory's success. Before the rocking-horse had quite come to a halt they were dragging out other ancient toys for their guest's inspection. Johnny found the puppet theatre, and Em demonstrated once and for all her contempt for crocodiles by letting it bite her nose. Then they put on an impromptu performance of *Snow White and the Only Three Dwarfs We Could Find*.

After that there was no stopping them. Johnny found a toboggan, and laid it aside against the coming of the snow. Daniel winced: he knew they wouldn't be here when the snows came. Em found a hobby-horse made from a sock and trundled it up and down as if riding a Derby winner.

There was a dartboard with real darts, none of that sucker-on-the-front rubbish but real heavy, pointy darts guaranteed capable of putting an eye out; and Daniel impressed the girls and astonished Brodie by landing a twenty, a double twenty and a bull's eye.

"I'm the Sultan of Araby," said Em, appearing in a turban and a curtain.

Johnny found a circular arrangement of pictures drawn on the inside of a cylinder with a series of slits in it. "What is it?"

"It's a zoetrope," said Daniel. "It's about the earliest way of making moving pictures. You turn the handle and look through the slit, and it looks like film of a very short boxing-match."

"*Rocky Minus Three*," said Johnny with a grin, and Daniel grinned back.

"Now I'm the Duchess of Thick Twist," announced Em, having changed into a wide flower-decked picture hat and a plum silk dress that probably belonged to her great-grand-mother. She looked like a blueberry muffin.

"Where are you getting this stuff?" asked Brodie, setting aside the wooden farm she'd been laying out and following the dumpy duchess into the next room.

"The dressing-up box," said Em, sliding a hand into hers. "Mummy used to keep things for us to dress up in. Mostly when we were younger, but ... " The little voice petered out.

Brodie squeezed her hand. "If I'm not too old to ride a

rocking-horse, you're not too old to dress up. What else have you got in this box?"

Em beamed and threw back the lid.

Next door they'd got the zoetrope going and Daniel was explaining how it worked when suddenly Johnny seemed to freeze. She jerked to her feet – they'd both been lying on the floor propped on their elbows – and stammered furiously, "I need to – go see – " She was gone before she could finish the sentence. He heard her scurrying along the landing. "Em, leave that now. Come and give me a hand ... "

But Em was enjoying herself too much to pay her sister any heed. She was going through the hats in the steamer trunk like a quick-change artist. "I'm a fairy. Now I'm a pirate. Now I'm ... er ... "

"Charlie Chaplin," prompted Brodie, although the likeness wasn't particularly striking. "Try this."

Em discarded the bowler hat and pulled on the mortarboard. "Now you're Daniel," said Brodie, and Em fell about laughing.

"What else is there in here?" She rooted, passed the child a policeman's helmet. "Now you're Detective Superintendent Deacon. No, scowl more – shout and stamp up and down a bit. Now you're ... "

She'd reached the bottom of the trunk. Among the velvet and chiffon her fingers found something cool and shiny. Somehow they recognised what it was while her brain was still otherwise engaged, watching an eleven-year-old in a cardboard helmet arrest a teddy-bear for failing to display a left ear.

She heard Johnny sharp at the door: "Come on, Em, we have to go now."

She heard Daniel in the next room: "Is everything all right, Johnny?"

She heard herself, an hour before: "I know how he did it." But she hadn't. She'd only known how it had been done.

Slowly, carefully, she pulled the silver foil out from under the dressing-up clothes and spread it on the bare boards. When it was all unfolded it was a couple of metres square, and one corner was missing.

She raised her eyes to find Em watching her, rigid, the helmet still on her head, the grin frozen grotesquely on her face.

Johnny, who'd almost reached them in time, who'd got as far as the door, now took three strides into the room, snatched her sister's hand and threw the helmet back in the trunk. She met Brodie's gaze with icy resolve. "I don't know what that is. It isn't ours." Then she turned and, dragging her sister in her wake, made for the door.

Daniel closed it as he came in. Sometimes, Brodie reflected distantly, in the space between heartbeats as the seconds stretched, he could be absurdly obtuse. But sometimes it was as if he was reading her mind.

Without moving from the door he looked at the foil sheet. Then he looked at Brodie, and she could see his mind whirring with the possibilities. Then he looked at the girls. He drew an unsteady breath.

"You could have *killed* him," he said.

# Chapter Twenty-One

Johnny wouldn't look at him, muttered in her teeth, "I don't know what you mean."

Brodie stayed where she was, kneeling on the floor. "He means, when you hung this across the road on the way to Nicky Speers' cottage."

"You heard him pass on his way into town," said Daniel. His voice was thin with shock. "You couldn't know he'd be coming back soon after closing time but it was a reasonable guess.

"I was in bed by eleven, I expect Peris was too. You crept downstairs – with the foil sheet folded into your back-pack – picked up a torch and a ball of string, then slipped away on your bikes. No one heard you go, no one missed you."

"I thought your father did it," said Brodie, her tone quiet and without emotion. It was too big a thing to shout at them for. Shouting is for leaving the top off the toothpaste and spending dinner-money on sweets. But these girls had tried to kill someone. End a life. If she started shouting she would-n't be able to stop. "I did wonder how a fat middle-aged man had scaled a five-foot wall, climbed into a tree and edged out along the branch to where I found the strings. But I figured you can do anything you want to do enough, and I knew he had all the motive necessary. It never occurred to me that you had too."

"When you heard the bike coming back," Daniel contin-ued softly, "out of sight up in the tree you let down the foil sheet. Nicky came round the bend and his own headlights blinded him. When he swerved they swerved too: he had nowhere left to go. He hit the wall at fifty miles an hour and his bones shattered."

"And you watched," said Brodie. She had to fight down a bubble of anger to continue. "You watched his body break.

You listened to him choke on his own blood. You folded up the foil, climbed down from the tree, and then you watched him dying. Hurting and dying. You watched and made no attempt to help."

Daniel's voice cut her off. "But he didn't die. He'll be all right. His bones will heal, in time. You didn't kill him. But you came so close. To ending his life and ruining your own."

Finally Johnny's chestnut head snapped up and she stared him rebelliously in the eye. "Our lives *are* ruined! Hadn't you noticed? He killed our mother!"

Daniel shook his head. "He didn't."

"And I say he did!" she yelled back. "Of course he did – who else? But that stupid policeman thinks our daddy did it, and now he can't come home! And Uncle Hugo's gone back to Africa, and even his stupid wife won't put her own stupid life on hold for a few weeks to look after us. We were a good family. An important family. We had money, people cared what we thought. And we're going to end up being fostered in a council house because a dirty farm-boy couldn't keep his kit on!"

"It doesn't matter," said Brodie tersely. "You can't take the law into your own hands. You're two little girls, for God's sake! If professional, experienced police detectives can't be sure Nicky Speers stabbed your mother, whatever made you think you had the right to punish him?"

Em hadn't taken much part in the argument until now. She wasn't good at arguing. Johnny argued and Em cried. She was crying now, great tears like crystal beads sliding down her face. "He deserved it!" she wailed.

"That's not your call," snapped Brodie. "Everyone who ever suffered from a crime wanted vengeance. That's *why* we have a legal system – because people who're hurt and in shock can't be expected to use good judgement. Society takes the burden off them, as much for their sake as the defendant's. Judging who's guilty and who's innocent, and what penalty is appropriate in all the circumstances, calls for cool heads. For people who're not emotionally involved. No one in their right mind would offer the adolescent daughters of a murder victim a say on sentencing. Even if they did, the death penalty wouldn't be available."

"I know," shouted Johnny. "We knew that if we wanted justice we'd have to see to it ourselves. The police weren't interested. We told them who was to blame and they let him go. Even after they found the knife they let him go. I mean, what do you need to arrest someone – that he committed his crime in the police station carpark during the tea-break? How could they *not* believe he did it? Because he *said* he didn't?"

Daniel came away from the door and stood with his hands in his pockets, regarding them sombrely. "Convicting someone of a serious crime, that he could spend a lot of his life paying for, is a painstaking business. It's not enough to think you know who did it. You have to make sure beyond any reasonable doubt. You have to prove that he was there when the crime took place, or at least that he wasn't somewhere else. You have to establish that he was capable of doing what was done. Then you look for some physical evidence linking him to the scene – the victim's blood or hair on his clothes, his skin under her fingernails, fibres from her carpet on his shoes. Scientific testing is so accurate these days that, although you can never prove a negative, you have to have misgivings if you can't connect the suspect with the victim forensically.

"Only after all these tests have been satisfied can you charge someone with a crime. And then he's entitled defend himself before an unbiased jury. If there's been an idiotic co-incidence that makes him look he did something he didn't, they're his last chance of being believed. They use their common sense. They consider the plausibility of witnesses, ask themselves who impresses them as truthful. They don't have to believe an expert witness if they think he's just going through the motions. Could the samples have been contaminated? Is there any other way the results could be misleading? Only when a dozen honest, sensible people with no axe to grind are convinced that he did what he's accused of doing does the question of punishment arise.

"Which makes knocking someone off a motorbike on the basis of personal dislike no justice at all. The police, after questioning him for hours and looking at the physical evidence, weren't convinced of his guilt. They may be wrong, but it's much more likely they're right. Nicky Speers is probably not responsible for your mother's murder. But you were almost responsible for his."

He drew a steadying breath. "Girls, you do realise we can't keep this between the four of us? You hurt somebody, badly. He isn't going to die, but it remains to be seen how good a recovery he'll make. Now, people will understand why you did it – that you were desperately upset and angry. But it can't be overlooked. I have to tell the police and they'll have to take it before a magistrate. Where it'll go from there I simply don't know. I'm sure the strain you've been under will be taken into account. People will deal with you sympathetically, make sure you get all the help you can use. Try not to be afraid. This too will pass."

"And look on the bright side," murmured Brodie. "You won't end up in a council house. At some point you'll be able to join your aunt and uncle in Johannesburg."

By now Em was weeping hysterically, great broken sobs she could hardly breathe around. Daniel knelt down and held her against his shoulder. She buried her face in him and her little body shook.

Johnny was at the point where any moment tears would breach the defences of her rage and put out the fires she was feeding on. She didn't want them to see her like that. She reached out and prised Em's hand off Daniel's sleeve, and said stiffly, "Then we'd better go and pack a few things." Ram-rod straight, she towed the smaller child away.

When the door closed behind them Brodie vented a shaky

sigh. "Dear God, what a stunner! I never even thought of them. Not till I found that foil sheet and realised that even if their father had taken it from here he wouldn't have risked bringing it back. The rest of it followed. Robert couldn't have climbed the tree – but his daughters could. Damn it, I even saw the green patches on the knees of their jeans!"

Daniel sank back on his heels. "They fooled me too. I thought they might be in danger: I never guessed they could be a danger to someone else." His eyes were wretched. "I was right *here*, Brodie. I was dealing with them every day; I was supposed to be looking after them. And I let them do something so bad that both they and Nicky will carry the consequences all their lives.

"I should have seen it coming. If I'd been half the teacher I think I am I'd have known their problems were out of my league. If I'd asked her Peris would have sent them to a child psychologist – they'd have got the support they needed and none of this would have happened. But no. I just can't resist playing Superman, can I, however ill-equipped."

There was a grain of truth in what he said, but he was being unnecessarily harsh on himself. This too was in character.

"You did what you were hired to do," she said gently. "All right, you didn't anticipate this. Neither did I; or Jack, or Peris. And if you'd asked for them to see a child psychologist they'd still be waiting for the first appointment. I doubt if anyone could have stopped this happening. You tried to help them. You *did* help them – think back to what they were like the first couple of days you were here. They were so traumatised they could hardly deal with the world. You reached them and brought them back."

"Maybe I shouldn't have!" whined Daniel, bitter with despair. "If I'd let them sink into a depressive morass Nicky Speers wouldn't now be strung together with splints and wire like a Sopwith Camel!"

Brodie rose and extended him a hand. "Nicky's going to

199

be OK. He's young, he's strong, he'll get over this. And the girls do have a point: if he'd exercised an iota of self-control he'd never have found himself in this predicament. Don't beat yourself up over Nicky, or any of them. None of what's happened is your fault. Stop trying to carry the world, Daniel – you'll end up so round-shouldered you'll never get a jacket to fit!"

Daniel managed a gruff little chuckle and let her draw him to his feet. The friendship of Brodie Farrell, even if he wouldn't have embarrassed her by saying so, was among his chief joys, and one of the reasons was this: that more than anyone he knew she could keep her feet grounded in reality and her eyes on the stars. When he felt buffeted by things he couldn't control Brodie was a sure anchor. He relied on her strength. But she never let him rely for too long before she pushed him back into the stream again. She had a keen instinct for when to help and when to let people help themselves. Her brisk, unsentimental kindness had got him through things he couldn't have endured alone. This was going to be one of them.

He said, "Should we call the police again? Even if Jack isn't back, maybe somebody ought to come and take charge of the situation?"

Brodie nodded. "I'll call, you stay with the girls."

But when they reached the door it was locked.

# Chapter Twenty-Two

"And that," said Brodie thoughtfully, "is something else we should have seen coming."

Daniel sighed. All at once he sounded very tired. "The idiots! What do they think this is going to get them?"

"Time," said Brodie. It was the obvious answer.

"To do what?"

"I suppose, to run away. Maybe they think they can find their father." She tried the door for herself, was no more able to budge it than Daniel had been. She didn't expect to, it was just one of those human compulsions. As a man, as a friend, she trusted him absolutely, would have followed him through the gates of hell if he'd asked her to. She just didn't believe that the door was locked until she'd tried it for herself.

"We could do that thing with a sheet of paper," she said, brightening. "Slide it under, push the key through, slide it back?"

Daniel looked doubtfully at the crack beneath the door. "I don't think it's wide enough."

Again, she had to try. She smoothed out a piece of newspaper that had been protecting china in a tea-chest. But he was right: even the paper wouldn't go through the gap.

"Your mobile phone?" he suggested. He didn't own one himself.

"In my handbag," said Brodie. "On the back on my chair at the kitchen table."

"Ah."

"You'll have to force the door."

He did own a television – at least, he did until it went up in smoke – so he'd seen this done. The beefiest male present braces his shoulder against the locked door and heaves, and it gives with such ease that you're left wondering if there's any point locking the damn things at all.

Well, Daniel was for once the beefiest male present. But the door was a baulk of solid timber and the frame was as thick as his fist, and when he put his shoulder to it and heaved the only thing that threatened to give was his collar-bone. "I don't think so," he said, stepping back.

Brodie huffed with exasperation. She wasn't used to being in situations she could do nothing about, but it rather looked as if this was one. "When are you expecting Peris back?"

"About six. She said to keep some tea for her."

Brodie looked at her watch. "It's gone six so she shouldn't be long. And Jack will get my message any time now. I asked him to meet me here."

"So we won't have to draw lots for who gets eaten."

She returned his grin. "Not yet, anyway."

A little time passed. They listened in vain for the sound of wheels on gravel. All the same, after about fifteen minutes Daniel said, "There's someone downstairs."

Brodie joined him at the door. "Maybe it's the monsters."

His gaze dropped. "Don't call them that."

She snorted with impatience. "What do you want me to call them? The post-traumatically-stressed poor-decision-makers? The morally challenged sub-adults?"

Daniel winced. "I know. But what they've done isn't the sum total of who they are. To call them monsters is to give up on them, to believe they're irredeemable."

Brodie flicked an irritable hand. "Whatever." She frowned. "What *is* that I can hear?"

"It's your mobile," said Daniel. "Maybe it's Jack."

But Brodie was intimately familiar with the tone of her phone, would have known it even through two floors of Georgian living-space and a locked door. She tried to focus on the distant sound, because if it wasn't her phone it was something else she knew and ought to recognise.

And then she did. She took a step back from the door and her eyes were afraid. "Daniel – that's the smoke alarm."

Jack Deacon shook his head decisively. "I don't see how that can be. I can put him places inside the last week. Four or five days, just maybe, but not a fortnight."

Dr Roy gave an accepting shrug. The body of Robert Daws seeped gently on the autopsy table while the pathologist took a slide out of his microscope. "In that case these little guys who live in ponds have suddenly taken a major step up the evolutionary ladder. They can now reach a stage in their development inside four, maybe five days that used to take them a fortnight. My goodness, they'll be making fire by the end of the month and celebrating Christmas inside a little aquatic St Paul's."

Deacon glowered at him. He was deeply suspicious of cleverness, never more so than when it was directed at him. "Are you saying the body of Robert Daws *had* to be in Frick Lake for a fortnight? Not could have been, not might have been, but must have been?"

"Yes," said the FME mildly. "I thought that was exactly what I said."

Deacon went on glaring at him until it struck him there was no point. Then he glared at Voss. "If Daws has been dead for a fortnight, who ambushed Nicky Speers? Who left a knife with Serena's blood on it in his garden shed? Who was wandering round Sparrow Hill in the middle of the night?"

DS Voss was surprised too, he just didn't take it so personally. "Maybe we were wrong about Nicky. Maybe it was his knife all along. Maybe when he thought you were onto him he drove into the wall deliberately."

"Then why lie?"

Voss shrugged. "If that's what happened, why not? – he'd lied about everything else."

"And what was he doing at Sparrow Hill?"

"Maybe he was looking for that knife."

"But he didn't use it in the main house. He used it in the cottage – Serena's studio."

"There was a lot going on that day," said Voss reasonably, "maybe he couldn't remember where he'd been. Or maybe he never was in the house. Maybe the girls imagined it. They've had a rough time, it's no wonder if they're having nightmares."

"And now I've got to go and tell them that their father's dead too," groaned Deacon. "Dear God, why does anybody ever want to become a policeman?"

Voss glanced round Dr Roy's preserve of rubber and stainless steel, smelling of disinfectant and, right now, pond water and decomposition. "It's the glamour, sir," he said woodenly. "That, and the women."

Deacon gave him a hard look. Then he found himself chuckling. "That must be it. Speaking of which, I still haven't called Brodie. Well, maybe she's still at Sparrow Hill. If not I'll call when I've got this done."

"Do you want me to come?"

The superintendent shook his head. "I'll take a WPC. You can ... you can ... " He looked at his watch. It was half-past six. "Here's a novel idea: you can have the night off. Catch up with some of those women who can't keep their hands off a man smelling of death and pond-weed."

Charlie Voss pursed his lips judiciously. "One night may not be enough." All the same, he was gone before Deacon could find something to throw at him that wasn't a bottled human organ.

"Run that by me again," said Brodie. Her voice was thin. "How I haven't got to call them monsters. How they're mostly misunderstood, and anyone can make a mistake, and ... "

"Later," said Daniel. "Call me a fool later. Right now, let's find a way out of here."

It was impossible to guess how long they had. Depending

on where and how it was set, a fire might smoulder for an hour without doing much harm, or it might race up through the chimney that was the main stairwell and into the attics with their stores of old treasures as dry as kindling in a matter of minutes. Neither of them felt like trusting to luck. Nothing that had happened so far suggested this was their lucky day.

They tried the door again, one at a time and both together. There wasn't a suspicion of movement. Neither the door, the frame nor the heavy iron lock would yield to anything less than dynamite. Brodie went to the window. "I guess this is Plan B."

It could have been worse. The attic windows were set into the hip of the roof: they wouldn't need fifteen metres of knotted sheets to reach the ground, had only to crawl along the gutter to the next window, get back inside and hurry downstairs.

"This isn't going to take both of us," said Daniel. "If the key's still in the door I can unlock it."

"*If*," said Brodie.

"Why would they take it?"

"Spite?"

But if it wasn't there she could still get out along the roof. If they could open the window. Generations of paint prevented the sash from travelling more than a few inches.

"Stand back."

Brodie looked round as the butt-end of a brass coal-scuttle swung past her ear and smashed the window, taking glass, glazing bars and very nearly Daniel with it. She hauled him back by his belt. "A *little* more warning would have been nice."

"Sorry. I was striking while the iron was hot."

They cleared the spears of glass from the frame and Daniel leaned out and peered along the roof-line. The next window was only five metres away. "I can do this."

"I have every confidence in you," said Brodie; but she held

onto his belt until he was safe on the roof and pointing the right way. "Don't forget this."

He gave the coal-scuttle a puzzled look. "To break the next window?" suggested Brodie. "Don't drop it. And don't take so wild a swing with it that you bounce yourself over the edge."

He looked back at her, his face a pale moon against the night sky as he crounched on his hands and knees in the gutter. "I can do this," he said again, insistently.

"Of course you can," said Brodie.

She watched from the window, though mostly all she could see were the soles of his shoes and his backside. When he swung the coal-scuttle again it sounded like the opening bar of a modern concerto, the bass boom of the brass threaded with the crystal timpani of shattered glass. He disappeared head-first, and a few seconds later she heard him at the door.

When it opened he looked less jubilant than she expected. "Hurry," he said briefly, "I don't think we have much time."

Dead on cue the electrics failed.

But the attics were not plunged into immediate blackness, though it took Brodie a moment to realise why not and another to see why this was not a good thing. A rosy glow was coming up the staircase.

Deacon collected WPC Meredith from the police station and headed for the Guildford Road. He tried Brodie's number again – ignoring the disapproving look of the young policewoman beside him, who habitually stopped drivers for talking on the phone – but there was still no answer. He didn't want to call Sparrow Hill because this wasn't something you could say over the phone. Better to wait until he got there. It was a ten minute drive, and he didn't know of any reason to hurry.

They edged cautiously towards the stairs. The heat hit

them before they got there and warned them what they would find. But it was like the door: they had to look to believe it.

The whole of the stairwell was filled with flame. How far down in the house it had its roots they had no way of knowing, but the last flight with its bare wooden treads was well alight, roaring like a train in a tunnel.

"We're not getting out that way," Brodie said with conviction. Somewhere in the last minute she'd taken hold of Daniel's hand, and didn't feel inclined to give it back just yet. "Is there another staircase?"

But he'd only been in the house a couple of days, up here only once before. "I don't know. Even if there is – ?"

"We could crawl along the roof and break in through another window," said Brodie.

They hurried back to the room they'd escaped through and Brodie leaned out of the window. There was one more dormer beyond it, but that room too was served by this corridor and these stairs. Possibly there were no others.

"All right," said Daniel, keeping his voice calm, "what are our options?"

"We roast on the stairs or make gravity pizza on the cobblestones below," said Brodie shortly. "Not a great choice."

His hand tightened on hers. "Not much of an answer either. You can do better than that. Do we wait to be rescued or try to escape? We could wait too long and waste time we could be using. But shinning down a drainpipe has its dangers too."

She moistened her lips and tried to think. Fear was getting in the way. "There are two people who should get here any time now. And there's a farm across the lane. When somebody spots the flames, help will be on its way. We don't want to break our necks just as the fire engine turns up."

He nodded agreement. "No, we don't. Well, if we're going to sit it out up here we want to keep the fire and smoke at bay as long as possible. That door that we couldn't break: it'll protect us. The curtains from the dressing-up box laid along the bottom will keep the smoke out."

Brodie pulled the red plush curtains out of the box and packed them against the crack. No light came through so possibly no air could either. "Mental note," she said. "Next time I'm trapped in a burning building, make sure it's with someone who has a thorough grasp of the physical sciences."

"That, or a fire extinguisher," said Daniel drily.

There wasn't much more they could do. They felt round for anything which might help if in the end they were forced to attempt an escape, but the darkness defeated them. There might have been a rope ladder stored somewhere in the room but it would be merest luck if they found it. Daniel found a rusty scythe, by the simple expedient of cutting himself on it – Brodie responded to his yelp of pain with a testy, "*Now* what?" – but nothing to help them down from the roof.

Listening at the door, Daniel thought the fire sounded closer but said nothing. "I don't understand. I *told* them Nicky would be all right. If they'd killed him maybe they'd have felt they had nothing to lose. But now they're in twice as much trouble. They can't think they can stay ahead of the police forever."

"They can," said Brodie. "Think it, I mean. You're right: they're not monsters, they're children. Children have a simplistic view of the world. They probably think they can run away with a travelling circus. *You* know they'll have to face the music sometime, *I* know, but they don't. They're thinking in the present tense. We were going to tell the police what they'd done and they had to stop us."

"By setting fire to the house around us?" His voice climbed incredulously.

"They don't understand cause and effect in the same way adults do. They can't picture the consequences of their actions. They left us to burn because they couldn't imagine what it would be like. When they sent Nicky spinning into a stone wall they didn't ask themselves what an impact like that would do to a human body, how it would feel. They think killing someone is like turning a switch: *bad* person, inconvenient person, turn him off."

"You're saying they're psychotic," Daniel said faintly.

"I'm *saying* they're children," Brodie said impatiently. "Johnny's fourteen. She has the body of a young woman, thinks she's all but grown up. But she has the mentality of a child and the emotions of a confused adolescent. That isn't her fault, she is what circumstances have made her, but don't lose sight of the fact that she's dangerous. She'll go through anyone who gets in her way to have what she wants."

For a moment Daniel said nothing more. Then: "You said, they watched."

Brodie couldn't see his face in the darkness. "What?"

"When they ambushed Nicky. They watched him smash into the wall. They listened to him choke on his own blood. If Poole hadn't come along when he did they'd have watched him die."

Brodie nodded; then, realising that wouldn't serve, said it aloud. "Yes. It wasn't real to them until they saw it. Like the Cheyne Wood Phantom – the kids got away with their hoax until Serena couldn't resist watching. She had to see the fear she'd caused. Johnny and Em had to see Nicky broken in the road in order to feel avenged."

"Reflections," Daniel said softly.

"What? Oh – yes. Well, they're the spitting image of their mother and aunt at that age. I guess the similarities are more than skin-deep."

"Johnny was terrified of history repeating itself," murmured Daniel. "That she and Em would go the same way as Constance and Serena – mad and murdered. I told her not to be so silly. But she knew. She felt it in her own blood. Not all ghosts are where they can be seen."

Then he drew a sharp breath and his voice went thin with fear. "But some are."

For a moment she didn't know what he meant. Then she

did. She smelled it before she saw it – the acrid scent of rubbish burning. Then a glow appeared in the middle of the floor. The fire wasn't just in the stairwell: the room beneath them was alight as well. The stench was two hundred years of paint and paper and the dust accumulated between the joists alight. The boards had held back both the smell and the fire as long as they were going to.

Then she understood what he meant. The first time she saw Daniel Hood he was unconscious in hospital with a hole in his chest and little burns over half his body. Maybe Johnny couldn't imagine how it felt to burn, but Daniel could. Daniel knew. And Brodie had forgotten. A wave of guilt swept through her. Unpleasant as this was for her, frightening as it was, difficult as it was to go on believing that the strong old building would keep the flames away until help came, for Daniel it was worse. It was a nightmare he'd survived only to find it waiting for him again. Brodie could imagine the consequences if they got this wrong – if they were still here when the fire came surging through, if no one noticed and help never came. But Daniel could remember, and there was all the difference in the world.

She couldn't see but she knew where he was – frozen by the door, between the blaze on the stairs and the timbers glowing brighter in the middle of the attic room. "Daniel," she said sharply, "come over here. We have to get out on the roof."

He made no reply that she heard. She tried again, peremptorily. "Daniel!"

The glow in the centre of the room was growing. Little tongues of flame were coming through. There was just enough red light now that she could see him. His back was pressed against the door and the livid light caught first one cheek, then the other as his head turned, desperate for escape and finding none. His eyes were white and she heard the breath saw in his throat.

Then as she watched the memory, the fear, overwhelmed

him and he slid down the door into a foetal heap at its foot, his knees drawn up, his arms around his head. A moan issued from him that was barely recognisable as a human sound. It might have been an animal in pain.

Even through her own fear Brodie felt her belly knot with compassion. He tried so hard. He got so far on guts alone. Now the courage was all used up, leaving him naked and defenceless before his worst demon.

If he'd been alone he'd have died there, too afraid of the fire before him to escape the greater one behind. But he wasn't alone. He was just the width of a room away from someone who cared about him, who wouldn't let him die in terror and agony while there was strength in her own limbs and determination in her heart.

There were two ways of doing this. Carefully, picking her way round the breach in the floor, trying to judge how far the weakness might extend so as to avoid crashing through charred boards into the inferno below; and fast. Brodie opted for fast. She had no way of knowing what damage the fire had done below them, but the longer this took the greater the risk. She sucked in a great energising breath at the window and crossed the room in three strides, hurdling the hotspot in the middle. She grabbed Daniel's wrist and yanked it away from his head.

"Up! Up, damn you! I'm not dying today, and neither are you."

# Chapter Twenty-Three

Brodie felt the growing heat at her back, ignored it determinedly. She bent down, shoving her face close to Daniel's, shouting in his ear. "I can't afford to die. I've got a little girl waiting for me. But I can't go back to her until you get your face off the floor and make the effort to come with me.

"It's four metres, Daniel. Thirteen feet. Three strides. A couple of seconds. It can't hurt you in a couple of seconds! Get up, and get moving, and do it *now!*"

At last – and it couldn't have been more than seconds but it felt like forever – there was movement in the pathetic heap at her feet. She waited no longer, but holding his hand in a grip of iron set off back the way she'd come. For a moment he hung back, terribly afraid, a dead weight she dragged behind her like a stone. Then he seemed to realise that if he had to quit his refuge then the sooner the better. Brodie felt him scramble to his feet behind her but couldn't spare the time to look. She kept moving, tugging him with her, shoving him aside when the hot-spot in the middle of the floor suddenly fountained fire.

So it was more than four strides and two seconds, but still they reached the comparative safety of the window untouched by the flames. But Brodie didn't stop there. She shoved Daniel through almost bodily. "Turn right. Right!" she screamed as he wavered. Then she was in the gutter behind him, pushing him on. He crawled to the furthest end of the roof before she would let him stop and collapse on the slates.

She sprawled beside him, lungs heaving – not so much with the smoke as the effort. Finally she sat up and peered at him by moonlight. "Are you all right?"

"No," he whispered. And as she searched him anxiously for signs of injury: "I'm ... ashamed."

Her womb clenched with pity. "You've nothing to be ashamed of."

"I could have got you *killed*."

"But you didn't."

"But I could have! I made you cross a fire-pit twice because I was too scared to do it once."

"I understand why," she said quietly.

"It's no excuse!" he cried, and she thought his heart was breaking. "You were safe. You put yourself in danger for me. And Brodie, if I'd been the one at the window, I couldn't have done the same for you!"

She put her arms round him. His whole body was shaking. "Daniel, Daniel. You talk as if there's only one kind of thing people can do for one another. You're my best friend. Not because I think you're Superman in a really good disguise" – she felt a tremor that could have been an embryonic chuckle – "but because you're a good man and I love you. You make me happy just by being around. I don't need you to leap tall buildings – or fire-pits – and stop runaway trains. I only need you to be who and what you are: my kind, gentle, understanding friend. Someone I can always talk to, however difficult what I have to say may be. Someone I can always trust."

"But you can't." His voice was muffled, by Brodie's shoulder and his own regrets. "How can you trust someone who falls apart at the sight of a few flames? Put your faith in me and I will let you down. I'd give anything for it to be otherwise – to think I could snatch you from the jaws of death. But I know better. When it matters, when it really matters, when it's a matter of life and death, you'll need me and I won't be there. You'll trust me to catch you and I'll let you fall."

"Daniel," she sighed, "your problem's what it always is – you expect too much of yourself. How many people do you know who *have* snatched someone from the jaws of death? That isn't what life's made up of. It's made of much smaller but maybe more significant things than that. You don't have to save someone's life to add value to it every day. And you can make it not worth living without ever threatening to end it. My life has been better in every way since I met you, Daniel Hood, than it was before.

"And suppose you're right, and one day I need you to catch me and you let me fall. Even as I'm hitting the ground I'll know you did your best. It isn't an empty cliché to say that's the most that should be asked of anyone, even by himself."

His heart was too full to reply. He returned her embrace tightly enough to bruise her; though Brodie would have suffered fractures rather than say so.

They sat together on the roof and waited in vain for signs that someone was aware of their plight, and watched the inexorable advance of the fire. It filled the attic rooms one by one, blowing flames out of the dormer windows like a slow broad-side. The surviving glass in the one nearest to them held back the blaze for longest, but finally it too shattered and belched out flame and roiling black smoke.

Brodie held Daniel's hand very tight and summoned all her courage. "When these slates get too hot to sit on, we jump. We'll break bones, but we may survive. If not, at least it'll be over quickly."

There was a silence. When Brodie looked at him Daniel said ruefully, "I can't even think of a way of saving you that I'm not brave enough to try." She hugged his arm and they waited for the last moment when the consequences of avoiding a decision outweighed those of making it.

With a roar and a rumble something huge and yellow turned in at the gate. Philip Poole's digger: Brodie could still smell it on her from their last encounter. Up to half an hour ago she had thought that mattered.

She had no idea what he intended, but Poole knew exactly what he was doing. He located them on the roof and positioned the digger below them. The bucket rose towards them. It couldn't reach the top of the high walls, but it halved the distance they had to drop. And he'd paused a moment in his own yard to half-fill it from the midden.

Poole leaned out of the cab, his ruddy face urgent. "The roof'll go at any minute. Jump!"

Daniel and Brodie traded a last look. "One at a time or both together?" he asked.

"Both together," she said firmly. "I'm sure as hell not coming back for you."

Still hand in hand they clambered awkwardly to their feet and jumped.

By the time Poole had backed away from the burning house, lowered the bucket and run forward to see what he'd caught, both Brodie and Daniel were on their feet, unhurt, squelching and odoriferous and wreathed in idiot grins. They hugged one another, and Brodie hugged Poole; and the farmer was sufficiently comfortable with the smell of his muck-heap that he didn't wish she wouldn't.

When they'd finished hugging and whooping Poole waved a bewildered hand at the blazing house. "What *happened*?"

"You are not going to *believe* what happened," said Brodie; and then another vehicle came screeching through the gateway, and because it was Deacon's car she put off telling him until they could tell them both.

Deacon tumbled out of the car and hurried over, staring up at the house in alarm. "Is there anyone inside?"

"No," said Brodie.

"Not now," said Daniel.

He looked at both of them, noticed the byre smell, noticed the digger with its bucket half-full of filthy straw. "You mean – *you* were inside?"

Before they could answer there was another mighty roar and the roof of the old house splintered and fell into the blaze. Great gouts of flame rose from the destruction. Daniel glanced at Brodie. Her jaw was clenched hard and her eyes were stretched. The distant wail of a fire engine speeding up the Guildford Road only underlined the fact that it would have been too late. If they'd been on the roof another two or three minutes they'd have fallen with the slates into the heart of the inferno.

His hand was too grimy to offer even to a farmer. He said simply, "We owe you our lives, Mr Poole."

WPC Meredith was looking round her, "What about Mrs Daws? What about the girls?"

"Peris went shopping," said Daniel. "Johnny and Em – " He ground to a halt, lacking the words.

Delicacy wasn't something that Brodie struggled with. "Johnny and Em," she said baldly, "locked us in the attic and set fire to the house. We don't know where they went after that."

"But *why*?" Poole's voice was thin as horn, appalled.

"Because they tried to kill Nicky Speers," said Deacon, "and you guessed. And you hadn't the sense to keep quiet."

Brodie stared at him in amazement. "How did you know?"

"I spent the afternoon at Frick Lake. We found Robert Daws' car in twenty feet of water. Daws was in it, and had been for a fortnight. If he didn't ambush Nicky, someone else did – someone else who hated the kid enough to kill him. Who else was there? If it wasn't Serena's husband it had to be her daughters."

"*When* did you know?"

He'd have had no trouble lying to almost anyone else. But her frank gaze disarmed him. He sniffed. "About thirty seconds ago?"

The straw from Poole's midden was only filthy but wet. Away from the fire the evening was growing cool and both Brodie and Daniel were beginning to shiver. It was not just the cold, of course, but the cold was a good excuse.

Deacon shepherded them to his car, though not before he'd spread a blanket on the seat. "Meredith will wait for the fire engine. I'll take you home, you can get cleaned up and change your clothes. Oh ... " He was looking at Daniel.

Daniel nodded, surprisingly cheerful. He'd come through nightmare into the balmy calm beyond. "Yep. Once again, Superintendent, everything I own is on my back as we speak."

"You didn't leave anything in the cottage?"

Daniel shook his head sunnily. "Moved it all into my room in the house. Even the telescope. I thought it would be safer there."

Brodie started to laugh. It was more than half hysteria, but it broke the tension of mind and muscle. "And this is why the name of Daniel Hood is whispered with reverence wherever clairvoyants meet." They giggled together like children while Deacon watched in disbelief through the rear-view mirror.

"I'll find you something for tonight," said Brodie. "We'll go shopping in the morning."

That reminded him. He looked over Deacon's shoulder at the dashboard clock. "Peris should have been back by now. She should have been back an hour ago."

Watching him, Brodie saw the wheels of thought turn and mesh behind the smutted glasses, slowly at first, gathering speed as they worked through the gears. His face went still and his eyes distant; then she saw concern creep in round the edges. In another moment it had turned to full-fledged alarm and his hand gripped Deacon's shoulder so hard the policeman nearly drove into the hedge.

Deacon tramped on the brake and turned furiously in his seat. "What the *hell* ... ?"

Brodie didn't spare him a glance. Her eyes were on Daniel and her voice was reedy with foreboding. "What is it?"

"She got back when she said, at six o'clock or shortly afterwards. Just as the fire started."

"Then why didn't she get help? Where is she?"

"She met the girls running from the house. They piled into the car and she drove away again."

217

Brodie frowned, still not understanding. "Whyever would she? Even if they asked; even if they asked nicely. She wouldn't just drive them away without telling you."

Daniel shook his head. "I don't think they asked nicely. I think they held a knife to her throat."

"That's absurd!" exploded Deacon. "Daniel, for pity's sake get a grip on yourself. Where would they get a knife? Why would they hijack their own aunt?"

Daniel tried to breathe steadily. "They got the knife where they got the other two, out of the kitchen drawer in the cottage. They hijacked Peris because they needed to be away from Sparrow Hill when you arrived and they're too young to drive."

"Other two?" The only knives Deacon could think of were the ones that killed Serena Daws. He thought he must have missed something. "You're not suggesting – ?"

"*Yes*," said Daniel. "Robert Daws didn't kill his wife. Johnny and Em murdered their mother."

# Chapter Twenty-Four

He felt their eyes like blows: slashing incredulity in Brodie's, cudgels of disgust in Deacon's. The car had ground to a halt and both of them were staring at him hard enough to make him flinch.

They seemed to expect him to apologise and say it was a bad joke. He wasn't going to. He'd never been more serious about anything in his life. He'd only now put the pieces together, but they fitted with a near-audible click that said there was no mistake. It explained the otherwise inexplicable. There were two knives because there were two killers.

Brodie found a voice first. "The girls," she said, as if she wasn't sure she'd heard him right. "You're saying the girls murdered Serena. Stabbed their own mother."

"Yes," said Daniel.

"*Why?*"

"Because they adored their father, and she hurt and humiliated him once too often. They heard their parents fight, saw Robert storm out, thought Serena had finally driven him away. One of them snatched up the knife he'd dropped and stabbed her."

"That's preposterous," snarled Deacon, turning back to the wheel.

"*Why* is it?" demanded Daniel. "You know what they've done since. They tried to kill Nicky. They tried to kill Brodie and me. Doesn't that make you just a little suspicious?"

Deacon spun round again, and might have grabbed Daniel by the shirt-front if he'd been a shade cleaner. "Don't get smart with me, sonny. I know what they've done. They hurt a man who was instrumental in the destruction of their family. Then they tried to silence two people who were stupid enough to tell them they knew. You're right, that's pretty extreme behaviour. But they found themselves in a pretty extreme situation.

If they lost control, maybe that's their fault – but maybe it's ours for not getting them the help they needed."

Brodie frowned. "That's not entirely fair. Daniel – "

"Oh, *Daniel*," the policeman spat angrily. "*Daniel* was taking care of it, was he? How could we possibly have done better than entrusting them to a man who wakes sweating twice a week and can't do his job without getting attacks of the vapours?"

Daniel rocked back as if Deacon really had struck him. White with fury, Brodie also reacted as if it was fists, not insults, that were being traded, pushing herself between them. "Jack – !"

But Daniel didn't need defending. He was resolute when he believed he was right. "Every word you say is true. But they don't alter the fact that two disturbed children who've certainly tried to kill three people, who I believe killed their mother, have now disappeared with another woman. Can we concentrate on finding them before they hurt Peris too? We can go into my shortcomings later."

Deacon went on staring at him, but no longer with the angry disbelief that was almost his trademark. He was weighing the chances of being right about Daniel's latest theory against the cost of being wrong. Then he picked up his radio.

Only when he had cars out looking for Peris's Volvo did he return his attention to his passengers. His brows lowered warily but there was no repeat of his earlier outburst. "How much of this do you know, and how much do you just think you know?"

"I don't *know* any of it," said Daniel. "But it adds up. The knives – "

"Serena was stabbed *thirteen times*," said Brodie carefully. "You really think her daughters did that?"

"I know it sounds incredible," Daniel said carefully. "And I may be wrong. I *hope* I'm wrong. But I don't think so."

After a moment Deacon said, "Explain."

"I think they told the truth about how it started. The fight, and what it was about, and how they watched from the window. Robert brought a knife in from the kitchen and slashed the painting. Serena laughed at him, and he threw it down and left.

"But the girls didn't run away at that point. They ran into the cottage and started shouting at Serena. They were hysterical: they thought she'd driven their father away. And they were devoted to him – everything they've done and said shows it. Even the way they relate to other people reflects their relationships with their parents. They're friendly with men, mistrustful of women. If they thought they'd lost Robert because of Serena's behaviour, I can see one of them snatching up the knife and stabbing her as she laughed."

"But there were two knives," Brodie pointed out. "And thirteen wounds. Can you explain that in terms of lost tempers?"

"Not really," acknowledged Daniel. "But they were very upset. The second girl found another knife in the kitchen drawer and joined in.

"I don't think either of them, alone, would have been capable of a sustained attack on their mother. But there were two of them, and two hysterical people constitute a very small mob. They behaved like a mob. They started taking out their fears and frustrations on their mother and they couldn't stop. When Serena tried to get help they smashed the phone.

"After she was dead, or at least past defending herself, they calmed down and realised how much trouble they were in. They had to disguise the fact that two knives were used. Once the police started thinking in twos someone would notice there were two of them. But if it was a solitary killer there was an obvious scapegoat across the road. It never occurred to them we might suspect Robert. Even when they told us he slashed the picture. They knew he hadn't hurt his wife, knew he never could have done, thought everyone else would know that too."

He paused a moment, marshalling his arguments, bracing himself for the hardest part. "But the wounds in Serena's body were clearly made by two different knives. Even they could see that much. So they took the bigger one and pushed it into the wounds made by the smaller. Then instead of two people stabbing Serena six or seven times each it looked as if one person had stabbed her thirteen times. They left the big knife behind and took the small one away."

Brodie was nodding slowly, her eyes on Deacon. "They wanted you to arrest Nicky Speers. They told us so. In their minds he was responsible for what happened. When you seemed reluctant they gave you a clue – that little drama in the early hours of Friday morning. They smashed the kitchen window to make it look someone had broken in, and made enough noise to bring Daniel and Peris running. I think Em was supposed to accuse Nicky then, but she got stage fright. Do you remember her face, and Johnny's? So they went away and rehearsed some more, then came back and finished the job."

"You questioned him," Daniel said to Deacon, "but you still didn't arrest him. The girls were incensed – particularly when they realised you suspected their father. They thought that once someone was arrested for Serena's murder Robert could come home. By now there was talk of a second knife, so they'd nothing to lose by planting it in Nicky's shed. You wondered how a fat middle-aged man scaled the wall behind the Speers' cottage? Well, he didn't, any more than he climbed the tree overhanging the lane. Two agile young girls did it instead. Everything happened less than a mile from Sparrow Hill. They could cycle it in a few minutes."

Brodie took up the story. "This next bit they admitted to. Of course, they didn't expect us to pass it on. When you released Nicky they decided they'd have to deal with him themselves. I was right about the mirror. But it wasn't a heavy Victorian thing – it was a sheet of aluminium foil hung from the branch of a tree. Nicky came along on his motorbike, saw what he thought was an oncoming vehicle and swerved into the wall. But someone was coming so the girls couldn't stay and watch him die. They pulled down the foil, stuffed it into a back-pack and cycled home. Philip Poole found Nicky in time to save his life.

"Johnny put the foil where she thought it would never be found. She didn't even tell Em, so when we were looking at the toys in the attic Em didn't know to steer clear of the dressing-up box. It was neatly folded at the bottom, but I knew it as soon as I saw it. There was even a corner missing – the corner I found tied to a bit of string up in the tree."

It was a struggle at times but Deacon was still following. "And that's when you let them know that you knew."

Daniel gave a self-deprecating shrug. "Put like that, it doesn't seem the brightest thing we've ever done."

"They wanted to pack some things," said Brodie. "We let them. Even that didn't seem particularly stupid until we went to follow them downstairs and found ourselves locked in."

"By which time," guessed Deacon, "they'd set the fire?"

Daniel nodded. "When we got onto the landing the stairs were ablaze. Soon after that the floor ... " The memory caught in his throat.

"The fire came up through the floor," said Brodie evenly, "and we had to get out. Philip saw the flames and came to the rescue. The rest you know."

Deacon switched his gaze to Daniel. "And you think that when the girls came running from the house Mrs Daws was just getting back. And they produced a weapon and made her drive them – where?"

"I have no idea," said Daniel honestly.

"London," said Brodie.

Deacon's eye narrowed. "Why London?"

She shrugged. "It's where runaway children always go, isn't it? They think the streets really are paved with gold. That damned Dick Whittington has a lot to answer for."

"They might also think they'd find their father there," ventured Daniel. "His head office is in the city. They may have thought, if he couldn't come home, that's where he'd go."

"Instead of which he was at the bottom of Frick Lake."

"They couldn't know that," said Brodie. "They thought he was avoiding the police because you suspected him."

"But if he left after the fight he didn't know Serena was dead," objected Deacon. "So why did he drive into a lake? The woman was a tramp, it can't have been that he couldn't face life without her."

"The woman was his wife," said Brodie, a touch sharply. "They seem to have made one another miserable for fifteen years, but they still meant something to each other. She wouldn't have been able to hurt him if they hadn't."

"She seduced a teenage boy so Daws killed himself?" Deacon's eyebrow canted doubtfully. "I don't think so. Daniel?"

But Daniel wasn't paying attention. He had his glasses off and the balls of his hands pressed against his eyes. The yellow hair spilled through his fingers. "Oh no ... "

Brodie's brow gathered. "What? Daniel, what is it?"

He exhaled slowly, his head tilting back against the headrest, his eyes shut. Without the glasses his face looked naked. "He came back. He saw his daughters putting the finishing touches to their handiwork.

"What was he going to do? Nothing? Live with the knowledge of what they'd done? Or call the police and report what he knew? Whatever else they were, they were his children – he couldn't live with doing that either."

"So he killed himself," whispered Brodie.

Daniel nodded. "He drove around in despair until he could bear it no longer, then he drove into Frick Lake. He hoped he'd never be found and the blame for Serena's death would rest at his door. If he couldn't deal with what the girls had done, he wanted at least to give them that."

He felt Deacon's eyes on him, braced himself for abuse. "I know," he said tiredly, "I need an analyst, things like that only happen in a seriously sick mind. Well, maybe they do, Superintendent. But this time it wasn't mine."

Deacon went on looking at him for what seemed a long time. Then he started the car again. As he drove he was thinking. He didn't leave them at Brodie's house but followed them inside. "You know these girls better than anyone," he told Daniel. "If you're right about them taking their aunt, what should we expect? Is it a hostage situation? Or have they made up some story to get her to drive them where they want to go?"

Fortunately there had been some things of Daniel's in the wash when he moved out. At least he wouldn't have to spend the next fourteen hours in women's clothes. He changed in Paddy's room, talking to Deacon through the open door.

"I don't think a lie would serve. Whatever they said – that they'd heard from their father, that they didn't feel safe in the house, whatever – I can't see Peris driving them anywhere without telling me first. She'd know I'd worry if they just disappeared."

Deacon agreed. "So she's a hostage."

"We know they take a fairly direct approach to getting what they want."

"I don't suppose there's any way you could be wrong about the fire." It was in Deacon's face and voice that he didn't see much doubt himself. He just wanted to have it on record.

A much cleaner Daniel tugged a sweater over his bright hair and shook his head. "I don't think so. They went downstairs, locking the door behind them, and within minutes we heard the smoke alarm. I'd believe in Father Christmas, the Tooth Fairy and God before I'd accept that was a coincidence."

"So they think you're dead." Deacon was filling the

doorway, a hand on each side. "So they reckon they haven't much to lose. They will hurt Mrs Daws to get what they want."

"Oh yes," said Daniel with conviction. "They've gone too far to turn back now. They'll do anything they think will work for them. The only thing keeping Peris safe is the fact that she can drive and they can't. If you stop the car, the only value she'll have is as a hostage."

"But we have to stop the car. We can't let them vanish." Deacon reached a decision. "Daniel, will you come with me? When we find them there'll be some negotiating to do. They may be more amenable talking to someone they know. I'll tell you what to say."

Daniel stared at him aghast. "They think I'm dead! They think they just killed me."

"Then it's important to show them they didn't, that you and Brodie are OK. And they mustn't find out we know about their mother."

Daniel's cheeks were the colour of parchment. "Hell, Jack, I don't know. A couple of days ago, maybe – I'd have said we had some degree of mutual respect, even friendship, I think if I'd had something important to say they'd have listened. But now? They locked me in an attic and lit a fire under me!" His voice cracked.

Deacon moved into the room as if his mere proximity might prove persuasive. It wouldn't be the first time. "If you don't want to do it, fair enough. You don't owe it to them. But you may be the best chance Peris has of walking away from this.

"Whatever else they are, they're two scared little girls who've done things even they can hardly believe. They acted on sheer instinct – it felt right, they wanted to do it, they were clever enough to get away with it. In the short term: they never even considered the long term. They didn't realise that at some point there would be consequences. Now they're on the run to nowhere, and when we find them they'll be trapped and desperate. I don't know what they'll do, but I can't see them giving up their hostage in return for a kind word and a clean hanky. Can you?"

Daniel so wanted to say yes. If he could say yes there was no further rôle in this for him. He had never wanted to be redundant so much in his life. But he wouldn't lie. He didn't lie about trivia, he couldn't lie when lives might be at stake. "No," he mumbled unhappily.

Deacon nodded. "Right now they must be terrified of the police. If I try to talk to them they'll pull up the drawbridge. They'll use Peris any way they can think of to keep us at bay. Unless we can get their trust. If we can convince them they'll be looked after, they won't be hurt, that despite what they've done people want to help them. I can tell them that but they won't believe me. A trained negotiator will say it just the right way, but they won't trust him either. Why should they? – they don't know him.

"They know you, Daniel. If they've learnt anything this week it's that you wouldn't lie to them. If you tell them they're all out of options, that things will be difficult for a while but they'll have help getting through it and if they can just look far enough ahead there's a better time coming, they'll believe you. They'll trust you. If you think they're worth saving, try. I'll be with you every step of the way."

Brodie too had washed and changed; and sprayed a little perfume around for good measure, so she was literally smelling of roses. She came looking for them in time to pick up the gist of the conversation. Unnoticed by either man, she froze in the doorway, implications pulsing through her like electricity. She could only guess how Daniel felt.

He shook his head microscopically and his voice was thin. "That's not fair. You can't put that on me."

"No," agreed Deacon quietly, "I can't. Only if you want to help."

"Of course I want to help! I *don't* want to be the reason it all goes wrong. I don't want Peris to get hurt because I guessed wrong about what would make them give her up."

"If it all goes pear-shaped," said Deacon, "it still won't be your fault. It'll be mine. It goes with the job: my decision, my responsibility. Nobody'll blame you, Daniel, I promise. But you could save that woman's life."

Every instinct urged Brodie to intervene. It *was* unfair – whatever Deacon said, failure was a burden that would bend Daniel double. But her cooler head said Deacon was right to ask. If someone's safety depended on it he had to use every weapon at his disposal, even if some of them weren't police issue. And then, how would Daniel feel if he might have prevented a tragedy and didn't even try?

She sidled past Deacon into her daughter's room and slipped a hand into Daniel's. She said softly, "It's your call. I'll support you whatever you choose. So will Jack." She faced the big man squarely, daring him to contradict.

Daniel mumbled, "You really think it would help?"

"I don't know," Deacon said frankly. "If I knew what was for the best in every possible situation I wouldn't be here, I'd be the goddamned Chief Constable. I think it might help. I think it might be the thing that turns the balance. Even if I'm wrong, if events have gone too far, I don't see how it can make matters worse. You could come and never be needed. You could try and make no progress. But they might respond to a familiar voice when the best negotiator in the world would only scare them more.

"I can't make you do this, Daniel, I won't even try. It's your decision: I won't fling it in your face whatever the outcome. But I'd be happier dealing with those girls if I had you with me than if I have to do it alone."

Jack Deacon always reckoned he had no particular talent with words. But he could hardly have pitched his sale better than that. Daniel felt the last shreds of choice blow away. He let his pent-up breath go with them. "I'll come."

Brodie nodded. "Then I'm coming too."

Deacon opened his mouth to protest. But the look she hit

him with had rocks in it, and said that if he wasn't ashamed to put pressure on someone that vulnerable then neither was she. Deacon shut his mouth and led the way out to his car.

# Chapter Twenty-Five

Deacon headed for the motorway. He didn't know the girls were making for London but so far no one had come up with a better suggestion. God alone knew what they hoped to achieve there. But then, they hadn't got into this much trouble by planning ahead.

So when the word came through on the radio that the Volvo estate car rented to Mrs Peris Daws had been spotted at motorway services twenty miles north of Dimmock they were only minutes away. Deacon pumped the accelerator and soon bright lights sprang at them out of a dip in the road, refuelling facilities for vehicles and people linked across the motorway by a high-level footbridge.

The Volvo was in a garage service bay, jacked off the ground and with one wheel removed. "*Smart* woman," muttered Deacon approvingly. He drove round the back, where a police car was parked in deep shadow, and got out to talk to the crew.

"Smart woman?" echoed Daniel, confused.

Brodie put it together for him. "She told the girls there was something wrong with the car. They didn't know enough to be sure she was lying, but they knew if there was an accident they'd be caught. So they let her bring it into the garage. And then ... " She didn't know what had happened then. They must have left or they'd have been detained by now. It wasn't immediately clear to her where they went.

Daniel nodded at the lights of the café across the bridge. "They went for a snack while they were waiting."

But Brodie shook her head. "Peris Daws isn't a timid woman. She's only co-operating because the girls will hurt her if she doesn't. Bet you anything they've got hold of another knife. But they can only control her like that close to,

230

if nobody sees the knife and she can't ask for help. They can't risk being in a crowd."

She was thinking aloud now. "Peris knows that too. She wants to cross the bridge. She offers to buy them drinks and stuff, but they're not falling for it. They can't stay with the car – the mechanic's going to be too close for too long. So they look for somewhere safe to wait. Out of sight, out of earshot, but not too far from the car." She looked around for inspiration. But dotted around the garage were a variety of permanent and temporary structures serving a variety of obscure purposes. It would be necessary to check each one. "Jack – "

He leaned an elbow on top of the car. "The mechanic didn't see where they went. He assumed they'd headed for the café. That's about twenty minutes ago – he told Mrs Daws to give him half an hour. But there's nothing wrong with the car."

"Like you said," agreed Brodie, "a smart woman. But the girls aren't stupid either. They didn't go to the café. I don't think they crossed the bridge."

Deacon nodded. "Constable Batty's had a good look round. They're not in the café or the shop, and he had a member of staff check the Ladies. Nobody remembers seeing them. And they aren't hard to remember – a black woman and two white girls."

"They could be in one of these buildings."

Constable Batty leaned down to look into the car. Whatever he was expecting to see in the front of Detective Superintendent Deacon's car, what he actually saw surprised him. He tried not to stare. "Why do you think that, miss?"

Deacon gave a gravelly chuckle. "Mrs Farrell is good at finding things, Batty. She reckons the easiest way to find something is not to look for it but to look *where it has to be*. So I'll take a wander round and see what I can spot. Daniel, do you fancy a stroll?"

Daniel could hardly think of anything he wanted to do

less. But it was why he was here, so he got out of the car and trailed off behind Deacon like a dog being taken to the vet.

Almost, Brodie went with them. But Deacon had to avoid startling the girls, wanted to be close enough to talk to them before they knew they'd been found. Three were more likely to attract attention than two. So Brodie stayed where she was, with Constable Batty and his partner, watching the Volvo.

"When we find them," said Deacon conversationally, his casual stroll in fact so purposeful that Daniel had to jog to keep up, "play it cool. We were worried about them. They were in a bit of a state when they left the house, we wanted to find them and tell them there's no damage done that can't be fixed. Don't accuse them of starting the fire – for now, it's something that just happened. Fortunately nobody got hurt."

"But they know that I know," objected Daniel.

"Of course they do. But we don't have to deal with that now. They're scared and feeling a long way from home: all we have to do is make them an offer they want to accept. Come with us and we'll look after you. Everything'll be OK. People have been worried about you. OK, you've been a bit silly, but come with us and we'll sort it out."

Walking round-shouldered, hands deep in his pockets, Daniel considered. "You may be underestimating them. Johnny in particular: she's a pretty robust individual. I can't see her quitting just because someone asks nicely. She had something in mind to come this far. She won't give it up unless I can offer her something better."

Deacon sniffed. "Do you know why most people obey the law? Not because they have an overwhelming moral commitment to it, or they're terrified of the consequences of not doing. Not because there's nothing they want that they can't get legally. The reason is, it's easier to keep the law than to break it. Things get complicated when you throw the rule-book out the window. You end up burning your house down to silence people who know what you've done – only then, where are you going to sleep tonight? So you make a run for it – but you can't drive so you have to kidnap someone who can.

"The longer it goes on, the more difficult it gets. Sooner or later you have to eat, sleep, change your clothes – and you don't have any money, and you don't know where anything is because you've left the only town you've ever known. Those girls are suffocating under all the complications. Offer them a square meal and a bed for the night, promise that nobody'll bother them until tomorrow, and they'll jump at it."

Daniel wasn't convinced. He knew, as perhaps Deacon did not, how incredibly single-minded children could be. They can focus on an object of desire to the exclusion of everything else. He couldn't see Johnny Daws meekly giving up her knife, and every vestige of autonomy for the next ten or fifteen years, in return for things she had before she started this. "What if they won't?"

Deacon shrugged. "They have to. The only question is when."

"And, who gets hurt."

The policeman cast him a sidelong glance. "If they start to cut that woman, Daniel, I'm going to forget they're just a couple of little girls. You put a knife to someone's throat, you forfeit the right to be treated with kid gloves."

Daniel stopped in mid-stride and stared after him until Deacon was forced to stop too. "You told me they'd be safe."

"They'll be as safe as houses once I get hold of them," the big man said testily. "But as long as they're waving lethal weapons around their safety is not my prime concern. Rescuing the innocent bystander: *that's* my prime concern."

It was hard to argue with his logic. Still, Daniel was a little shocked. Teachers are generally less sentimental about children than those who see less of them, but it was difficult to talk about two young girls that he knew, that he'd taught, as if they were dangerous criminals. Even though they were. He said hesitantly, "You're not thinking ... snipers ... ?"

Deacon laughed aloud – too loud for a man who was trying to pass unnoticed. "You're a hoot, Daniel, you really are. No, I wasn't thinking snipers. And I've got the carpet-bombers on hold for the moment, too. Come on, let's find the little horrors before we worry too much how we're going to grab them."

But as they walked on he murmured, "Besides, there aren't many situations that snipers can resolve that a couple of big Rottweilers can't." The startled jerk of Daniel's yellow head in the half-darkness was all the reward he asked.

They passed among the sheds and stores, trying doors as they went. Daniel's nerves cranked a little tighter with every one. When they found the right door it was unlikely Johnny Daws would instantly leap out of it with her knife between her teeth. Still, the tension racked him until he couldn't think straight.


After a minute Brodie turned to Constable Batty. "I'm going to have a look round the main concourse."

He said mildly, "We've done that. And there's another crew on the other side watching out for them."

"I can go places you can't."

"A WPC did that."

She breathed heavily at him. "I can't sit here doing nothing any longer. I'm going to have a look across the bridge. All right?"

As she got out of Deacon's car another pulled up and Detective Sergeant Voss emerged. Learning what was going on he'd chased up the motorway to join in. Charlie Voss was made for discreet surveillance. With his shock of sandy hair, freckles and amiable open countenance, he looked more like a curate than a detective. His car looked less like a police car than an entry in a Demolition Derby.

Batty brought him up to date. "The superintendent's checking out the sheds. Mr Hood went with him."

"Good."

Brodie was aware of a sub-text. "Why do you say that?"

Under the sandy brows Voss's eyes were awkward, hoping she wouldn't press him. But she waited for an answer, so he had to come up with something he could say in front of a junior officer. "Because the chief's a copper, not a social worker. If they don't come quietly, if things get hectic, somebody's got to try and remember they're just two little girls."

"I'm heading across the bridge," said Brodie. "Coming?"

"OK."

She needed a hat. If she was going to be out in the open she didn't want Johnny spotting her before she saw Johnny. As the most striking thing about her appearance was the thick black hair curling down to the middle of her back, the easiest way to disguise herself was to put it up under a hat.

Unfortunately, this was Deacon's car and the only hat she could find was a waxed brown thing with a brim that he used to keep rain off his notebook. Pulling it on, Brodie gathered from Voss's expression that the effect was not so much *Vogue* as *Angling for Idiots*. "Come on," she growled.

The motorway hadn't always come this far south. The last section opened some thirteen months before and the services weren't finished yet. Finishing touches were still being put to the bridge. The clear plastic tunnel from which those who didn't get out much could watch the traffic thunder beneath was awaiting its last section of weather-proofing, over the north-bound fast lane. A red and white plastic barrier kept travellers from straying too close to the rail.

As she and Voss reached the gap a little boy in jeans and a backward baseball cap, arms full of take-away food, emerged from the ambling crowd and paused at the plastic barrier, gazing down at the racing lights. Brodie glanced round automatically but couldn't see who he belonged to. She frowned disapprovingly. However long you'd been driving, however tired you were, you didn't send small children to fetch supper from a thronged motorway services. Anything could happen to them. There could be any number of dangerous lunatics stalking a place like this.

Then she remembered there were at least two, and they were children themselves, and concerned herself a little less with the boy in the baseball cap.

But as they passed him Brodie suddenly linked her arm with Voss's – causing him to look at her in surprise and trepidation – and putting her face close to his said in an urgent murmur, "Keep moving. Say nothing."

Voss had meant to do just that until his superintendent's girlfriend suddenly attached herself to him. Now he was having trouble remembering which foot had to move next. "You've seen something?"

"Yes. *Don't* look now. The little boy with the baseball cap, that we just passed?"

"What about him?"

"He isn't a he. It's Em."

Deacon had had the foresight to switch his mobile phone onto the vibration setting. Even so, when it went off against his breast he started like a shying horse. He took the thing out and answered snappily, "Yes?"

"Voss here, sir. I'm with Mrs Farrell on the bridge. We've just passed Emerald Daws and she's heading your way."

Daniel saw the detective's eyes widen though he didn't know why. "Did she see you?" asked Deacon.

"No. Mrs Farrell's wearing a" – for want of an adequate description Voss settled for a generality – "hat."

"Any sign of the others?"

"No. But Em's got enough food for three. They must still be on your side."

"Then where the hell are they?" He scanned the jumble of buildings around him like a convoy captain looking for submarines. "Stay where you are, I don't want them doubling back over the bridge and disappearing into the crowd. Put Brodie on."

Brodie took the phone. "Jack?"

"Can you still see Em?"

"Yes."

"Follow her. At a distance – just close enough to see where she goes."

She gave Voss his phone back and hurried after Em, anxious not to lose her in the two-way throng of travellers.

Em reached the far end as Brodie approached the centre. Instead of continuing towards the garage she turned right. Brodie stopped and, pulling out her own phone, called Deacon. "She's just left the bridge. Can you see her yet? – she's wearing a grey denim jacket and a baseball cap back-to-front."

"Got her," grunted Deacon with quiet satisfaction. "OK, Brodie, we'll take it from here."

With Daniel jogging to keep up, he strode across the cracked and empty concrete towards the solitary child, still a hundred metres away. He glanced towards the garage, but though the big estate car was down off the jack now Em wasn't heading for it. Johnny *had* found somewhere quiet to wait.

Em was on a path that wound round the end of the bridge and down to what was effectively a builders' depot beneath. There were no buildings, just pallets of breeze blocks, stacks of shuttering, some scaffolding, a couple of cement mixers and an elderly caravan. During the day the area would be alive with labouring men, yammering power-tools and casual obscenities, and at night the builders left here those things that were too big to bring each morning. They'd erected a pallisade of steel-mesh fencing to keep it safe, but that was months ago and the corners had gone bow-legged like cowboys.

Which wouldn't have mattered if the caravan had been secure, because they could have stored valuables inside. But Deacon could see from here, by the security light hanging under the bridge, that although the door was padlocked the hinges had parted from the wall. Anyone could have squeezed through the fence, got into the caravan and helped himself to the contents.

Or spent a quiet half hour where no one could see him and even people looking for him would not find him. "They're in the caravan," said Deacon.

Daniel peered but saw nothing. "How do you know?"

"I'm a detective," growled Deacon. He used the phone again. But obviously he didn't get the result he wanted, because he scowled at the thing and shook it. Then he put it away. "I can't raise Batty and Vickers. You'll have to fetch them. Tell them to cover the far side of the compound. I'll stop anyone leaving this way. Go!"

Though he was a young man in reasonable health, Daniel was not much given to physical exertion. His work didn't require it, and his hobby called more for stillness than speed. Like all people without a car he thought nothing of walking quite long distances, but it took something seriously unpleasant behind him to make him run. Deacon's impatient frown sent him scurrying towards the garage like the electric hare at a greyhound track.

Deacon enjoyed putting the fear of God into people. He watched Daniel accelerate with the pleasure of a man who has bred a Derby hopeful. Then he looked back to where Em was squeezing through the buckled corner of the builders' compound.

You study, you train; you amass experience; you learn from your own and others' triumphs and disasters; you reach a point where you know, and so does everyone who matters, that precious few people could do your job any better. And still, sometimes, you need luck on your side. Out of nowhere, faster than he could see it coming, Deacon found himself in that situation, and when he needed the luck it wasn't there.

As she squeezed through the gap in the fence Em caught

her denim jacket on a spike. She put down her shopping, slipped out of the coat and turned back to free it. That's when she saw Deacon watching her.

Their eyes met over a distance of twenty metres. For a long second Deacon clung to the desperate hope that she wouldn't recognise him. She'd seen a lot of big men in overcoats over the last fortnight, he'd spent a lot of time in her house but not that much with her, could she really take one look at his face in the chiaroscuro world under the bridge and know who he was?

When that second ended he had his answer. Em opened her mouth in a scream of piercing intensity. Then she grabbed her coat and leaving the food on the ground ran for the caravan.

It was too soon. An Olympic sprinter couldn't have brought help yet. For three minutes Deacon would be on his own. He'd spent longer alone facing down more dangerous quarry; but he doubted if the compound was any more secure on the far side than on this. As he squeezed himself like toothpaste through the gap at this corner the girls could be squeezing through the gap opposite and hurrying away before anyone could intercept them.

He had two options: stay on the outside ready to give chase – knowing that, though his job involved more strenuous activity than Daniel's, his bones were twenty years older and his body five stones heavier, and it was years since he'd run down a fugitive in a fair race. He could probably make them leave Peris but he wouldn't catch the girls. Or he could force his way into the compound and keep them in the caravan until help arrived. Whatever his decision, he had to make it now, before Johnny could react to her sister's scream.

If he kept his distance she might not use whatever weapon she'd equipped herself with. But if she did, the closer he was the quicker he could stop it. Jack Deacon had never achieved his successes through caution. That was the way of strategists, of tacticians, of policemen who did their best work in offices with calculators. He got his results by grabbing problems by the throat before they had time to get worse. While Em was still running towards the caravan Deacon was on one knee, thrusting his shoulders into the gap.

In a peculiar way, though the people were moving in slow-motion, events now moved very fast. The caravan door banged open and Peris hurtled through it as if kicked, landing on her knees in the mud with her arms tied behind her. Johnny stood in the doorway, chestnut hair flowing in the traffic's slipstream, the harsh white light glinting off the knife in her hand, like an icon of Joan of Arc.

Deacon tried to reach Peris before Johnny could but only succeeded in doing what Em had done – attaching himself to the fence by his clothing. He struggled and felt himself held. Freeing himself, the way Em had, would take only a few seconds. But he didn't have them.

Seeing his predicament, instantly understanding that it put him at her mercy in a way she could not have dreamed, Johnny leapt lightly from the step of the caravan and walked towards him, he thought, like a dancer, disdaining to leave a footprint in the mud. Deacon tried to get to his feet, and heard the expensive sound of fabric ripping, but was still held half on his knees when she reached him.

Until that moment he hadn't believed, heart and soul, that Juanita and Emerald Daws had done all they were accused of. The pieces added up, it made sense, it explained things that had refused to fit any other pattern, but a part of him had resisted belief. They were children, for God's sake! They'd got it wrong, misunderstood; there had to be some mistake.

Now, with Johnny standing over him, feet apart, the knife balanced in her hand, he knew there was no mistake. He didn't know if she was mad or bad, but he could see it in her eyes that killing had become easy. Jack Deacon looked at a fourteen-year-old girl and was afraid.

He kept the fear inside where she couldn't see it. "Now

then, young lady," he said with what he hoped was an amiable bluffness, "don't you think this has gone far enough?"

Peris Daws, still on her knees, looking at the ground, was babbling in a low, fast monotone. "Everything's all right, Superintendent. Don't worry about me. We went for a little drive, me and the girls. We'll be back before long. Why don't you go wait for us – ?"

It was patently absurd, and would have been if the woman hadn't got her wrists tied behind her back. She was chattering with fear. But Deacon knew what she was doing. She was trying to save his life.

Even Em knew what was coming and tried to prevent it. She gave a high-pitched whine, wringing her cap between her hands, and sobbed out the most surreal statement ever heard on a murder inquiry. "Don't, Johnny – you'll get us into trouble!"

Johnny glanced at her and back at Deacon with a tolerant smile. "Kids!" It took an effort but Deacon smiled back.

Then she turned the knife in her hand and drove it into him until the point hit bone.

# Chapter Twenty-Six

At its end the bridge rested on a squat tower which hid from Daniel's view, and also from the constables, events taking place in the builders' compound. Between pants he explained the situation as he'd left it, and Batty and Vickers sprinted off back the way he'd come.

As Daniel followed at his own pace, nursing a stitch, he saw three figures, in ascending sizes like plaster ducks, appear from behind the tower and stroll nonchalantly towards the garage. A second later they saw the policemen homing in on them and, abandoning nonchalance as a failed strategy, changed direction and began to run. The smaller ones dragging the other between them, they made for the broad fan of stairs onto the bridge. The crowds that had earlier presented a problem now offered their best chance of escape.

They did not know that the far side of the bridge was already closed against them. The policemen slowed and spread out, discreetly herding them that way. Dragging Peris with them, the girls disappeared into the illusory safety of the steel and perspex tunnel. The policemen met behind them, waving people off the bridge but not letting anyone else on.

In another minute the girls would realise they were trapped. Daniel had no idea how they would react but he wouldn't put money on tearful apologies. He wondered where Brodie was, hoped she was well out of the way.

Then he wondered where Deacon had got to. There was no longer any point him watching the compound. Daniel was puzzled that, even now the girls were on the bridge, Deacon still hadn't appeared. With growing unease he started down the spiral path.

As he rounded the foot of the tower the compound came into sight. So did Deacon – at least, something bulky in a dark raincoat lying along the foot of the mesh fence. Daniel's heart leapt and he picked up speed again, running recklessly down the steep path. He thought he was going to find the detective dead. He couldn't think how the girls had eluded him except by driving a knife into his heart. Even as he ran Daniel wondered how he would break the news to Brodie.

When, at the sound of his gasping, slithering approach, the still mound along the fence raised its head and said in a thick voice, "I need some help here," relief made Daniel go weak at the knees.

"Jack," he panted. "Are you all right?"

"No, I'm bloody not," grated Deacon. He was on his side in the mud, holding his thigh very tightly with both hands. "I'm bleeding like a stuck pig."

There are some advantages to being small: Daniel wriggled through the fence without difficulty. He knelt by the injured man and moved his hands away to see the extent of the damage. Bright arterial blood erupted from the wound. "Yes," he said quickly, slapping Deacon's hands back in place.

Another side-effect of being small was that, with no hips to speak of, he needed a belt to keep his trousers up. Tightened round Deacon's thigh it made an effective tourniquet. The bleeding slowed to a trickle.

"All right," said Daniel unsteadily. "You're going to be OK. But I need to get help. Where's your phone?"

Deacon shook his head. "She threw it onto the road."

Of course she had. She'd smashed Serena's to stop her summoning help, why would she leave Deacon his? "Don't worry, I'll find one. I'll be back in two minutes. You stay here." Then Daniel looked at the man lying, shocked and in pain, in the mud at his feet and managed a rueful smile. "Sorry."

"Just go, Daniel," gritted Deacon.

When he climbed back up to the carpark Daniel found a

crowd gathering. He borrowed a mobile phone to call for an ambulance, then he called the police as well. They knew there was an incident in progress, had not known they had an officer down.

When that was done Daniel faced a dilemma. He could guess why the crowd had gathered and still felt an obligation towards those at the heart of it. But perhaps Deacon needed him more.

Then he got lucky. A woman came up to him, scrutinised his pale and sweaty face and saw Deacon's blood on his hands. "Are you hurt? I'm a nurse."

Daniel breathed a sigh of relief. "I'm fine. But there's an injured man under the bridge. He's bleeding. I've fixed a tourniquet and called an ambulance, but could you stay with him till it arrives?"

"Of course." She backed out of the ever denser cluster of people, leaving him to concentrate on the extra-curricular activities of his pupils.

He pushed through the crowd until he found Constable Batty holding it back. He gave an abridged version of what had befallen Deacon and what he'd done about it. "Where are the girls? Mr Deacon wanted me to talk to them."

Batty gave a short, entirely humourless laugh. "I don't think that's a good idea." When he stood back and Daniel could see past him, he understood.

After she lost sight of Em, Brodie waited on the bridge. She saw Deacon disappear beneath her and Daniel run towards the garage. Soon afterwards the two constables appeared. But they stopped at the far end of the bridge and a crowd started to collect. There were too many people in the way for her to see why.

She backed up a little and called to Charlie Voss. "What's happening? I can't make it out."

Voss had acquired reinforcements: a couple of uniformed officers cordoning off this end of the bridge. A crowd was gathering behind them too. Voss beckoned to her. "I don't want to have to shout," he shouted.

"It's the superintendent," he said quietly when she reached him. "He's hurt. Johnny got close enough to stab him."

The colour drained from Brodie's face. "Is it bad?"

Voss shook his ginger head. "I don't think so. Daniel stopped the bleeding and called an ambulance. I don't think there's anything to worry about."

Brodie drew some deep, steadying breaths. "So where are the girls now?"

Voss wasn't sure why she wanted to know. He'd seen the steely glint in her eye as the fear passed and he didn't entirely trust her to leave the crisis management to him. But he couldn't refuse to answer. "They're on the bridge, coming this way. I'm trying to get the public clear without them noticing."

And it would work, until the two-way stream of humanity around them dried up at which point someone much dimmer than Juanita Daws would realise something was amiss. What would she do then? Put her knife to her hostage's throat, probably, and start issuing demands.

She wouldn't get them, of course. Deacon wouldn't have let her off this bridge and Voss wouldn't either. The girls were too dangerous to turn loose. There might never again be as good a chance to corner them as there was here and now.

"Where's Daniel?"

"On the other side," said Voss.

"Jack wanted him to talk to them."

"I know," said Voss. "I don't think it's a good idea. If a policeman with over twenty years' experience isn't safe from them, I'm not letting a civilian anywhere near them."

On the bridge the trail of pedestrians thinned and petered out. For a moment neither of them could see the girls. Then Voss pointed. "There." His voice dropped half an octave. "Damn!"

Brodie hadn't seen them because they were not where she was looking, walking up the centre of the perspex tunnel, wondering why everything had gone quiet. They knew. They'd worked it out while there were still a few people covering their movements and acted with the boldness that was their hallmark, that shouldn't still have been taking people by surprise.

Where the perspex weather-shield was incomplete they had kicked aside the barrier and dragged their hostage to the edge. The wind whipped their hair as they manhandled her under the rail. Nothing now stood between them and a ten metre fall among vehicles moving at seventy miles an hour. With her hands tied behind her Peris had no means of holding on. Johnny and Em were either side of her, each holding her aunt's arm with one hand and the railing with the other. If they let her go she would fall. If they jumped she would fall. If she grew faint and swayed, they would not be able to hold her.

There was no longer any question of rushing the girls, or waiting until they tired. Talking, thought Voss, was the only way this could end without a disaster. He reached for his phone.

Across the bridge Daniel said quietly, "I have to talk to them. Let me through."

"No," said Constable Batty.

"It's why I'm here – why Detective Superintendent Deacon wanted me here. Let me do what I came for."

Batty was resolute. "They have a knife and a hostage, and all three of them could fall in less time than it takes to say it. If you try to intervene they could kill you too. I'm not risking it. We'll have a negotiator here in twenty minutes."

"They can't hold on for twenty minutes! She's a big woman and they're two young girls, and the first one who weakens will take the others with her. They want to talk: it's why they're out there. They know me. They may trust me when they won't trust anyone else."

Batty was unconvinced. But Constable Vickers regarded Daniel thoughtfully. "It *is* what the chief had in mind."

"The chief may possibly have *changed* his mind since getting stabbed," retorted Batty tartly.

"You wouldn't get close enough to get stabbed, would you?"

"Mama Hood didn't breed no heroes," averred Daniel.

Constable Vickers looked at his colleague. "We have to let him try. There's nothing to lose."

Batty was unconvinced. Just then his radio crackled, demanding his attention. He spoke for a moment, then shrugged. "OK. If you want to do this, we're to let you through."

Daniel started onto the bridge. "If I seem to be making things worse I'll come back," he promised.

By now the footbridge was deserted but for the four of them. His hurried steps rang hollow on concrete. He was aware of eyes on his back as he walked, people wondering who he was and why he was being allowed over the bridge when they weren't. He felt conspicuous, and had no idea what he would say to the girls when he reached them.

Brodie clutched Voss's forearm and her lips moved in an almost silent prayer. No one further away would have known what she was saying but Voss heard and was shocked. "For God's sake!"

She hadn't meant it for his ears, but she still hoped they would jump before Daniel reached them. "Don't you understand?" she demanded fiercely. "He's going to lose them. All of them. Johnny's waiting till he's close enough to see their faces and then she's going to let go. If she can't have her own way, she'll do as much damage as she can before she kills herself."

"She can't hurt Daniel," said Voss, uncomprehending. "She hasn't got a spare hand."

"You damn fool," swore Brodie bitterly, "she doesn't need a *knife* to hurt him! She just has to make him think they could be saved so it's his fault when they die. *I* know they're going to jump, you know they're going to jump. But Daniel thinks they're only going to jump if he gets this wrong. It's going to haunt him for the rest of his life."

Johnny let him get almost within arm's reach before stopping him with a jerk of her head. "That's close enough."

Daniel looked at Peris and his heart stumbled. The woman was deeply, numbly afraid and he could do nothing to comfort her. Her life was in the hands of a disturbed and desperate adolescent, and she knew Johnny was capable of killing all three of them just to make a point. She knew the girls had only to relax their grip and she would fall to her death. Her chest had cramped up so she was breathing off the top of her lungs, hasty ragged gasps that caught in her throat and rasped between her teeth. Her face ran with sweat and her eyes were rimed with white. Daniel flicked her a tiny uncertain smile, and somewhere she found the courage to return it.

"Tell me what you want," he said, his voice thin. "Tell me what you want and let's end this."

Johnny was poised on the cusp of triumph and despair. A word, an expression, could send her either way. Behind Peris's back she gave her sister a look Daniel couldn't interpret; but Em shuddered and clung tight to the rail, round tears like marbles spilling down her paper-white cheeks.

"I want you to get everyone out of the way so we can go back to our car," said Johnny. "I don't want anyone to follow. Leave us alone and I'll let Peris go when we're safe."

Daniel moistened his lips. "Fine. I can get that for you. Come back inside."

Throwing her head back Johnny barked a terse laugh at him. "Daniel, if you want to be believed you need to lie more. The police aren't going to let us off this bridge. You can promise the moon but you can't deliver. If we come inside they'll rush us – and if Peris gets hurt, or if you do, that's a risk they're willing to take. Letting us get back on the motorway isn't."

Daniel gave a troubled shrug. "Maybe you're right. I don't know. I only know that if you fall you're going to die, and Peris is going to die, and there has to be something I can get for you that you want more than that."

"I want my daddy," whined Em. She was shaking visibly in the wind.

Daniel tried again. "I know you're scared. You feel trapped, you think there's no way back. But there's always a way back. For you, now, it's just a couple of steps, from outside the rail to inside the rail. I won't try to grab you. Nothing will change except you'll be safer and warmer while we look for an answer. What do you think, Johnny? Can you trust me that far?"

He saw her eyes cloud uncertainly as she thought about it. About the paucity of options. About the unavoidable reality that she was on a high ledge over a fast road with policemen at each end. Her gaze slid towards Em, aware that it was not only her life and Peris's at stake but her sister's as well.

When her eyes came back she'd reached some kind of a decision. She said, "Do you know who killed my mother?"

It was the last thing Daniel expected. He stumbled for an answer. It wasn't his conscience that got in the way: with lives on the line he'd have lied like a trooper, earnestly and fluently and entirely without remorse, if he'd had the skill. But since he was old enough to make a moral distinction between what was right and what was merely expedient Daniel Hood had departed from the truth the way most men part with teeth: grudgingly and as seldom as possible. He was as fluent as a man playing the piano-accordion with one hand behind his back. All he had to say was "No," and he couldn't say that convincingly. "Er – "

Johnny gave a tired, knowing smile. "Yes. You do."

Daniel ceded the unequal struggle and nodded. "I suppose I do."

"*How* do you know?"

He sketched a one-shouldered shrug. "I had some time to think. Between getting locked in an attic and having more immediate problems to worry about."

Johnny's smile turned impish. "Sorry about that. But I couldn't let you give us up. I'm really not going to prison, Daniel. You do know that, don't you?"

He found himself shaking with trepidation. "Think about this, Johnny. Don't make a mistake that can't be put right later. Ask yourself what your father would want."

For the first time in the six days he'd known her Johnny's gaze flickered, less than assured. "We did it for him. Because she hurt him. Will he understand, do you think?"

"I'm sure he'll try," Daniel managed. "Whatever's happened, you're still his daughters. I know you love him; I'm sure he loves you."

"He loved her, too," Johnny said distantly. "My mother. And she betrayed him with a dirty farm-boy, and then she *told* him. She hadn't even the decency to lie! She told him to his face what she was doing, and when he started to cry she laughed at him."

Her voice soared with anger as the dam over-topped again. "Laughed at him! With the tears streaming down his face. My daddy's the kindest man in the world, and he still loved her after everything she'd done, and she broke his heart and laughed in his face. He ran into the kitchen and came back with the knife. I thought he was going to stab her. I wanted to shout, let them know we were there, but I couldn't. And he only slashed the damned painting. Then he ran out to his car."

"You thought you'd lost him." In that instant their world had convulsed, destroying everything that mattered to them. Distraught, their hearts ground in the complex machinery of adult relationships, they felt helpless and inconsequential. Until, left without alternatives, with the fetid waters of the last ditch closing over their heads, they decided to fight back. To fight for what they cared about, and to fight dirty.

"I thought I was never going to see him again," Johnny said thickly. "I couldn't bear it. I thought ... I don't know what I thought. Maybe, that if she was gone he'd come back. I snatched up the knife he'd thrown down and lunged at her. I didn't even know if I was hurting her – I didn't know Em had found another knife and joined in – until suddenly she was on the floor and there was blood everywhere."

"And you panicked."

She raised her head and her proud tawny eyes transfixed him. "No. Then I calmed down and saw what we had to do. If she didn't die we were in trouble; if she did we were two sad little girls who'd just lost their mother."

It would have been less disturbing if she'd been more emotional. But she spoke as if her mother's death had been inevitable. Daniel told himself it was a defence mechanism, only by keeping it at arm's length could she deal with it at all, but it seemed as if she hardly cared. She'd stabbed her mother again and again until she stopped moving, then calmly worked out how to shift the blame elsewhere. It may have been displacement activity, to occupy her mind that would otherwise be overwhelmed by what she'd done, but her attitude appalled him almost as much as her actions.

He fought to keep his voice level. "Did you always mean Nicky Speers to take the blame?"

"Oh yes," affirmed Johnny. "As soon as I saw we had some explaining to do. So I had to hide the fact that two knives had been used. Do you know about that?" Daniel nodded mutely. "We didn't do that until she was dead," Johnny said primly; and if she saw the sick look on his face she chose to ignore it.

"I could have made it clearer. I could have left something of his with her. But I thought it would be too obvious. The police should have suspected him without a row of muddy boot-prints leading across the road. It was only when people started talking as if my daddy might have done it that I realised how stupid the police were, and that I'd have to make it plainer."

Daniel shook his head slowly. "Superintendent Deacon wasn't too stupid to follow your trail, Johnny, he was too smart. He knew it didn't make sense."

"And blaming my daddy did?" she demanded indignantly.

Daniel went to answer, thought better of it. He was on dangerous ground now, because he knew something about Robert Daws that his daughters didn't, and though they would have to know it would alter the situation massively and unpredictably if they found out now. And he wouldn't have to say much, not to Johnny. It might be enough for him to think it. Her father was the only thing in the world this girl held in genuine and abiding regard. She had to be rendered harmless before she discovered he was dead, because at that point she'd go nova.

"Johnny," he said instead, "can we talk about this later, when everyone's safe? Let Peris go. There's nothing more she can do for you." He swallowed. "Nothing that I can't."

Johnny looked incredulously at him then laughed out loud. "Don't be ridiculous!"

"I mean it," he insisted, surprised and a little offended. "I'd be a pretty good hostage. You know I'm not going to come over all Sylvester Stallone. I'll stay with you till you're ready to leave here."

"That's not a hostage, it's a baby-sitter. Oh, go home, Daniel," said Johnny dismissively. "We've nothing left to talk about."

Her arms were growing tired. She wasn't sure how much longer she could resist the wind tearing at her. Trying to make it easier she shifted her stance, linking her arm through Peris's to hold the rail with both hands.

Peris felt her move and thought she was going to fall. Her eyes found Daniel's and clung to him and she whimpered. He wanted to grab for her, knew he mustn't. One sudden move and they'd all be gone.

Johnny jerked her aunt's pinioned arm. "Shut up, you bitch." Beneath her the lights of the speeding vehicles blurred one with the next in a river of light. The temptation to just let go and let it bear her away was mounting.

"They're going to do it." Freeing himself from Brodie's talons, Charlie Voss fumbled urgently in his pocket. "They're going to jump."

She put her hand to her mouth, whispering through the fingers. "What do we do? What *can* we do? Rush them?"

He was already dialling. "No. We'd never reach them." He spoke tersely into the phone. "We have to stop the traffic. Get the signs turned on. When they go, I don't want them going through someone's windscreen."

Daniel didn't know what else to say, what else to try. "Johnny – look at me. Look at me! Don't look down."

After a moment some weary impulse of obedience made her do as he said. He nodded shakily. "Good. Now listen to me. You're not doing this. We're going to find another way."

Johnny shook her head, the chestnut curls whipping her face. "It's too late. Even if we got off this bridge I don't know where we'd go. We set out to find my father, but I don't really know how and I don't know how I'd face him if we did. I told you, he still loved her."

"Daddy loves us," said Em's little voice, cold and surprised. "We're going to be together."

Johnny looked at her with compassion. "I'm sorry. I don't think so."

"You *promised*!"

"I thought I could make it work. But it got complicated and I'm too tired. I'm sorry, Em. I think it ends here."

"Please ... " Daniel was almost in tears. "Tell me what you want. Anything! I'll find a way ... "

Em sobbed steadily, her face against Peris's sleeve. Some of the sobs were words. "I want my daddy – "

He might have got somewhere with Em. He might have convinced her he could deliver things that her sister knew were impossible. He opened his mouth to try, then shut it again. Suppose she believed him. Suppose she scrambled quickly under the handrail to dash her tear-streaked little face against his chest. Johnny couldn't hold Peris on her own: the woman's body would veer out over the drop and she would fall. Daniel wanted to save them. He wanted to save them all. But he couldn't sacrifice Peris to save her kidnappers.

"I want my daddy," wailed Em.

Daniel bit his lip. They didn't know. That wasn't within his gift either, but they didn't know. If he could carry it off. If he could lie and not betray himself. "All right," he said carefully, "that we can do. Would it help? If the police brought him here? Could we all leave together?"

From the quick, startled-deer glance she gave him it seemed the possibility hadn't occurred to Johnny. She thought about it now. She'd been without hope, ready to die; after that, the prospect of being reunited with her father was bright enough to eclipse everything that waited behind it. Or almost.

"The police think he's a murderer," she said, thinking aloud. "If they knew where he was they'd have arrested him."

Daniel was ashamed of himself. That was something else he mustn't let them see. "*I* know where he is. Where he's been for the last fortnight. I can arrange it for you to see him. That's a promise." The fact that none of those statements was an actual untruth gave him no comfort at all.

Johnny's expression remained doubtful. Yet this was why she'd taken a hostage – because she believed it could buy her what she wanted. Only now the deal seemed on could she see the flaws in her reasoning.

Em couldn't. Em thought they'd somehow turned defeat into victory and were going to get everything they wanted; and if she didn't quite understand how, well, she hadn't understood how they'd got here either. "Yes!" she gasped, pale face suddenly aglow. "My daddy. Bring him here. I want my daddy. Bring him here *now*!"

"It'll take a little time," stammered Daniel, wrong-footed by the abrupt change of mood. "Not long. But you're going to get cold out there. You don't want to get cold and fall before he gets here." He dared a step forward. "I'll help you get Peris inside."

Em was too excited to listen. "How long? I don't *want* to wait! Tell them to bring him. Tell them now." Already she was dancing and shuffling on the parapet, oblivious of the life she held in her small cold hand, certain she'd miss him if she wasn't ready to greet her father at once. "Now!"

Johnny wasn't excited. Johnny was utterly still, her eyes clamped on Daniel's face, boring a well to test the truth. He flinched under the intensity of her gaze, and she drew a deep, tremulous breath. Her voice was an accusing ghost. "You *liar*!"

He knew then that it was over. That they would jump – at least, that Johnny would and Em would follow as she always did – and there was nothing he could do to stop them. With both hands, with people running to help, he couldn't hold them all.

So there was a choice to be made. It wasn't a difficult choice. Two of them were here of their own volition, one was not; two were free to save themselves, one was not. But exercising it would be difficult. Because the other thing he saw in Johnny's face, besides shock at his deceit and hatred of the deceiver, was the absolute determination that, even if she could no longer win, she would see him choke on the ashes of his victory.

# Chapter Twenty-Seven

Of the kind of time measured objectively by watches, only minutes had passed since the girls pushed their hostage under the rail and joined her on the outside of the bridge. Daniel had been pleading with them only a few minutes, and it was less time than that since Detective Sergeant Voss ordered the traffic to be stopped. It was just beginning to slow. Voss understood that it took time. Hundreds of vehicles travelling at seventy miles an hour can't be stopped in their own length without risking more lives than he stood to save. But regardless of what his watch said, there *felt* to have been time enough. He felt to have spent half his life on this damned bridge, watching the unfolding of a tragedy he was powerless to prevent.

If someone had asked her, Brodie would have said she cared little for the fate of two mad children who thought their own unhappiness could be redeemed by other people's blood. She cared more for the terrified woman in their hands; but she had known Peris Daws for mere days, had spent barely an hour in her company, could sympathise with her plight without feeling it as a wound to her own heart.

But Daniel was her friend, one of half a dozen people in the world whose well-being genuinely concerned her, and she knew that what was about to happen, that she would need a stiff drink and a hug from her daughter to put behind her, Daniel would agonise over in mind-destroying detail for months to come. It was who he was: he could suffer for England. Other people's tragedies pierced him to the core. In the wake of the imminent disaster he would flay himself, and his pain would hurt Brodie in a way that the events themselves would not. She stood at Voss's side, aching to be at Daniel's side, frozen by the knowledge that any action of hers could only hasten what he dreaded.

Across the bridge Jack Deacon was imposing on his Good Samaritan. With the tourniquet doing its job he was feeling steadier. He was consumed by the need to know what was happening on the bridge, that he'd had to leave in the hands of Charlie Voss and a couple of constables he wouldn't have trusted to see his cat across the road. "Help me up."

The nurse, whose name was Mrs Parsons, misunderstood and gave him a reassuring smile. "No, Mr Deacon, you stay where you are. The paramedics are big strong lads, they won't have any trouble lifting you."

"I don't care if they're the front row of the London Irish," snarled Deacon, "I'm not sitting in the mud waiting for them when matters of life and death are being decided thirty feet above my head. Help me up. I want to see what's happening."

Mrs Parsons continued to protest until he started clawing his way up the wire-mesh fence, at which point she decided it was better to help than watch him fall and start bleeding again. When he was on his feet she pulled the mesh aside and they moved out of the shadow of the bridge to watch the drama enfold.

"Good Lord!" she exclaimed. "Are they going to jump?"

Deacon nodded grimly. "I rather think they are."

"But – they're *children*!"

Deacon sighed. "No, Mrs Parsons, they're a couple of little psychopaths. We think they've killed one person already; we know they've tried to kill others. Maybe you shouldn't watch this. I'll be all right now."

The woman looked at him like slapping his face. "If they fall there may be something I can do."

Deacon looked at the traffic, only now slowing perceptibly. "I doubt it."

Brodie, who was closest, saw Daniel lean forward and speak to Peris. Even in her terror the woman looked perplexed. But it must have mattered because Daniel insisted on an answer.

Brodie nudged Charlie Voss. "Something's happening."

Daniel spoke to Johnny then. Whatever he said, the effect was electric. She swayed away from the rail as if he'd struck her, one hand going to her mouth as if to stifle a cry.

Voss saw Peris's face split in a wail of terror as, cut adrift, she began to swing. He saw Daniel grab for her, and though she was heavier than him he braced himself against the rail and hung on, stubbornly denying the claim of gravity.

Deacon saw clear air between the girls and their hostage, then they were falling. There seemed to be time for him to wonder where he'd seen that before, and remember it was the solid fuel boosters dropping away from a Space Shuttle launch vehicle.

Mrs Parsons saw two young girls fall ten metres into heavy traffic. She saw one bounce off the bonnet of a red jeep and land on the white line, and the other crash in the middle of the fast lane. The driver of the truck that went over her had neither time nor space to avoid her; but by then it was probably all over anyway.

From both ends of the bridge policemen were running. Batty grabbed Daniel and Vickers grabbed Peris; together they hauled her to safety. Then they had to break Daniel's grip on her shoulder-bag. His hand was fisted so tight on the strap that he couldn't let go.

By the time Brodie reached them, Daniel and Peris had sunk in a heap on the concrete. When Constable Vickers freed her arms Peris flung them round the young man and held him as if he were more in need of comfort than she. All Brodie could do was stand over them, waiting for a bit of Daniel to emerge from the clinch so she could touch him too.

It took a while, but finally Peris mastered herself and put him down. Batty helped her to her feet and, draping his tunic round her shoulders, guided her gently from the scene.

Before she went, though, she took Daniel's chin in one hand and made him look at her. "I heard *nothing*," she said, and though her voice shook with reaction her resolve was iron. Then she went with the constable.

Ten metres below the traffic rumbled and slewed to a halt. Even before it was stationary Mrs Parsons was dancing between the mudguards to reach the casualties.

A cursory glance was enough to establish that Johnny Daws was beyond help. But Em had bounced on something a little more yielding than tarmac, and though her eyes were wide with shock they weren't blown yet. "This one," the nurse shouted to the paramedics.

Deacon reached her first, slumping leadenly beside her. He wasn't a doctor but he'd seen a lot of injured people and a few dying ones, and he didn't think the paramedics needed to rush. His craggy face softened in a smile. "Hi, Em."

She recognised him. Her answering smile was unshadowed by any recollection of enmity. "Hello, Mr Deacon."

"That was a bit of a fall."

For a little while she seemed to drift, sometimes closer, sometimes further away, mumbling. He stroked the floss of pale hair back from her brow and told her she was going to be all right. At length she gathered her strength and looked him full in the eyes. "Where's my daddy, Mr Deacon?"

"Your daddy's fine, Em. I saw him just a few hours ago. Try to rest. I bet, when you wake up, he'll be there."

She smiled again, gratefully, and shut her eyes; and when the paramedics scrambled down the bank with their stretcher there wasn't the hint of a pulse left in the small broken body.

Brodie took Daniel home. She left Paddy with Marta, not wanting her to witness his distress. She kept saying to him, "You saved Peris. She'd be dead but for you." But he would not be comforted. He huddled on the sofa, his knees drawn up to his chest, his head on his arms, mute with grief. At other times he roamed the flat like a caged beast, unable to rest.

259

Brodie crumbled sleeping pills into half an inch of brandy and kept prompting him until it was gone. She stayed with him until unconsciousness stilled him.

Deacon phoned from the hospital around noon the next day. He had some heavy-duty stitches in his leg and a drip in the back of his hand, and he was uncomfortable and impatient with weakness, but when Brodie tried to commiserate he brushed it off. He hadn't called to talk about himself. "How's Daniel?"

"Not great," she admitted. "I had to slip him a Micky Finn to get him to sleep last night. At nine this morning he looked like a zombie; by ten he was bouncing off the walls again. He's gone out. He mumbled something about seeing the builders, but I think he was just desperate to get out of the house."

There was a pause. Then Deacon said, "I don't want to alarm you, Brodie, but I don't think he should be on his own. He probably thinks he doesn't want company right now, but it's what he needs. He needs to know he's not to blame for what happened."

Brodie was slow to respond. When she did her voice was different: not louder but sharper, with an acuity he knew would be matched by the intelligence in her eyes if he'd been present to see. "Jack – what is it you're not telling me?"

He parried with a question of his own. "What has Daniel said?"

"Nothing! Until right now I didn't know there was anything else *to* say. But something happened, didn't it? – something more than what I and everyone else saw. And Peris knows, and you know, and Daniel's torturing himself over it but for some reason he can't tell me. Why? Why does he think last night was a calamity when I saw him save a woman's life?"

"He wanted to save them all," said Deacon.

"And I wanted to marry Richard Gere," snapped Brodie. "Being a grown-up means recognising what's possible.

Daniel's a grown-up too – he isn't crucifying himself over something that was never within his grasp. What happened? What did he say?"

Now Deacon's tone sharpened. "What makes you think it was something he said?"

So she was on the right lines. "Peris made such a point of telling him she heard nothing that it had to be a lie. The woman nearly died. She saw her two nieces kill themselves, knowing they meant to take her with them. But when she was safe, the first words she spoke were to tell Daniel that what passed between them would go no further. Why? Why did it matter so much to her? Why did she think it would matter that much to *him*?"

Deacon said quietly, "You have to understand, Brodie, there are things I don't know. That I can't know, because if I did I'd have to do something about them. If you want to know more you'll have to ask Daniel." He thought for a moment. "If it's any help, you can tell him that – even though I don't know what happened – I do understand."

Brodie was doing what she did best: reading between the lines. Sometimes it was possible to guess what was missing from the shape left by its absence. She was getting an idea of what was being kept from her more from what Deacon wasn't prepared to say than what he was. "And you're happy with that?"

She heard him shrug. "Happy's hardly the word, but I don't have any problem with it. Any other outcome would have been worse. Remember, there was no future for them. Both parents are dead, and how and why would have dogged them forever. They could have spent the rest of their lives behind bars. I wouldn't wish that on my worst enemy.

"And suppose they were released at some point. How long would it have been before someone else upset them? They'd have done it again. Someone else who's only crime was to cross them would have ended up maimed or dead. It's my professional judgement that the world's a safer place without them."

She couldn't fault his logic. But somehow Brodie was still shocked to hear him say it. "What about your superiors? Will they feel the same way?"

"My superiors," he said tersely, "will hear nothing of this. All they need to know is that Emerald Daws was dying with a massive head injury, she was lapsing in and out of consciousness, nothing she said could be relied on. If they press me I'll say I couldn't make any sense of it. If you like, you can tell Daniel that too."

"And then he'll tell me what it is that you won't?"

"I don't know," said Deacon honestly. "But he needs to."

Brodie was still mulling over the conversation as she drove to the shore. If she wasn't entirely sure what it had been about, she did know how important it was. To Daniel; but also, and more than she would have guessed, to her. Deacon had called up spectres she couldn't just banish to an unused corner of her mind.

Work on Daniel's house was progressing at its customary pace. Mr Wilmslow told her he hadn't seen his client for days. Brodie's sense of unease grew as she walked towards the pier. From there she could see the length of the shingle shore until it vanished under the bluff of the Firestone Cliffs to the east and into the blue blur of distance to the west. None of the handful of people on the beach looked like Daniel.

She was returning to the car when she saw him – under the pier, propped against one of the timber piles, watching her. She leaned back against the car and crossed her ankles, waiting for him to come to her. After a minute he did.

"I wondered where you'd got to," Brodie said softly.

"Not far," said Daniel. Walking in the fresh air seemed to have eased his agitation. Apart from the hours of drugged sleep, this was the quietest she'd seen him since last night.

He leaned against the car beside her, hands in his pockets, chin on his chest.

Brodie said quietly, "We need to talk."

He shook his head once, with conviction. "No."

"Tell me what happened. On the bridge."

"You saw what happened."

"I saw it. I want to know what I wasn't close enough to hear."

A tremor shook him from head to foot. "Who says – ?"

"Daniel," she sighed, "you know you're going to tell me eventually. Peris knows. Jack knows – "

"Deacon?" That startled him.

"Yes. I could get it out of either of them, but I'd rather hear it from you."

He couldn't look at her. His gaze veered unhappily between his shoes, the English Channel and the black finger of the rotten pier. After a long moment he said, "I killed them."

"Of course you didn't kill them," Brodie said shortly. "They jumped off a bridge. They were *always* going to jump – everyone but you knew it. They had nothing to come back to."

"Maybe." He shuddered. "I don't know. All I know– "

She drew a calming breath and, without looking at him, gazing out to sea, said it again. "Tell me what happened."

He knew it was over. That they would jump and there was nothing he could do to stop them. He couldn't hold them all.

He scanned Peris desperately for something he could hang onto. The light coat she was wearing would tear under her weight. Her hands were behind her back, her arms too plump to grasp. Across her chest –

"Peris," he said urgently, "this is important. Your bag: is it leather?"

None of them understood. Johnny frowned. Em paused in her excited little jig and put her head on one side. Peris stared at him wildly, her face contorted by fear. "B-bag – ?"

"Is it leather?" he said again. "Peris! Your bag. Is it real leather?"

"Y-yes. Yes."

Leather was strong. Plastic would break, but a leather strap across the woman's shoulder might hold until help arrived. Easy to grab, easy to grip: if he braced against the rail with all his strength he could stop her falling until bigger men arrived to pull her inside.

What he couldn't do was hold her on the ledge with two other people pulling her off.

"I had to make them let go," he mumbled. "I couldn't hold them all. And the girls could have come inside anytime they wanted. I didn't – I didn't – It's not as if I pushed them ..."

"*Tell* me, Daniel," said Brodie, gently insistent.

"I had to ... shake them. I thought, if I could jolt them enough they'd let go of her. I knew they might jump. Damn it!" He rolled his eyes skyward, refusing even the scant solace of ambivalence. "I knew they *would* jump. It didn't have to matter. I couldn't see any other way to save Peris."

His voice cracked. He hung his head, panting softly until he could continue. "I had to distract them. It was her only chance, if I could make them forget about her for a moment. And there was only one thing I knew that they didn't ..."

That was it, that Deacon had refused to tell her. Brodie felt the strength leach from her body into her shoes. "You told them about Robert."

"I told them he was dead. That he drove his car into a lake because he couldn't live with what they'd done. That, after the fight, he came back and found them pushing knives into their mother's body."

There was a long silence between them. The tide made glockenspiel noises on the shingle. A dog barked quarter of a mile away; nearer at hand Mr Wilmslow hit his thumb with a hammer and swore.

Daniel said softly, "Say something. Please say something."

264

Brodie didn't know what to say. She'd known something was racking him. Knowing what it was hadn't, as she'd hoped, put everything right. Instead, for a moment the rules of physics seemed to have been suspended. She felt as if she were turning inside out, the resilient core that was her sense of identity, of knowing who she was and how the world fitted round her, seeping out through her pores.

Daniel did that? Daniel?

But why was she appalled? She knew what those children were, for God's sake they tried to kill her! When she thought they'd killed themselves what she mostly felt was, Fair enough. Back on the bridge she'd prayed for them jump as soon as possible, before Daniel could take responsibility for their deaths. And now? Clearly at least some of the responsibility was his. How much? And how much did it alter how she felt about what happened, about him? She didn't know. She didn't know.

"Brodie? Anything. *Please.*"

There was all the difference in the world between wanting something to happen, hoping it would happen, even praying for it, and taking steps to bring it about. It wasn't murder, he hadn't pushed them; but he'd pushed them into it.

She found a voice, even if it was one she barely recognised as her own. "You knew what would happen. You took away their last reason to live. You *made* them jump."

He shook his head miserably. "I'd have saved them if I could. I couldn't. The only one I had a chance of saving was Peris, and that was the only way I could see."

"You weren't concerned that the price was too high?"

"*Concerned?*" His voice broke on despair. "Brodie, they were going to kill her! She'd never done them any harm, but they were going to kill her just to make a point. And then they were going to kill themselves. If I'd done nothing, all three of them would be dead. But Peris is alive. I think – I *think* – her life is my justification."

"Justification?" It came out half a snort, half a sob. "I dare say it is. I dare say a court would think so. Jack wants you to know, incidentally, that there's no question of that. As far as he's concerned the matter's closed."

Daniel's eyes on her face were hollow and hot. "You think I care about that? About what a court might think? About what Jack thinks? Brodie, you know me better than that! I did what I thought was right. After that, the only opinion I care about is yours."

"Why?" she demanded angrily. "You don't need my approval. Why does it matter to you what I think?"

"It always matters to me what you think," he said simply.

Just in time Brodie tasted the tartness of her retort and bit it back. Why was she trying to punish him? If she knew one thing about Daniel Hood, it was that he was more than capable of punishing himself for transgressions, actual or only perceived. If he thought he'd got something this wrong he would crucify himself. She'd always thought she was the pragmatic one in their partnership. Daniel was gentler than her, truer than her – but also less likely to take the path of least resistance than anyone she knew.

He hadn't acted as he had because it was the easy option. He'd believed there was no alternative. Brodie had known as soon as she saw them on the bridge that the girls would jump. She couldn't have saved them and Daniel couldn't. He *had* found a way to save Peris. If it had been Brodie on the bridge the woman would have died too. But when she tried to say that, even in her own head it sounded like a criticism. She hated the tiny, insistent voice deep inside her calling him a murderer.

This wasn't why she was here, and it certainly wasn't why Deacon had sent her. He'd been worried about Daniel wrestling with his conscience alone. Well, he wasn't alone any more: now he was having to defend himself against the one person he might have expected to understand. Or, in the absense of understanding, to take his part anyway. Because that's what friends do: support one another, even when the cause is questionable, out of sheer love.

Daniel was in pain and she wanted to comfort him. She wanted to tell him that everything was all right. And she couldn't. She'd have lied, happily, if she'd thought she could get away with it. But this was Daniel, and he'd know if she lied, and her lies would hurt him more than the truth. More than the silence.

She tried to explain. "I *know* you did what you believed was best. By any rational assessment it was. If you'd done anything else, three people would be dead now instead of two – one of them a woman who wanted to live and didn't deserve to die."

Daniel's voice was so low it was barely audible. "But you don't believe it."

For most of her life Brodie had been a polite, compliant sort of person. She'd yielded to pressure, turned the other cheek, made peace not war, tried to meet other people's expectations. When the reward for all this was to have her husband leave her for another woman, she changed. Radically. Now when she was pushed she pushed back; even when it was least appropriate.

"What do you want from me, Daniel?" she demanded harshly. "Forgiveness? You don't need it. Not mine, not anyone's. You did what you thought was necessary. Jack thinks it was necessary too, and I'm damn sure Peris does. All right: if it had been my decision maybe I'd have made it differently. Maybe I'd have watched all of them die rather than choose who was to live. But it wasn't mine, it was yours. What matters is that you can live with it."

That came out more brutal than she intended. She wished now she'd settled for a soothing lie. Even if he suspected it might have been less painful than the naked truth.

She shook her head wearily. "I'm sorry. I'm not sure I understand it myself. My brain knows they weren't capable of being saved. But my heart and my womb say that a child is a child, you have to fight for the worst of them. I think you were probably right. I *feel* you were wrong."

Brodie knew she was twisting the knife in his side. She felt dreadful. But in the moment of her death Johnny had managed a last act of malice: she'd thrown up a wall between them. And the wall was growing, and already Brodie couldn't see over it or past it, and she was afraid it would be there between them forever.

She didn't dare ask what Daniel was thinking. She couldn't look at him. She thought she was losing him, and it mattered more than she would have thought possible, and still there seemed to be nothing she could offer, neither lies nor the truth, to heal the rift.

On the whole, when he wasn't actively infuriating them, people liked Daniel Hood, but they always thought he was weak. He was small and fair, with an amiable expression behind thick glasses, and there was something childlike about his enthusiasms, his thought-processes, even his obstinacies.

But Brodie knew him better than most. She knew he was stronger than he looked. Strong enough to hold his own course almost regardless of what the elements threw at him. She hoped desperately that he'd be strong enough now: that when he got over the horror he'd believe in the rightness of his decision firmly enough not to need her validation. She could accept what he'd done if that was enough for him, if he could manage without her approval. She had no way of knowing if that was possible.

For the longest time they stayed where they were, not speaking, leaning against the car, side by side, no part of his body touching hers, gazing numbly out to sea. Finally Brodie sighed brokenly. "Oh, Daniel."

"I know," he murmured.